Paul Heyse, Mary Wilson

The Dead Lake and other tales

Paul Heyse, Mary Wilson

The Dead Lake and other tales

ISBN/EAN: 9783743360754

Manufactured in Europe, USA, Canada, Australia, Japa

Cover: Foto ©Andreas Hilbeck / pixelio.de

Manufactured and distributed by brebook publishing software (www.brebook.com)

Paul Heyse, Mary Wilson

The Dead Lake and other tales

COLLECTION

OF

GERMAN AUTHORS.

VOL. 15.

THE DEAD LAKE & OTHER TALES BY P. HEYSE.

IN ONE VOLUME.

THE DEAD LAKE

AND

OTHER TALES

BY

PAUL HEYSE.

FROM THE GERMAN

BY

MARY WILSON.

Authorized Edition.

LEIPZIG 1870

BERNHARD TAUCHNITZ.

LONDON: SAMPSON LOW, MARSTON, SEARLE & RIVINGTON.
CROWN BUILDINGS, 188, FLEET STREET.
PARIS: C. REINWALD & Cⁱᵉ, 15, RUE DES SAINTS PÈRES.

CONTENTS.

A FORTNIGHT

AT

THE DEAD LAKE.

THE DEAD LAKE.

Summer was at its heighth, yet in one corner of the Alps an icy cold wind revolted against its dominion, and threatened to change the pouring rain into snow flakes. The air was so gloomy that even a house which stood about a hundred paces from the shore of the lake, could not be distinguished, although it was white-washed and twilight had hardly set in.

A fire had been lighted in the kitchen. The land-lady was standing by it frying a dish of fish, while with one foot she rocked a cradle which stood beside the hearth. In the tap room, the landlord was lying on a bench by the stove, cursing the flies which would not let him sleep. A barefooted maid of all work sat spin-ning in a corner, and now and then glanced with a sigh, through the dingy panes at the wild storm which was raging without. A tall strong fellow, the farm servant of the inn, came grumbling into the room: he shook the rain-drops from his clothes, like a dog com-ing out of the water, and threw a heap of wet fishing nets into a corner. It seemed as if the cloud of dis-content and ill-humour which hung over the house, was only kept by this moody silence from bursting into a storm of discord and quarreling.

Suddenly the outer door opened, and a stranger's

step was heard groping through the dark passage; the landlord did not move, only the maid rose, and opened the door of the room.

A man in a travelling suit stood at the entrance, and asked if this was the inn of the dead lake. As the girl answered shortly in the affirmative, he walked in, threw his dripping plaid and travelling pouch on the table, and sat down on the bench apparently exhausted; but he neither removed his hat heavy with rain nor laid down his walking stick, as if intending to start again after a short rest.

The maid still stood before him, waiting for his orders, but he seemed to have forgotten the presence of any one in the room but himself, leant his head against the wall, and closed his eyes; so deep silence once more reigned in the hot dark room, only interrupted by the buzzing of the flies, and the listless sighs of the maid.

At last the landlady brought in the supper; a little lad who stared at the stranger carried the candle before her. The landlord rose lazily from his bench, yawned and approached the table leaving to his wife the charge of inviting the stranger to partake of their meal. The traveller refused with a silent shake of the head, and the landlady apologized for the meagreness of their fare. Meat, they had none, except a few live ducks and chickens. They could not afford to buy it, for their own use, and now travellers never came that way, for two years ago, a new road had been made on the other side of the mountain, and the post which had formerly passed their inn now drove the other way. If the weather was fine, a tourist, or a painter who wished to sketch the environs of the lake now and then lodged with them; but they did not spend or expect much, neither was the selling of a few fish very profitable.

If however the gentleman wished to remain over night, he would not fare badly. The bedrooms were just adjoining, and the beds well aired. They had also a barrel of beer in the cellar, good Tyrolese wine, and their spirits of gentian was celebrated. But all these offers did not tempt the guest; he replied that he would stay for the night, and only wished a jug of fresh water. Then he arose and without casting a single look at the people seated round the table, and silently eating their supper, or taking any notice of the little boy of ten, although the child made the most friendly advances, and gazed admiringly at his gold watch guard, which sparkled faintly in the dim light. The maid servant took another candle from the cornice of the stove, and showed him the way to the next room, where she filled his jug with fresh water, and then left him to his own thoughts.

The landlord sent an oath after him. "Just their usual luck," he grumbled, if any guest ever came to them, it was always some idle vagrant who ordered nothing, and finally took his leave without paying for his bed, often disappearing in company with the bed-clothes. His wife replied that it was just those folks, who regaled themselves on all that larder and cellar could supply, and tried to ingratiate themselves with the landlord. This gentleman was ill in mind or body, as he neither ate nor drank. At this moment the stranger again entered the room, and asked if he could have a boat, as he wished to fish on the lake by torch-light, as soon as the rain had ceased.—The landlady secretly poked her husband in the side, as if to say;

"Now, you see! he is not right in the head; don't contradict him for heaven's sake."

The landlord who was fully aware of the advantage to be gained by this singular demand, answered in his surly manner, that the gentleman could have both his boats, though it was not the fashion in these parts to fish at night, but if it amused him he was welcome to do so.   The farm servant would prepare the torch immediately—so saying, he made a sign to the tall fellow who was still occupied in picking his fish bones, and opened the door for his guest.

The rain had not ceased and the water was dashing and gushing from the gutters. The stranger seemed insensible to any outward discomfort; he hastily walked towards the shore, and by the light of the lantern which the farm servant had brought with him, he examined the two boats, as if he wished to make sure which of them was the safest. They were both fastened under a shed, where different fishing implements were lying under some benches. Then sending back the farm servant under some pretext or other, he sought on the shore of the lake for a couple of heavy stones, which he placed in the largest of the two boats.—He drew a deep breath, and stood for a moment with his eyes fixed on the dark water, which as far as one could see by the light of the lantern was furrowed by the drizzling rain. The wind had ceased for a moment, the surf foamed, and dashed round the keel of the small boats; from the house, one could hear the monotonous sing song of the landlady who was lulling her baby to sleep. Even this sounded melancholy, reminding more of the cares of motherhood than of its joys, and heightened the dismal impression made by the forsaken aspect of this corner of the world.

The stranger was just returning to the house, when he heard on the road coming from the south, along which he had also travelled that morning, the cracking of a whip and the crashing and creaking of wheels which were drawn heavily up the hill through the deep and sloughy ruts. Shortly afterwards a lightly covered carriage stopped before the inn. Lights were brought to the door, a female voice asked questions which the landlady answered in her most amiable tones; then two women got out of the carriage and carefully carried something wrapped up in cloaks into the house. The farm servant helped the coachman to bring his horses under shelter. A few minutes later every thing had relapsed into the former silence.

It had all passed like a vision before the stranger, neither awakening his curiosity, nor, still less, his interest. He once more looked up at the dense clouds to see if there was any chance of their dispersing, and then entered the house where lights were now shining in the room opposite the tap room, and shadows were flitting to-and fro behind the curtains. He gave back the lantern to the man, and some orders about baits and fishing hooks which he would require in the morning, and retired to his room.

There he lighted the candle, and placed it in a bent candlestick, which stood on the rickety table.— Then he threw open a casement to let out the stuffy and damp air, and for a while looked out on the splashing and spirting gutter in which a cork was restlessly dancing. Further off no object could be discerned; the inky darkness of the cloudy sky hid everything from

view. The wind howled in a ravine near the lake, like
some caged beast of prey, and the trees near the house
groaned under the weight of the gushing rain. It was
an unfavourable moment for standing near an open
window but the stranger seemed to be listening intently
to the dismal sound of the storm which raged without.
Only when the wind drove the rain straight into his
face, he moved away, and paced up and down between
the bare walls of the little room, with his hands crossed
behind his back. His face was quite calm, and his
eyes appeared to be looking beyond what surrounded
him, into some distant world.

At last he took writing materials, and a small portfolio from his travelling pouch, sat down beside the
dim candle, and wrote as follows:

"I cannot go to rest, Charles, without bidding
you good night. How weary I am, you must have
perceived when we met, unfortunately for so short a
time, six weeks ago. *Then* I ought to have spoken
to you, and we might have come to an agreement on
this chapter on pathology, as we have done on so many
others: Had I done so, I could now have quietly
smoked my last cigar, instead of tiring us both, with
this dull writing, but the words seemed to cleave to my
lips. We should have probably disputed about the
matter—Each of us would have maintained his own
opinion, so I thought it useless to spoil the few hours
we had to spend in each other's society. I am well
acquainted with your principles, and know that if you
were here, you would endeavour to reconcile me to
existence. But you would wrong me, if you thought
that I had caused this dissension between life and myself which nothing but a divorce can appease. I would

willingly live if I *could*. I am not such a coward, or so fastidious that a few 'slings and arrows of outrageous fortune' should drive me distracted and make me take the resolution to leap out of my skin in the full sense of the word. Who would throw over the whole concern, and fume against the inscrutable Powers because many things are disagreeable to bear? Are not the decrees of the eternal powers equally unfathomable and indisputable? But here lies the fault—I can play the part of a wise man no longer. The desperate attempt to save reason at least from the general wreck of soul and mind has failed. Just now when I watched an old cork which had fallen into the gutter, and which lashed by the rain was helplessly whirling about in the dirty puddle, the thought struck me that this cork was my own brain which had stolen from out my heated skull, and was now taking a shower bath. If such an absurd fancy could take possession of my mind for a whole quarter of an hour, then must the last prop of my reason be fast giving way.

"I have the highest idea of the self-sacrificing duties of a man towards his fellow-creatures, yet I cannot calmly see the moment approach when the asphyxiated soul is to be buried alive, watch the loss of self-consciousness, and finally sink lower than the most miserable brute. This, my dear Charles, would require the dullness of a sheep patiently awaiting the butcher's knife, though it feels a worm gnawing at its brain.

"But I quite forget that this will seem but a confused outpouring of words to you, who are only aware of a portion of my calamities. You only know what the rest of the world is acquainted with—that my adopted sister died, this day year, that her father followed her a few days later, and her mother in the spring of this year.—You also know that my family consisted of only these three—that I loved them dearly —that, in fact, except yourself, they were the only beings to whom I was much attached.

"Under any circumstance their loss would have wounded me deeply, but I should have ended by overcoming this grief. Even had they been severed from me at a single stroke, I could have bravely outlived it. Truly the death of one man is always irreparable but his life is never indispensable. Science, my profession, my youth, would have healed the wound.— Now, it is still open, and the blood which flows from it cannot be stanched, for these three precious lives would have been spared, but for me!.....

I must begin from the beginning, Charles, if I wish to make these sad words clear to you.—You know, I believe, that I hardly ever saw my own parents, that after the death of my father, I should have been brought up at the orphan asylum, if those generous people had not taken pity on the son of the poor surgeon, and adopted me. My foster-father was one of the most opulent merchants of the town.—When he gave me a home, he was still childless after eight years of marriage. He hoped that my presence would cheer him, and his wife, and enliven the quiet dull house. Unfortunately, at first, I but ill rewarded the kindness of the worthy couple, though I was greatly attached to them. I was a reserved, irritable, and unamiable lad, with a great tendency to ponder over everything. My behaviour vacillated between a moody silence which lasted for days, and sudden and passionate outbreaks of temper. Even now I feel deeply ashamed when I think of the truly angelic patience with which my foster-parents bore my perverseness, and tried to moderate my violent temper without ever showing how sorely I disappointed their hopes.

Suddenly all was changed. When I had lived about two years in their house, my adoptive parents saw their heart's desire fulfilled. A child was born to them, the most beautiful and gifted creature I have ever seen. As if by magic, everything grew bright— even I, was changed, and became a good-humoured and sensible lad. I was quite infatuated about the little girl, and watched her like a nurse. For hours together I played with her. I taught her to speak, to run, forgot my dearest occupations, and all my schoolfellows when with her.

"My behaviour towards her parents also completely altered. These excellent people, instead of no longer caring for my society, now redoubled their kindness towards me, and seemed to regard both of us as their children and as having an equal right to their affection.

"As time went on, my fraternal love for the little Ellen only increased with my years; the more so, that a curious similarity in our characters became more perceptible every day. She was not one of those soft, pliable and easily managed girls who give no more trouble to their mothers, than to their future husbands. She would suddenly change from the most extravagant gaiety, to the deepest melancholy—if one can use the term, melancholy, in speaking of a child. In those moments, she would steal out of the garden where she had been romping, and laughing with her little companions, and come to my little room, sit down with grave face, opposite to me, at my writing-table, and read the first book she could get hold of.

"From my school-days upwards, I had always been heart and mind, a naturalist, and had no other thought, but that I would study medicine as my father had done. I used to show her all my collections, even the skeleton of a large monkey which stood in a corner behind my bed, and to hold most unchildlike conversations with the little girl; at other times she would communicate her childishness to me; I cooked for her dolls and physicked them after having first carefully bedaubed their faces with the tokens of the measles and I filled her little garden with all sorts of medical herbs from my herborium. We never shewed much tenderness towards each other. Only once I kissed her lips; it was when I left for the University at nineteen years of age.

"Though I deeply felt the pain of leaving my adoptive home, yet I fancied it would not become me as a man to show any emotion, still my voice failed me when my dear mother embraced me with tears in her eyes. Little Ellen stood pale, and silent by her side. I turned to her with some joke and jestingly gave her different directions about the care of my zoological collection, (preserved in camphor and spirits of wine) which I had entrusted to her charge. Then I drew this child of eight into my arms to bid her farewell. As I kissed her, I was startled by a sudden shudder which ran through her frame, as if an asp had bitten her. She staggered back with closed eyes and nearly fainted away. She quickly recovered however, and next day wrote me a childishly merry letter.

"Since that day I only once touched her lips again, and then they were cold and closed for ever.

"How the six years of my University carreer passed, how I found life at home when I returned for the holidays would be useless to relate. It would be a long, and monotonous narrative. Some estrangement arose between me and my foster-sister, partly through my fault, for science and study monopolized my attention more and more. From year to year this strange girl grew more reserved in my presence. Only in her charming letters could I discover a trace of the old intimacy of our childhood.

"Her outward development did not fall short of its early promise.

"She was fullgrown at the age of fourteen; somewhat slender, but quite formed. The small portrait of her which I once showed you has but little resemblance. Her character, if I may so express myself, was even more mature than her person, and only betrayed itself in her movements. A stately calm, an indifference, scarcely concealed for many things which generally appear alluring at her age, isolated her a good deal. Then again, when she wished to please, her smile, the gentle and timid yielding up of herself had a charm not to be described. Few knew her real value, her genuine upright soul; and among those few, her brother was not. I was then too much engrossed by my studies, too eager to solve the mysteries of physical science, to care about the secrets of that young heart. Strange to say although I was always of a sensual disposition, and certainly no paragon of virtue, and having eyes to see could easily perceive, that all my conquests, compared with that remarkable girl, appeared like housemaids beside a young princess, yet it never entered my head to fall in love with her. When I wrote home, it was always to my foster-mother, and she had to remind me sometimes, of what was due to my little sister.

"She once wrote that the child who was as reserved as ever, did not show what she felt, although my neglect seemed to hurt her, and one day when I had forgotten even to mention her in my letter, she had cried the whole night.

"I hastened to repair my negligence, and wrote her a most penitent letter half in earnest, half in jest, accusing. myself of the darkest crimes towards my faithful little sister, protesting that she was a thousand times too kind to me a petrified egotist whose very heart had been turned to stone, among skeletons and anatomical preparations. Her answer was full of loving kindness, and after that our fraternal intercourse seemed re-established on the old footing.

"Then she was fourteen years of age. On her fifteenth birthday, I passed my examination for a doctor's degree and we exchanged merry congratulations by telegraph.

"Then I travelled during a year with you for a companion, and you will remember that the letters I received from home often made me slightly uneasy.

"My mother wrote that Ellen was not well; she did not complain, but her altered looks only too visibly testified to her sufferings. The old family physician looked rather grave about it. Now I was well acquainted with this good old gentleman. He was a strict adherent of the old school, and greatly prejudiced against the stethoscope, otherwise he had the reputation of much experience in diagnostics, and of great caution, and attention.

"Still this could not tranquillize me, and my parents who believed me to be the greatest medical genius in the world, expressed a strong desire, that if I could possibly get away, I should hasten home and have a consultation with the old doctor. So I determined, as you know to quit my studies in Paris—to hurry home, and decide for myself if all was as it should be.

"When I arrived, Ellen advanced to greet me, looking so well, and lively, that at the first moment, I asked with playful indignation, if this was the august patient to attent to whose delicate health, a celebrated young physician had been summoned from a great distance. Poor child! the pleasure caused by my having set aside every other consideration for her sake, gave that delusive air of blooming health. I soon perceived that the old doctor had not looked grave without cause. I was decidedly however opposed to his opinion that she was threatened with pulmonary disease. After a most careful auscultation, I had found her lungs to be perfectly sound, whereas the palpitations of her heart seemed to be somewhat irregular; this symptom proceeded from a morbid state of the nervous, and blood system. Accordingly the first treatment which was principly directed against everything stimulating and enjoined great quiet, seemed to me the reverse of salutary. I prescribed steel, wine, and strengthening food, to rectify the poverty of blood, and declared that the remedies by which the old doctor hoped to ward off the disease were as bad as poison in her case. Her parents, of course, sided with me, particularly as the apparent success of my treatment during the first weeks of my stay with them corroborated my statement. Ellen felt more lively, and stronger, her sleep and appetite returned, and while the old practitioner withdrew deeply hurt, and mortified, I enjoyed the first pleasures of fame though it still stood on a very precarious footing, and I felt the happiness of having delivered those dear to me, from a heavy care.

"I never intended to establish myself in that town. I knew that I could only reside in a large capital where I could find better assistance in my studies. I, therefore, carefully entrusted Ellen's treatment to the second doctor. of the place, a very humble man, rather irresolute, and dependent on others, who in presence of so young, and far travelled a colleague, meekly resigned any opinion of his own, and promised to keep strictly to the enjoined course of treatment; and now and then to write and inform me of the progress of the cure. The parents saw me depart with heavy hearts, but my welfare, and their duty with regard to my success in life, outweighed any wishes of their own, and Ellen eagerly seconded my desire. I had already lost too much of my precious time on her account, she said; she felt much better, and now that she knew my orders, no one should induce her to do anything I had not sanctioned. I still see the smile with which she bade me good-bye, while the repressed tears choked her voice. Alas! Charles, it was the last time that I saw a smile light up that dear face!

"So I departed entirely blinded, and at the commencement of my stay at M—— I was so completely taken up with the exercise of my profession, that in the letters from home I only noticed the favourable particulars; especially as Ellen's frequent accounts of herself, which almost formed a sort of diary, lulled me into so perfect a security, that I fancied, the care and anxiety which now and then appeared in her mother's letters to be only caused by the exaggerated fondness of a mother's heart.

"My colleague full of respect for my green wisdom, did his best to interpret every graver symptom in favour of my diagnostics, and so I lived on, a rose coloured mist blinding my eyes, till the darkest night suddenly closed around me.

"Ellen's letters which in the later weeks had become rather dispirited suddenly stopped. In their stead I received a letter from the doctor, about six months after my departure saying that another consultation with me seemed to him most desirable. In the last few weeks several symptoms had suddenly changed, so that he dared not proceed in the former manner without further orders. My adoptive parents also eagerly intreated me to come to them.

"But even in spite of all this, I still lingered, certainly not for any frivolous reason; the life or death of some of my patients, just then, depending on my stay. At last a telegraphic despatch startled me into activity. A vomiting of blood had taken place: If you do not come instantly, wrote her mother, you will not find her alive.

"Late at night I arrived at their house feeling as if I myself were dying. On that dreadful journey the scales had suddenly fallen from my eyes, and with the same ingenuity which I had formerly exercised to confirm my own errors, I now sought out every argument expressly to torment myself with the conviction that I alone was responsible for the loss of this much cherished being. I tottered up the wellknown stairs. Her mother met me on the landing, tearless, but with a disturbed look in her eyes. It seemed almost like a relief to me, when she exclaimed: 'you are too late!'—I had dreaded to meet the eyes of my poor sister, as a murderer dreads the dying look of his victim. And yet it was more painful to see the calm face, which reclined on her pillows, smiling, and free from reproach.

"No one accused me; they still believed in me, and laid the blame on different incidents, but I felt crushed under the weight of my despair, and the wildest self-reproaches.

On entering the chamber of death, her father looking like a corpse, staggered heavily into my arms, and losing all self-command, burst into such convulsive sobs, that the people passing in the streets stopped to listen. Then the sight of all the old servants who had adored her; of her mother so completely *changed*—even to this day my hair stands on end when I think of that dreadful scene. The mother beside herself with grief called for wine, for I was to drink Ellen's health —she supposed the 'so called good God' would not object to that. But when the servant brought it, the father taking the glass from the plate dashed it against the wall, crying out: 'broken! dead!' A hundred times, till his voice was choked by tears.—At last his wife led him away and I was left alone with the dead.

"Enough of this dreadful night. I need only add that by dissection, I obtained a full confirmation, of that, of which the quick penetration of the old physician had foreseen the danger.—Could it have been averted? Who can say with certainty whether a conflagration can be stayed or not, if he does not know what feeds it, or from whence the wind blows. I had poured fuel on the fire which had snatched away this innocent life.

"You may imagine that I did not close my eyes that night. The morning found me still sitting, racked with pain and fever, by the bed-side of my sister, when the door opened, and her mother entered the room. She had recovered the noble and gentle serenity of her features, now that the first delirium of despair had passed. She kissed me, with overflowing tears, and even in *my* burning eyes the tears welled up. 'My dear son,' she said 'I here surrender to you a small packet which I found in her writing-table: Your name is on it.'

"It was her diary, beginning with her twelfth year, up to a few days before her death—On every page I found my name; on the last were these words, 'I am dying, darling—I have known you and been permitted to love you. What more can life bring me? I now have no other wish but that you should know that I only lived for you, and through you!'—And this to her murderer!!

"All the events that succeeded; the death of her father, the short widowhood of her mother, who pined away till she was at last re-united to her darling ones, all this, sad as it was, could no longer move me, the darkness within me was so great—What mattered it if one spark more died out or not? *That* I never could forget or overcome—That all hopes of ever being happy again were at end, was a conviction deeply impressed on my heart.

"I repeated to myself a hundred times, that I had

acted for the best according to my belief, that every one of my colleagues had experienced a like misfortune, that we were only responsible for our intentions—But in spite of all this, did these three lives weigh the less on my soul? Could I absolve myself, were all the judges in Heaven and earth to proclaim me free from guilt? I had destroyed the only joy of my benefactors, and had miserably deceived them.—I had neglected this precious life, and how could I henceforth expect any man to entrust his life to me?

"I know what you would oppose to this Charles— You have often told me that I was too sensitive for a doctor's profession—That every one who consults us knows beforehand that we are only human,—not omnipotent, and omniscient Gods, and takes his chance.

"The best doctors are those who never let their feelings interfere, and never paralyse their energies for the future, by useless regrets for the unalterable past. I quite agree with you that these are most sound maxims. But I know enough of disease to foresee that mine is incurable. -

"When the first stunning pain had somewhat subsided, I said to myself, that I *must* bear it as well as I could, and at least try to be of some use as a subordinate, having forfeited my rights as a master.— I threw my whole energy into theoretical studies—I collected, dissected, and observed—I might, perhaps, have reconciled myself to this new existence, if the past had not thrown a shadow over every thing. Now I loathed and revolted inwardly against all this groping on the boundaries of human knowledge. A general, after losing a battle upon which depended the destiny of a whole nation, will hardly like, as long as the war

asts, to sit in a corner of some quiet library, and study
.actics and strategy. Then I believed that time would
:ure my wounds and make life, at least, supportable to
ne, even if it should be for ever sunless and gloomy.

"I had tried aimless wandering and had only ex-
)erienced the truth of that hacknied saying that shift-
ng of scenes can never change Tragedy into Comedy.

"Only once it seemed as if I might be allured back
.o that part of my life alone worth living for—my pro-
'ession!

"It was on a steamer between Marseilles and Genoa
—We had left the coast far behind us—suddenly the
Captain came up in great consternation, and asked if
.here was any doctor among the passengers. A lady
1ad been taken ill, and was lying in the cabin writhing
vith pain—I was just lying down to sleep, determined
10t to meddle in this matter, when I heard moans and
:xclamations from the cabin which would not let me
·est. I asked the Captain to take me down, and after
;earching the ship's medicine chest; found some re-
nedies which soothed the pain. The lady would not
et me go, but insisted in a strange medly of Spanish,
ind French on my passing the night on a sofa in the
idjoining cabin. At last she went to sleep, and my
;yes also closed, weary with gazing through the open
1atchway at the moon-lit sea.

"All at once, I felt something like an icy cold hand
Irawn across my face. I started up, believing it to be
he spray which was dashing off the wheels into the
:abin—but to my intense horror, I saw the figure of
£llen standing beside me, just as she had looked when
ying in her coffin, only her dim widely opened eyes
vere fixed on me, and her white finger was laid to her

lips, as if to say: 'Do not betray me.' Then she approached the couch of the stranger, lifted one of the green silk curtains and after gazing for several minutes on the sleeping woman she sadly shook her head, and looked gravely at me as if to reproach me for caring for another when I had left *her* to die. For one moment she sunk down at the foot of the bed as if greatly exhausted: then beckoning three times to me she glided through the hatchway like a streak of mist. Since that night I have never again approached a sick-bed. You know, Charles, that I was never of a visionary nature, that I do not believe in spirits. Of course I know as well as you do that this was only a delusion of the senses. An apparition caused by the over excited state of my nerves. But does this alter the main point? Did I suffer the less because I knew it to be owing to the power of my nerves over my reason? How can one, whose senses are at variance with him, hope to gain peace? and how is *he* to live, who hopes no longer?

"I have become a superfluous guest at the banquet of life, and so I prefer taking leave of it, and only press your hand once more before disappearing. My existence is now no longer necessary to any one—not even to a dog.

"None but a healthy and cheerful egotist could tolerate a life which subsists only for itself. Pardon me, my dear friend, I know that you will now and then miss me, but you would surely prefer; never to meet me again, than to recognize me some day in a mad-house; clothed in a straight waistcoat, and muttering soliloquies.

"This letter has nearly attained the dimensions of a volume, but as it is the last I shall ever write, its length

may be pardoned. I shall seal this enclosure with a
steady hand, for I am only about to do that which I
must, that which I believe to be for the best.

"Here in this solitary inn, they will only suppose
me to be some crazed Englishman who insists on
fishing by torch-light, in the middle of the night. To-
morrow when they see the boat driven on the lake
without me, they will say, I have only suffered for my
folly, by falling asleep, and tumbling overboard. Let
all my acquaintances suppose the same. And now
good night. I own that on the point of going to sleep,
I feel some curiosity, and hope to have many things—
made clear to me.—It is a pity that I shall not be able
to impart my observations to you, as we have always
done when studying together on terrestrial subjects.

"I am also desirous to witness what dreams may
haunt us in eternal sleep, if a dead man can witness
anything.

"Nothing further has any interest for me—My will
was deposed six months ago in the court of justice—
You are my executor—I thank you once more for your
faithful and firm friendship—Let this be my last word.

"EBERHARD."

He did not read over what he had written but
immediately folded it, put it in an envelope, sealed it,
and wrote the address—Then he again looked out of
the window—The storm had gradually subsided. He
lighted a cigar and pacing his room, he watched the
long-legged spiders crawling about the low ceiling,
and observed the effects of tobacco on them, by blowing a thick cloud of smoke over their backs. But he
soon grew tired of this interesting occupation, and

stared vacantly at the white washed walls that surrounded him. Suddenly a clamour arose in the adjoining tap-room. He heard through the door a gruff
voice which belonged neither to the landlord, nor to
the farm servant, complaining of some unreasonable
demand. "Yes it was always so, just those women who
cried and lamented if a baby had a cold, did not feel
the least compassion for two poor horses, but would
drag them from the manger, and after a journey of
fifteen miles, in this cursed weather; mostly uphill,
and over those dreadful roads, would force them to
trot for ten miles further, and the whole night through,
regardless as to whether they could move a limb on
the morrow or not. But he would not stir; no, not if
they were to lay down a hundred kronenthalers on the
very spot. He was not in the service of a knacker, but
had to deliver up his roadsters in the same condition
in which he got them; and besides to say the truth he
wished for some rest for himself, and did not care to
break his limbs on the way or get drowned in a
puddle.

A timid female voice which had now and then
interrupted this speech with beseeching words was
silenced by this conclusion, which was accompanied
by a fierce oath, and a heavy thump of the fist on the
table. The landlord intervened in his abrupt way by
seconding the coachman, and ordering some beer from
the cellar. Then the two men began to converse on
other subjects, the coachman chiefly abusing the bad
roads which ruined horses and carriage. The landlord
fully agreed with him, and asked him how it was that
the ladies had preferred coming by this side of the
dead lake. The coachman informed him that a land-

slip had made the other road quite impassable, at least for twenty-four hours. The rest of the passengers had been contented to wait at the station, but these ladies had insisted on continuing their journey on this dangerous road; perhaps because of the child, which never ceased to wail and moan. At this moment the door opened, and the men's rough tones were suddenly hushed. A melodious woman's voice was heard whose touching accents seemed to quiet even these coarse fellows. At least the coachman, who on her renewing her prayer to him to prepare for their departure, answered quite civilly, and without any superfluous oaths, that it was almost impossible to gratify her wishes, and gave his reasons. She appeared to acquiesce in their importance, and after a moment's silent reflection, asked if any messenger could be found who for a considerable gratification would undertake to summon the nearest doctor, otherwise the child would probably not live through the night. In saying this her voice trembled so much that the involuntary listener was touched to the heart. He walked to the casement, hoping to drown those soft tones in the rushing sound of the rain. At this moment however the clouds above the lake dispersed showing the moon's clear and silvery crescent and the sudden stillness forced him to hear the rest of the parley.

The landlord called his servant, and asked him if he would take a message to the doctor who lived six miles distant, in the small market-town which was situated in a neighbouring valley. The man replied that he had no objection to the long walk, or the bad road, if the lady gave him a liberal fee; but he knew that it would be useless for Hansel the forester's assistant had told him that very day, that his friend Sepp had to wait another week to have the ball extracted from his thigh, for the doctor himself was ill, from a fall from his horse, and his apprentice had an unsafe hand, as he was renowned for drinking too much brandy. Then the sad and gentle voice of the lady asked, after a silence of several minutes, if it would not be possible to procure a litter, and carry the child to the nearest place where a doctor resided, she herself would help to carry it; she only required a couple of trustworthy men, and a guide with a lighted torch.

That could not be done either, the landlord answered;—they had no litter on which the child could be carried comfortably, and then they could not all leave the house; however he would speak to his wife about it.

He was just reluctantly leaving his bench by the stove, when the landlady herself rushed into the room, and cried out that the nurse begged her mistress to come to the child—that departure was now not to be thought of, for the child was dying.

The listener in the adjacent room turned from the window as if drawn by some magic power; he took a few steps towards the door, then stopped and shook his head with a sigh. He tried to recommence his walk up and down the small room; but at every second step, he stood still to listen for some further sound. His cigar had gone out. Mechanically he approached it to the candle to light it, but before he was aware of what he was doing, his breath had extinguished the feeble flame. He remained staring at the dying sparks in the wick—one moment more and the last would disappear. Possibly in the next room a little flame far more valuable than the miserable light of this penny candle was on the point of relapsing into the darkness of night.

Well let it die out; what right had any one to meddle in the matter. Perhaps by trying to kindle it again, it would only the more surely be extinguished by his clumsy hands. What can it signify? Why try to save a human being's life, who may, some day or other, wish that he had never been born, and who may perhaps also see the hour, when he shall have to bid good night to his dearest friend——

Again he listened, and held his breath not to lose a sound of what was passing in the next room. He fancied he heard a child's plaintive moaning, then the lady's gentle voice trying to soothe it, passionate weeping, and then silence. He could stand it no longer in the solitude of his room. He only wished to hear how the child was going on. He began to think himself a barbarian, to be quietly hiding in a corner, when even these rough peasants showed some sympathy. Hastily opening the door, he groped his way through the dark empty tap-room, and across the passage. The door was ajar, and a ray of light streamed through the chink. He now distinctly heard the child moan and the mother quieting it. "We ought to prepare some tea for the poor child in order to bring on a perspiration," said the hostess, "We must try and find some."—"The elder berries, in the drawer up-stairs, would not do badly in case of need," answered her husband; then silence reigned again, only interrupted by the sighs of the house-maid, who knelt in a corner, repeating one pater-noster after another.

"Put another feather-bed on the child," advised

the coachman; "it has caught cold; see how its little hands twitch convulsively—it is freezing."

The farm-servant, who stood near the stove, was just going to lay another log on the still glowing embers, when he was arrested by a firm hand which was laid on his shoulders. He turned round and perceived the stranger standing before him. "I forbid you to put on another chip of wood;" he said, in a voice which denoted that he was accustomed to be strictly obeyed; "and you all," he continued, turning to the rest of the idle spectators, "get out of the room; do you hear? the air here is bad enough to stifle even a healthy man." They all looked at each other—only the mother and nurse of the child had not perceived the entrance of the stranger. The mother knelt beside the bed with one arm clasped round the moaning child as if to defend it from assassins. The nurse stood by her, and stared in helpless despair on her little charge— on its wandering eyes, and fever parched lips, from which now and then a low wail escaped. She started back, as if death in person was approaching her, when the stranger stept up to the bed, laid his hand on the burning brow, and took up one of the little thin arms to feel the pulse.

The shriek of horror which the nurse involuntarily uttered, awakened the mother from the lethargy of despair. She looked wonderingly at the stranger, and a sudden ray of hope brightened her face.

"Madam," he said, "will you entrust your child to one entirely unknown to you, who though he has not the presumption to promise to save its life, yet knows what in these cases, is prescribed by our feeble science."

She could not answer him; this unlooked for aid

in her direst distress overpowered her. "Take this," he said, drawing a card from his pocket-book, "my name may not be known to you, but the title which stands before it will show you, that others too have trusted to my skill; with what result, has nothing to do with the present case."

The young woman remained in her former position, but she stretched towards him the arm not engaged in supporting her child's head, and said: "The Almighty seems to have sent you, He has had compassion on me. I fully confide in you!"

"Then order a pitcher of fresh spring water from the well, and a tub to be brought. The rest I will manage myself."

He hastily opened both windows, and took the feather-bed from off the child, only covering it lightly with a large plaid. Then he called in the farm-servant who was standing in the passage, with the rest of the people, grumbling, and waiting for the result of the stranger's despotic interference. He asked if no snow or ice could be procured in the neighbourhood. "Yes," growled out the man, "there was some to be had; but one must climb for about an hour through the woods, to get to the crevice in a rock, where the snow never melted summer or winter, as the sun could not reach the spot. To-morrow morning he would go and fetch some!"

"You don't seem to undertand me," resumed the doctor; "here I lay down this kronenthaler; it is now half past nine o'clock; the moon is up, the storm has ceased—whoever brings me in the course of an hour, a load of snow or ice has gained this reward. To-morrow you may bring down a whole glacier, and will not get a penny for it." "All right," said the farm-servant with a short laugh, and walked away. The nurse had in the meantime brought in the cold water and an empty tub. Without another word, the stranger lifted the child from the bed, stripped off its clothes, and telling the mother to hold it, he poured the icy cold water over it. He then dried it quickly, laid it again in its bed, and wrapped a wet towel round its head. The child which a moment ago had struggled and screamed in his arms, now seemed relieved. The eyes ceased to wander, and turned towards the mother with a wondering, but calm look—then she closed them with a deep sigh.

"The child is dying!" the nurse screamed out, and burst into a fit of crying. "I thought that would be the consequence of the cold water, and the open windows. Ah, Madam, how could you suffer this?"

"Silence," said the stranger imperiously, "or you will have to leave the room. I hope, Madam," he continued, in a gentler tone, "that you do not expect a miracle from me. The illness we have to combat, cannot be vanquished in one night. The child has a virulent typhus fever, and our chief care must be to prevent the brain from being affected. But do not let every new symptom alarm you. As far as I can judge, no aggravating circumstances exist. You see the child has again opened its eyes. Nature already feels that we are assisting it. How old is the child?" "Seven years and a few weeks." "A fine child, so well deve-lopped; what anguish you must now suffer."

Tears streamed from the poor mother's eyes; she pressed her face against the little white hand which lay on the dark plaid. All the agitation of the last weary hours, dissolved in these refreshing tears.

At last she arose, and with a grateful look at the doctor, she sank into a chair which he had placed for her beside the bed. He too took a seat at the foot of it, and gravely but calmly observed the little girl. They were both silent. The nurse, ashamed of her thoughtless outbreak, went to and fro to renew the cold compresses. Without, all was still; the last clouds had disappeared and a ray of moonlight stole in, and shone slanting through the narrow casement, lighting up the small white hand of the young mother who was softly stroking the little hand of her child. The only sound which broke the silence proceeded from the streamlets formed by the rain, which were now rushing past the house, the regular dripping of the gutter, and the whistling of the coachman who was bedding his horses.

Suddenly the child raised herself on the pillows, looked at the stranger with widely opened eyes, and said: "Is this Papa? is he not dead? I want to give him a kiss, Mamma; has he not brought something for his little daughter? I want to sit on his knee. Where is Sophy? Oh! my poor head! Papa please hold my head. I am thirsty." Then the small fair head sank back on the pillow, and the eyes closed as if in pain. Eberhard rose and held a glass of fresh water to her burning lips. "Thank you, Papa," said the child. Then she became very quiet, only the twitchings of the feverish half opened mouth betrayed her sufferings.

"I must explain to you," the lady began, turning to the silent doctor, who had now resumed his seat," how it comes that my poor darling has those strange fancies. Unfortunately I must reproach myself with having caused this violent shock: The father of my poor little girl was an Austrian officer. A few months after our marriage, I had to part with him; his regiment was ordered to Italy, where the war was commencing. Shortly afterwards news reached me that he had been amongst the first victims of the bloody battle of Solferino. Since that time I have always felt the greatest longing to visit the spot where my dear husband found repose after his short career, and though no cross marks his grave, at least to inhale the air in which his brave heart breathed its last. Even my little girl expressed the same wish as she grew older, and understood me when I told her of her father's death. Many things deterred me from realizing this plan, particularly the fear that the long journey might overfatigue, and agitate the child, who always had a very excitable imagination, and a tender heart: and now I have to suffer severely for having indulged my desire. If you had seen how eagerly she listened to the words which I translated to her from the account of the old serjeant, whom I found watching the monument on the field of battle. Her cheeks burned, and her eyes glistened; her emotion was far beyond her years. When we turned back she shivered, and in the following night, complained of headache, and did not sleep for an instant. She did not mention her father again till this moment, when she mistook you for him, and fancied he was sitting at her bedside. Perhaps it would have been better, had I remained where I was, but I dreaded the Italian doctors, and did not believe the danger to be so imminent. In my own carriage, for I had taken post-horses on leaving the railway, I thought we could easily arrange a comfortable bed for the child. The weather too was warm, and she herself eagerly desired to be taken home. The storm reached us just at the worst part of the road; and we were most thankful when we reached this inn. But what would have become of us without your help?"

She turned from the gloomy and taciturn man to dry her tears. Then they again sat silently opposite each other. He felt tempted to entreat her to go on speaking. Here was something in her voice which soothed him, and was as cooling balm to his feverish soul, but he saw that her thoughts were again occupied with the child, and he had nothing to tell her. He only gazed more earnestly at the young woman by the dim light of the candle and of the moon. He remarked that her brow, and the shape of her eyes which had a distinguished melancholy and gentle expression in them, resembled those of his adoptive mother, who had so often looked at him with thoughtful affection. Her figure was round and supple, and every turn of her head and of her slender throat was full of grace.

The abundant auburn hair hung negligently over her shoulders. All about her showed the habits of one accustomed to wealth. Wealth enobled by a cultivated mind, and refined taste, but which had lost all charms for her, in the danger which threatened her most precious treasure.

The door was now cautiously opened, and the farm-servant dragged in a large tub filled with ice; then wiping the perspiration from his forehead, he triumphantly pointed to the clock which showed that ten minutes were still wanting to the stipulated hour, pocketed his well earned money, and officiously asked if anything else was wanted. "No, he could go to bed now," the doctor answered. He then tore a piece of oiled silk from the lining of his travelling pouch, made a bag of it to hold the ice, and showed the nurse how to lay it on the forehead of the child. Her mistress interfered—"No," she said, "you must now lie down, and rest, Josephine; you have not slept for thirty-six hours."—"Neither, Madam, have you," observed the maid, "and I do not need it so much as your honour, for at least I have swallowed a few morsels of food."

"Do as I tell you," resumed the mother; "I well know how useless it would be for me to attempt to sleep. Perhaps I may be able to take some rest in the morning, if the night passes well."

"Allow me to feel your pulse, Madam," said the doctor, and then without another word he suddenly left the room.

The two women looked after him in astonishment, and the maid, an elderly fat woman, with a round face, strongly marked by the smallpox, and good natured brown eyes, availed herself of his absence, to sing the praises of their unknown deliverer, quite as eagerly as she had previously abused him. "He had something so peculiar about him," she remarked; "he appeared to be ill and yet kind heartedness was written on every feature—and how cleverly he managed everything; how well he supported our child's head, just as if he had been a nurse all the days of his life. And then he is so very handsome and quite young, only now and then when a stern expression comes over his face, he looks so grave and gloomy, as if he had never laughed; and at other times he shuts his eyes, as if he were in great pain, and wished to conceal it."

At this moment the subject of her remarks returned,

carrying a large glass of milk in his hand. He gave
it to the lady as one would offer some medicine to a
child. "Drink this, Madam," he said; "it is new milk
and will do you good." "You require strength to ful-
fill the task you have undertaken, and here nothing else
is to be had. It would be very beneficial to the child,
if she could be induced to swallow a few drops.
Approach the glass to her lips, and persuade her to
try it; you have succeeded. We must do all we can
to keep up her strength, so that another attack may
not overcome her. Now follow my advice. and lie
down on that bed; I will watch the child, and the maid
also can well spare a few hours more of sleep. When
midnight has passed, I will awake you and then the
maid can lie down." She still objected. "Do as I
tell you," he said passionately, "or I will think that
you never really felt the confidence you showed me."

She turned towards the bed where the child, relieved by the ice compresses, lay apparently asleep and
stooping over its delicate little face kissed its closed
eyes. "I will obey you," she said, with a faint smile,
"if you promise to awake me, in case my child should
grow worse."

He silently pressed her hand and took her seat by
the bedside, while her maid helped her to lie down on
the second bed, which stood in a corner, after having
removed a load of coverings.

When a quarter of an hour had passed, the faithful
creature, softly approaching the doctor, who sat absorbed in his own thoughts, stooped, seized one of his
hands, and before he could prevent it had pressed it
to her lips, whispering: "God be praised, she sleeps!
Oh sir, you can work marvels! For four nights, my

mistress had not closed her eyes. First the grief, and agitation before we reached that unfortunate battle-field; and then, anxiety about her child. If you but knew what an angel my mistress is. If I were to tell you all. . . ."

"Leave that for another time," he interrupted; you have nothing else to do now, but to lie down, and not to stir till I call you. To-night you are useless, and to-morrow you must be up early. Here are pillows, and coverlets enough. Arrange a bed for yourself beside the stove; and now good night. Don't contradict me. Do you wish to awake your mistress by uselessly arguing the matter?"

The good woman obeyed with a timid humble look, pulled a feather-bed into a corner of the room, and in a few minutes her regular breathing, proved that she too had needed rest after the hardships of the last few days.

A short while afterwards, the moon disappeared behind a cloud, and only the faint reflex of the starry sky was to be seen, on that part of the lake which could be overlooked from the room in which the lonely watcher sat by the sick-bed. He now for the first time felt a desire to take some food, and to quench his thirst. He drank the remainder of the milk which still stood on the table. As he put down the glass he fancied he saw the lady on the bed make a convulsive movement. He approached her softly. In an uneasy dream, she had put both hands to her eyes as if to wipe away tears; now she slept quietly, and her hands slowly sank down again. Motionless he gazed on that fair face, on which every dream was reflected as the shadows of dissolving clouds on the calm surface of a lake; sorrow, anxiety, then hope! Now she smiled, and the delicately chiselled lips parted, disclosing two rows of pearly teeth. The next moment her brow darkened, an imploring look appeared on her face; she stretched out both her hands and clasped them together; he then remarked on one of her fingers, two wedding rings, and wondered whether the second one belonged to the father of her child, or if some other man were now in possession of that small hand. He was roused from these thoughts by a moan from the little girl. He only arranged the coverlet which had fallen on the ground and wrapped it round the small feet of the young woman who had not taken off her boots. Then he returned to his occupation of changing, every quarter of an hour, the ice that had melted and now and then refreshing the parched lips of the child with a few drops of water.

Towards midnight a violent wind arose on the lake, and the young man shivered as the window was still open. He seized the first wrap which he found among the luggage, and covered himself up with it. It was a long soft burnouss lined with silk which belonged to the young woman. He pulled the hood over his head; and a sweet scent was wafted from it; as the silk touched his face a peculiar feeling of languor came over him; he closed his eyes, but a confused maze of ideas passed through his mind, and he could not sleep.

Suddenly his eyes opened with an expression of terror in them. He started from his chair, and trembling violently, he stared at the lake. Conspicuous on the dark surface of the water, something white glided slowly; it had the shape of a veiled figure, and seemed to move towards the house. The moon had appeared again, and lit up a faint streak of mist which had strayed from the mountain tops, and was swept across the lake. When it reached the current of wind that blew from the ravine, it dissolved, and the surface of the water was as clear as before; but the only one who had seen this airy apparition still stood as if rooted to the ground and stared at the spot where it had disappeared. A cold perspiration bathed his brow, his breath came shortly and quickly, and his eyes, which started from their sockets, remained fixed on that spot, as if he expected to see the vision appear again the next moment.

A hot little hand touched the clammy ones of the horror-stricken man. "Is it you, Papa?" asked the little girl; and sat up in her bed. Two small thin arms were stretched up to him and before he was aware of it, the child clung to his neck and hid its burning face on his breast. "Don't leave us again, Papa," she said, "or Mamma will cry again, and I must die."

In an instant the nightmare which oppressed him, vanished. He clasped the slender little figure in his arms, as if it were a protection against the malignant powers. He held her so for some time, and while the child caressed him, he felt the blood flow more calmly through his veins. He kissed her little face, stroking her damp curls, asked: "What is your name, my child." "Are you my Papa," she said, "and do not even know that I am your own little Fan? Ah, yes, I know that they have shot you, that is why you have forgotten me. Did it hurt you much?"

"To-morrow I will tell you all about it," he said,

and gently laid her back on her bed; "now, you must keep quiet, and not awake your Mamma."

The child obediently lay down, and closed her eyes, but she held fast the hand of her faithful guardian, and now and then looked up at him with a wondering but wide awake expression. He too stedfastly gazed on the innocent face, as if fearing that were he to turn round, the terrifying vision would again appear.

So he watched by the sick-bed till day dawned. When the bare rocky peaks which rose above the lake, blushed in the first morning light, sounds of life, broke the stillness of the house.

The farm-servant crept shoeless along the passage, and cautiously peeping into the sick-room, pointed to the now empty wooden tub and asked if another supply of ice were wanted. The doctor nodded his head, and he disappeared. Then came the landlady and offered her ready services, but Everhard declined them. The generosity of the strange gentleman had worked wonders with the inmates of the house. Only the coachman, who had not got over his intoxication of the previous day, stumbled, cursing, and growling, with heavy boots, down the stairs, and through the passage; so that the lady asked still half asleep, if it were time to start. "Not yet," answered Everhard, "you can sleep on for another hour." Then he rose hastily, and went out to prevent the noisy fellow from again approaching the sick-room. When he returned after a few minutes, he found the young mother seated at the bedside of her child.

"Why are you up already?" he asked reproachfully. "Already?" she replied, "you wish to put me to confusion. Have you not succeeded in deceiving me, and taken my place through the whole of the night. Why did you not let me share the night-watch with you?"

"Because I could easily dispense with sleep, which was most needful for you. And then there was nothing to be done which required help. Be of good cheer; we have every reason to be satisfied with this night."

"Then the danger is over! thanks be to heaven!"

"I cannot give you that certainty," he answered; "you have promised to trust me, and can only do so, if I conceal nothing from you. But I can give you the assurance that all the symptoms are as favourable as can be expected in this illness. The inmates of the house are well disposed towards us, and will do their best to help us."

A ray of pleasure brightened her pale face. "Oh! my friend," she exclaimed, "if it were but possible!" She held out her hand to him, and tears stood in her eyes.

He stooped to kiss her hand, but in reality to hide his emotion. "Could you have believed me capable of forsaking you, before the child's life was saved?" he asked. "Do not thank me, not imagine that I am sacrificing anything by remaining here. I have already brought you the greatest sacrifice I could offer, all the rest is a relief to me."

She looked up inquiringly. "I am keeping you from other duties?" she asked.

"No," he answered gloomily; "ever since last year I have been an idle, and restless man. Led by motives, which cannot interest you, I once gave myself my word of honour, never to exercise my profession as a doctor again. Yesterday, I broke this word for your sake. If you will permit me to continue my attendance, you will free me from reproach, and so we shall be of mutual service to each other."

After a pause during which he had felt the pulse of the child, he resumed, "She now sleeps quietly; if you wish to apprize your friends of your present abode, you have time to do so. The coachman, who is meanwhile getting ready, will post your letter at the next station."

"I have no one, who would feel anxious at my non-appearance," said the lady, and blushed slightly; "I live so very retired!"

"No one?" he repeated, with surprise, and involuntarily his eyes fastened on the two rings.

She remarked his glance, and understood it instantly. "The second ring," she said unconstrainedly, "is not the sign of a second marriage. It belonged to my husband, who feeling death approaching, drew it from his finger and begged a comrade of his to bring it to me. Since that day, I have refused all solicitations to change my condition, and have only withdrawn from my dear husband's family, because a near relation of his, imagines that he has some claim to my hand. I have vowed to live only for my child, and to the memory of the dead, and this vow is sacred to me."

The nurse now awoke, and reluctantly sat up on her couch, but she jumped up briskly, when she saw her mistress and the doctor already actively employed, and hastened with great zeal to relieve them; protesting that it was all the doctor's fault, as he had strictly forbidden her to watch.

"Bathe the child," said Everhard; "I will now leave you for half an hour; bathe the child as we did yesterday, and let it drink some milk which you can now get fresh from the cow. And here comes a fresh supply of ice. You see the attendance could nowhere be better than it is in this desolate nook of the world. Fortunately an apothecary's shop is not needed in this case. Good-bye; we shall soon meet again." He bowed slightly and left the room. Then he walked down to the shore, loosened one of the boats which were chained up in the shed, and with a few powerful strokes launched the light bark into the open lake. The sun had not yet risen above the surrounding heights, overgrown with dark pines, and the calm and sultry air lay heavily on the dark surface of the water, and oppressed the chest of the young man who was fatigued by the sleepless night. He looked down into the depths below him and noticed that close to the boat the water seemed transparent as crystal, and nearly white, while the lake beyond, though the sky was bright and clear, appeared like a black unfathomable chasm. He recollected what a woodcutter had once told him, that the lake was bottomless—that its waters sank deeper and deeper till at last they reached hell; and so when the evil spirits there found their abode too hot for them, they went to bathe in them.

He pulled in his oars and looked up at the nearly perpendicular shores which were covered with dark fir-woods up to their very peaks. These had exchanged the glow of early morning for a dull greyish tint. And now the sun had burst forth with great power, and tried to gild the ravine, which looked like a cauldron of dark iron. But only a dazzling white light was reflected on the smooth surface of the lake. The dense woods which surrounded it absorbed every ray of sunshine. No cheerful light coloured and enlivened the dreary landscape. A small patch of green grass, near the inn, on which a red-brown cow grazed, and the blue smoke which curled up from the chimney were the only objects that awakened the consoling thought, that even in this wilderness human beings had found a home. An islet, covered with birch-trees, lay near the opposite shore. Everhard rowed up to it, tied the bark to a post, and stripped off his clothes to enjoy an early bath.

Suddenly the thought struck him, with what intention he had arrived yesterday. He shuddered. It seemed to him as if his resolve would be fulfilled, even against his will; as if he had pledged himself to that perfidious depth, which would claim him for its own. One moment he felt tempted to put on his clothes again, and to row back as fast as he could, but ashamed of his weakness, he shook off these fancies and boldly jumped into the water.

The cold Alpine waves closed round him like ice just melted by the sun, and he had to exert all his knowledge of swimming, to keep his blood, by continual movement, from congealing. When he stepped out of the water, and leaning against the stem of a young birch, his feet buried in the soft moss, dried himself briskly, he felt happier than he had done for many a day. He looked towards the house. In the room, where the child lay he could see some one moving near the window. The distance was too great to distinguish the figure, still less the features, yet it pleased to him to think that among the inmates of that house, there were some who needed him, and had placed their hopes in him.

Meanwhile the child in the sick-room raised herself in her bed, looked searchingly round the room, and said: "Has Papa gone away? is he again dead? I want him to sit beside me." Her mother kissed the child's forehead and begged her to remain quiet. "That good gentleman is not your Papa," she said; "you must not call him so. He is the doctor, who will make you well again, if you are a good child, and do all he tells you." "Not my Papa," repeated the little girl meditatively. She seemed to relinquish her first idea with difficulty. "What is his name?" she resumed. "Will he leave me?"

"Here he comes," said the fat nurse, who had tears in her eyes, on hearing her darling speak calmly and sensibly, for the first time for several days. "Just look Ma'am, how fast he rows, as if he were impatient to get back to our child. Well, I call that a doctor! To-day he looks even handsomer, than he did yester-day, with his fine black beard and pale face. Only his eyes have a stern expression, that would frighten one if he were not so kind."

They now saw him leap from the boat but he did not speak to them, as he passed the door, and they heard him give some orders to the landlady. A few minutes later he entered the sick-room, at once ap-proached the bed of the child, and talked kindly to it. This presence seemed to exercise a sort of charm on the little girl. She breathed with more ease, and closed her eyes at his persuasion.

The stillness in the sick-room was so great that they heard the splash of the fish leaping in the water.

After some time he rose, and whispered, "She sleeps; the fever has abated. I hope she may be able to rest for a few hours, and I will take care that no one disturbs her. I will now lie down for a short while, till the chicken broth I have ordered for our little patient, is ready.

"How can I ever express my thanks to you for all your kindness, and solicitude," observed the child's mother with much emotion.

By not thanking me at all he replied almost gruffly, and left them.

When he entered his room, he found the letter he had written the night before still lying on the table. The large red seal now, seemed offensive to his eyes, yet he could not make up his mind to destroy it, so he put it by, in his portfolio. He then threw himself on his bed, and tried to sleep, but the thick coming thoughts, beset him like buzzing flies. He fancied he heard the child's voice, and that of its lovely mother, and raised himself on his bed to listen. At length after much musing and reflection, he fell into an uneasy sleep disturbed by dreams.

At noon, the landlady entered his room, and seeing him asleep, tried to creep away noiselessly. But he was up in a moment, and inquiring if the soup were ready, followed her into the kitchen. "Where is the broth?" he asked, and approached the hearth whence a tempting odour arose from the different pots and pans. The stupid maid who was stirring something in one of them, let fall her wooden ladle in amazement, and stared open-mouthed at the stranger as he lifted the lid of one of the pots, and examined its contents with a critical eye. Then he asked for a plate poured some of the chicken broth into it, and carefully took out the herbs which floated on it.

When he turned to carry away the soup, he saw the young mother standing at the entrance. "Is this right?" she asked with a charming smile, "instead of sleeping I see you have turned cook."

"I only cook for my patients," he replied, "the care of preparing dinner for the healthy, I leave to our hostess, who will do honour to our confidence in her, and needs no help of mine. Is our patient still asleep?"

"She awoke a moment since, and has just asked for you."

When he entered the sick-room, the child sat upright in her bed, and greeted the doctor with a smile. Then she willingly swallowed a few spoonfuls of the soup which he offered her. She did not appear to be hungry however, but only to do it because he wished it. She listened eagerly to all the doctor said. He told her that in the morning he had watched the fish disport themselves in the lake, and promised her that they would go and catch some of them when she could leave her bed.

After a while she again seemed to lose consciousness. Her blue eyes partially closed, and the small head sank back on her pillows.

"Be of good cheer," said the doctor; "the progress is slow but sure. Your maid must continue to change the ice frequently. Meanwhile we will go and have dinner. It is ready."

"Leave me here with my child," she whispered. "No," he replied, curtly. "You must breathe the fresh air. We do not want another patient, and your pulse is much agitated. When we have dined, we will relieve the nurse."

He walked on without another word, and she dared not oppose him. In the shade before the house, close to the window of the sick-room, the cover had been laid for two. Just as they came out, the landlady brought a dish of fish, and placed them on the table, these were followed by a roasted fowl. During the repast they hardly spoke a word to each other. Both were lost in thought. Now and then, he would persuade her, not only to take a few mouthfuls on her plate, but to eat them. "I shall be offended," he said, gaily, "if you eat nothing. We doctors enjoy the reputation of being great gourmands. I hope I have not disgraced my profession in this instance?"

"Pardon me, if I cannot yet bear the brightness around me," she said. "My heart has been too deeply troubled. I have passed through such heavy storms, that the ground still trembles beneath me. To-morrow I will behave better." Then they both relapsed into silence, and gazed at the lake, over which the mid-day heat was brooding. A cricket chirped in the quiet little garden; and within the landlord snored on his bench by the stove. From the shed by the lake, the gurgle of the waves against the softly rocking boats was heard, and from the sick-room the nurse humming a nursery rhyme, the same with which years ago she had lulled the child in her cradle to sleep.

. . . .

The quiet day was followed by a restless night. The fever increased in violence; the child moaned continually, and could hardly be kept in her bed. At midnight she grew calmer.

The doctor hardly stirred from the house; only in the evening, he refreshed himself with a cigar out of doors. Then he took a turn round the house, and every time he passed the window of the sick-room, stopped for a moment, and spoke a few words of encouragement to the mother who would not quit the bed-side. In the night, while watching with her—the nurse had been sent to bed—he suddenly said: "How much your child resembles you. Just now, in this dim light, when you stooped over her and the little girl looked up to you with that peculiarly spiritual and pre-cocious expression which illness gives, I could almost have fancied that you were sisters. Ten years hence, she will be your very image." "Perhaps you are right," answered the young mother, "but the resemblance is only outward: all her mental qualities she inherits from her father. I often wonder at so great a likeness in such a young child, and *that* too a girl. Her truth-fulness her self-denial, her courage often make me feel as if my lost husband had been given back to me in this child."

"You are mentioning qualities, which during our short acquaintance, I have remarked that you possess in a high degree."

She shook her head, "If I seem courageous, it is only owing to my natural cowardice. When you first saw me I was quite broken-hearted with misery, and anxiety, but I dared not give vent to my feelings, for I knew that I should break down utterly at the sound of my own voice. My husband could look the most fearful events calmly in the face; and so it is with the child. He could make any sacrifice without thinking of himself."

"And you; I should think, you did not spare your-self in the first days of this trial."

"A mother's heart feels no sacrifice," she answered, "but before my child was born I often had to strive with myself, and force myself to do what was distaste-ful to me for the sake of others. It is not so with the child, though youth generally is, and well may be, the season for egotism. I could tell you a hundred traits of her excellent disposition. I have often felt anxious about her, for so precocious a tenderness of feeling is said to be the presage of a short life. Who can tell whether it may not be realized."

Everhard looked out on the lake, and seemed not to have heard her last words. Suddenly he said; "you have probably a portrait of your husband: Will you show it to me?"

She took off a delicately worked Venetian chain, which she wore round her neck, opened the locket which was fastened to it, and handed it to him.

He gazed at it for several minutes, and then silently gave it back to her. After a long pause he said, "Was it a youthful attachment?"

"Not quite what is generally so called. I was, cer-tainly very young when I made his acquaintance. Be-fore I saw him no man had ever made any impression on me; but I hardly knew how dearly I loved him till a month after our marriage took place. I only learnt to appreciate him fully during the short period of our union, and my love grew into a passion when I had lost him for ever. Had you known him, you would have become friends; he never had an enemy."

Everhard had risen and was pacing the room with noiseless steps. He stopped before the table and took up a volume which projected from a travelling bag. They were Lenau's poems. On the fly leaf was inscribed the name of Lucille.

"Does this poet please you?" asked the doctor.—

"I hardly know whether he repels, or attracts me; and although I generally have a clear perception in such things, yet I cannot quite discover in his thoughts, what is genuine and what is artificial. He suffered much, yet it often appears to me, as if by continually irritating them, he purposely re-opened his wounds. I hardly know why I took this book on my journey; perhaps as a sort of consolation."

"You seek consolation with a poet so weary of life?"

"Why not? *He* died mad. When I think of that death, the grief for my husband's seems easier to bear, for what a glorious death was granted to *him!* Young, loved by all, he died heroically for his country! I carry his image undefaced in my heart, not distorted by illness, and the last agony, nor estranged from me by insanity. How dreadful must it not be to see one dear to us deprived of his senses. Do you not feel the same?"

He was silent for a moment, and then replied by another question: "So you would have thought the death of your husband desirable, if he had been doomed to life long insanity?"

"Spare me the answer. I cannot give you one truthfully, without pain."

"So much the better," he said. She did not understand him. A few minutes later he left the room.

He returned an hour after midnight, and insisted

on relieving the mother from her watch by the sick-bed. She could not resist his imperative manner, and only begged him to let her, and the nurse, relieve him alternately. He promised to do so; and this time kept his promise. In the morning when Lucille awoke, she found the nurse alone, and heard that the doctor lay on a straw mattress in the tap-room to be near at hand in case of need.

.   .   .   .   .   .

A week had passed since these events, and Everhard again sat in his little room at the crazy table, and the candle cast the same dim flickering light, as on that first occasion, only the moon shone so brightly through the casement, that one could easily have dispensed with any other light. Everhard had just perused the letter written on that dark and gloomy night, and was now adding a postscript on the blank page.

"A week older, Charles; and yet a week younger! When I look at my face, and compare it with the aged features which appear to me in these pages, then I find that I have made the most retrograde movement, and have again arrived at an age, at which even you did not know me; at a time when I never thought of death, though I touched it daily with my dissecting knife; *then* I had no more thought of it, than a child's doctor has of catching the measles. I have now studied the morbid symptoms in my letter, as coolly as I once did the strange countenance of number So and so in the hospital.

"You will be glad to hear that I have surmounted my last crisis, but I, when I search my thoughts, can only deplore this.

"Everything was ready for my departure, my trunks so nicely packed, the last leave takings exchanged; I heard the shrill whistle of the engine,—suddenly I am told that I have missed the train; and so I remain, not at home, nor abroad, but sitting at the railway station in a most provoking position. It seems ridiculous to have to stay and unpack, after all these preparations for departure. How it all happened I will tell you in a few words, lest you should think that cowardice overcame me at the last moment, that I regretted to leave this life, and persuaded myself that after all it was the best. No it was not that which played me this trick, it was my old passion, my profession! I found it of more importance to save a young life, than to despatch my own, so prematurely old. The child in question was well worth the trouble, that I can tell you. And as for the mother! don't fancy that I have fallen in love; you would be mistaken. Or do you call love, the feelings of a poor devil of a miner who after having been buried in a coal-pit, is brought to life again and rejoices in the first breath of fresh air. Do not be afraid that I shall give you a description of this young woman's charms. Whether she be handsome, amiable—what is usually so called; clever, or whether she possess all those qualities the description of which generally fills columns, I know not. All I know, is that in her presence, I forget my existence; the past, the future—all I feel is that she is there beside me and that I would desire nothing more to all eternity, than that she should remain so. Do you recollect how strange it once seemed to us, that the same passionate poet, from whose brain proceeded 'Werther' should have expressed such tame feelings as these—

'Gaze at the moon,
'Or think of thee,
'I fancy 'tis the same.
'All in a holy light, I see,
'And know not how it came.'

"And now to my shame be it spoken, I experience
the same feelings in myself. This lunacy, as we jestingly
called it, has taken such possession of me, that my only
desire at present is, that through all the future years of
my life, I might live as in one long night, surrounded
by the pale veiled halo which now calms my soul.

"This is but a dream. Ere long I must insist on
my little patient's departure to more civilised regions,
where she will be better provided for during her convalescence, than she can be here, where chicken-broth
is the landlady's sole culinary achievement. Then I
shall become unnecessary, and can bid farewell to
the Dead Lake, and once more try to live in a world
which after these events will seem doubly desolate to
me. Was I not right in deploring the departure of the
train? By this time I should have reached my destination. But why should not the journey be only post-
poned for a fortnight; especially as the one I had
intended to take does in no wise depend on the weather,
or the company. I can tell you the reason, Charles; I
know that you will not despise me for it. My courage
is gone! Is it so very despicable that I now dread that
gloomy depth, into which a week ago I was willing to
plunge; now that I have found a place of rest up here
in the daylight? And though in a few days I shall be
again roaming about, like the wandering unsettled
savage I was, up to this last week, yet nothing can
ever efface from my heart the feeling that somewhere
between heaven and earth there is a corner where I

could live in repose; where, like that Matricide, in Sophocles, I had found a sanctuary from which, awed by the holiness of the refuge even the furies keep aloof, and dare not sully the threshold.

"Unfortunately, it is perfectly clear to me that from her, I also must keep aloof. This woman even if I ventured to offer her my unamiable society for the remainder of her life, could but politely decline. She has made a vow to remain faithful to the memory of her dead husband. What is a vow? Ought it to be a chain to bind and check our very existence, after we have outgrown our former selves. In the course of seven years the physical part of man is completely renewed, and is our spiritual part, surrounded by new flesh and blood to remain the same, because some misanthrope doubted his own power of revival. Have I not also broken my vow never again to approach a sick-bed. And I even deem this to be rather to my credit than my shame. But the vow of this woman is raised far above the fickleness of human wishes and resolves. She wishes me well; I could find no truer friend in need than she would prove. She would make any sacrifice but this for me, who have saved her child; but her whole existence, her heart, and soul are rivetted to the memory of her own passed happiness, and to the future happiness of her child—and for me, to whom the present alone is of importance.... I have carefully avoided the question as to where she lives, in what town, under what circumstances in what neighbourhood. I will part from her without knowing anything of this, lest I should be tempted to seek her, and endeavour to make the impossible possible.

"A few days more of the happiness of this singular

position—in this solitary wilderness among the mountains, far from all the littlenesses and miseries of the world, and as if we were in heaven, where there is neither giving in marriage, nor parting—then come what may; what must!.

"In truth it is a strange and cruel remedy which fate has employed, making a deep incision in my heart, in order to convince me how little I was ripe for death; how much strength and feeling there was still in me, how much I could yet endure!

"Enough of this for to-day. We live here totally deprived of all postal communication. When, and where, I shall close this letter and forward it, the Gods only know, if indeed they concern themselves with our correspondence.   "Farewell!"

He laid down the pen and listened. From the sick room, the child's soft prattle was heard and though free from the restless and rambling tone of fever, yet it was an unusually late hour for the child to be awake. He also heard the soft voice of the mother calming it by a few soothing words. When Everhard entered the room the child was already fast asleep.

"She has just been dreaming of you;" turning towards him with one of her charming smiles; she told me, she dreamt that you had given her a white lamb, with a red ribbon round its neck, which took food from her hand. She had possessed it for some time when it suddenly occurred to her that she had not thanked you for it; so she begged me to call you that she might repair this neglect."

"And why did you not call me?" asked the doctor.

"I told her that her uncle Everhard would never

listen to any thanks. That Mamma too had received a gift from him for which she never, never could thank him sufficiently. The best way to thank him, was to be a good child and go to sleep again. You should have seen how earnestly the dear child tried, after this, to go to sleep. You see she is asleep already and her forehead is moist. You have more influence, over her than any other person has."

He thoughtfully contemplated the childish face.

"I regret that I am not a princess," Lucille continued with a slight blush; "for then I could offer you a place at my court, and beg you to accompany me on my travels in the capacity of Court Physician. I cannot imagine what we shall do without you—at every cold little Fanny catches, we shall miss you sadly. And yet I am content with my station in life. A princess would perhaps presume that she could repay you for your devotion to her child by offering you an establishment. I cannot regret the feeling that I can never repay you for all your generosity." She stretched out her hand to him, which he pressed, strangely moved, to his lips.

"Madame Lucille," he said, without continuing the subject, "it is now eleven o'clock; it is my turn to watch, and you are relieved."

"No," she answered gaily, I am not quite so obedient as our little Fan, or rather, sleep does not so readily obey my call. You must allow me to remain awake for another hour, and if you are not tired, you shall read aloud to me. I have seen a volume of Gœthe's works in your hands. I admire him above all other poets, and wish to get more fully acquainted with him, for I must confess to my shame, that on looking through your volume the other day, I remarked that most of its contents were unknown to me.

"As you please," he said, "but most of its contents will remain for ever new to you, were you to hear them ever so often. At least that is my experience of them."

He fetched the book, the first volume of the poems, and without selecting any particular poem began at the first page. He lowered his voice but read without any studied art of delivery. Never had he so keenly and clearly felt the charm of the everlasting spring which emanates from the blossoms of the poet's youthful ardour.

He dared not look at her whilst he read fearing to meet the mute enquiry in the eyes of the young woman; but when he came to "the hunter's evening song," he with difficulty faltered out the words,

> 'Gaze at the moon,
> 'Or think of thee,
> 'I fancy 'tis the same.
> 'All in a holy light, I see,
> 'And know not how it came!'

Suddenly he stopped, let the book glide on to the bed of the child, and rose hastily.

"What has happened?" she asked, startled. "Go and rest," he replied with averted face. "Wake the nurse; she can take my watch for this night. The atmosphere here oppresses me, I must breathe the fresh air, I already feel better, since I have risen. I will go and take a row on the lake."

So saying he disappeared, leaving her with all her feelings in a state of tumultuous disturbance at the enigma she dared not solve.

. . . .

The next day at their early meeting, they succeeded in assuming the gay and unconstrained tone which had hitherto existed between them. The child assisted them in their efforts. The night had been quiet and refreshing, and a bath which had been prepared for her, under Everhard's superintendence; in an old washing tub of the landlady's had greatly revived her, and had sent her off into another long sleep. Towards evening the doctor brought home from his walk different kinds of ferns, gentians, and also gaily coloured pebbles which he had found near the rocks. He sat down by Fanny's bed-side, and told her all about the birds, and other small animals which he had met in his wanderings over the heights. He was pleased at the intelligent questions the child put to him, as she sat up in bed and admired with wide opened eyes the treasures he had laid on her coverlet. The mother sat beside them working at a piece of embroidery. From the kitchen without was heard the crackling of the fire on the hearth, over which the child's soup was being prepared. Everhard did not relinquish his night watch this time, but no more was said of reading aloud. Neither was there any mention made of it during the following nights, and indeed no occasion for it presented itself. The night watching had now become almost unnecessary, so the doctor could, without further apprehension, remain a good deal in his room. Even in the day-time, now that the child was allowed to be up for several hours, he seldom appeared. But often under pretext of fishing he would row over to the islet from whence he did not return till late in the evening, or he would roam through the pine woods and the ravine, and climb up to the ice cavern.

The farm-servant who hearing that the lady wished

for the last strawberries of the season had climbed up there, to look for some, reported on his return that he had met the doctor seated on a rock, and looking like a man in a dream. He had bidden him good day, and the doctor had started up, and with a silent nod of recognition, had disappeared in the wood. He was evidently touched in the head, the farm-servant continued; I always said so from the moment I saw him sitting quite crazed like in the tap-room, and refusing all refreshment.

This continued during several days. In proportion to the progress of the child's recovery did the doctor's melancholy, from which the sudden call of duty had roused him, appear to increase. Those days were full of gloom; he felt how necessary it was to abridge them. One forenoon he started without waiting for dinner, not caring to meet the sad inquiring look in Lucille's eyes. He climbed up the steep ravine with the firm resolve to arrive at a final decision. In spite of the fierce noon-day heat, he pursued a road which he had recently discovered, and which led towards the south across the rocky ridge of the mountains. He knew that if he continued his walk he would reach before night fall a Romanic* village which was separated from the dead lake by nearly impassable tracts of ice and snow. Once there, and he had achieved all that now seemed impossible to him, all leave taking was spared him and he was as one dead to those to whom he had now become useless.

This seemed to him the best plan, and he relied on his strength of will to carry it out. But when the

* A part of Switzerland on the frontiers of Italy.

The Translator.

last glimpse of the lake had disappeared and he found himself surrounded only by the sterile wilderness of rocks, he felt so wretched that he could not proceed, but flung himself on the ground, in the shade of a projecting rock, and buried his face amidst the moss and heather. He eagerly sought for all the reasons which should prevent his departure, and make his return necessary, his papers, his diary which he had left in his room; the anxiety his sudden disappearance would cause Lucille. Then he reflected that he was in duty bound to provide for their departure, and for their safe journey to the next town. He made a solemn vow that all should be done that very day. He would send down the farm-servant to order a carriage as soon as he had returned to the inn. In twenty-four hours everything would be accomplished, and the separation irrevocable. After that he did not care what happened.

When he had firmly settled this in his mind, he felt relieved, and hastily arose to reach the inn without further delay. He resolved to be cheerful and to enjoy the few hours that remained to him of her society as if they were to last for ever. He regretted having embittered many a day by the thought of the approaching end. He plucked a bunch of scentless Alpine flowers and ferns—it should be his farewell token to little Fanny. So thinking he rapidly descended the steep mountain, and reached the last firs in the ravine when the greatest heat of the day was over. Below him lay the lake. Not the slightest breeze ruffled its calm surface which clearly reflected the small meadow on the opposite shore; the firs on the steep slope above it, and beyond these, the bare grey rocks and crags. Then he looked towards the fisherman's house. His quick eye discerned every shingle on its stone laden roof—in the yard, the old hen followed by her yellow brood, and the linen hung out on ropes to dry. Those who lived beneath that lowly roof were nowhere to be seen. Generally at this time of the day, everyone dozed over some slight work, so Everhard was much surprised when he saw the door of the house open, and a perfect stranger step out into the bright sunshine. He was a tall young man dressed in a light summer costume. His face was partly shaded by a broad brimmed straw-hat, and only a fair moustache of a military cut was visible underneath it.

The newcomer stood still for a few minutes, looked around him as if to examine the weather, and then eagerly talked through the open door to some one who had not yet appeared. A few minutes later Lucille joined him, without a hat, only holding a large parasol to protect her delicate complexion from the sun. She accompanied the stranger to the shed on the lake, and a moment after Everhard saw them both issue from it, in one of the boats, and take the direction across the smooth lake towards the islet. The stranger wielded the oars so dextrously that they soon reached their destination. Then leaping on shore he assisted Lucille to get out. They walked along the shore wending their way between the birches and the high bulrushes, apparently with the intention of making the circuit of the small island. Everhard's heart throbbed so wildly that he had to lean against the stem of a fir-tree till the first giddiness had passed.

Who was the new comer who seemed so intimate with her, that she followed him on his boating excursions, and thus granted him what she had ever refused to Everhard her friend and helper? Who was this stranger that she leant on his arm, and while walking by his side, and gaily conversing with him seemed even to forget her child, and abandoned it to the care of the nurse? Well whoever it was, he had arrived just in time to wake them all out of the dream into which the solitary stillness of the place had lulled them.

Doubtless the sight of this old acquaintance brought back to Lucille's remembrance all that she had forgotten at the bed-side of her child; her intercourse with the outer world; her friends, and admirers, recollections to which Everhard would ever remain a stranger, and which summoned her back to a life in which he could have no share. So much the better! It could but facilitate the execution of his resolves, and confirm the urgency of a separation.

He felt it was impossible to share her presence with a third. He strode down the precipitous path, and reached the house greatly exhausted, and his knees knocking under him. He remarked a travelling carriage which stood beside the shed, and in the stables in which a cow was kept during the winter, two horses were tied to the manger. Without heeding the landlady who was dying to tell him the news, he walked straight into the room where the child sat at the table playing with a new doll.

"Uncle Max is here," she cried out to him, her face beaming with joy. "He has brought me a doll that can move its eyes; then he dined with Mamma, and now they are both on the island. They will soon return however, as Uncle Max means to take us away in his large travelling carriage, but Mamma said that she would not move a step without your special consent."

"Fanny," he said, and took the child's curly head between his hands, "you won't forget me, though I cannot offer you a beautiful doll, but only a simple bunch of flowers?"

The child looked up surprised; "Mamma said that after the good God, I should love you best, because you have saved my life. I love you better than all other people; but Mamma I love best of all."

He stooped over the fair face, and kissed the child's truthful loving eyes, and her pale lips.

"You are right, little Fan," said he, speaking with difficulty, "she deserves your love. Here is my bouquet, and give her my compliments." He turned towards the door.

"What are you going away! the child called after him; won't you come, and tell me some nice story."

"Another time," was all he could say. The nurse who just then came in, tried to detain him, and wondered at his disturbed appearance, but he passed her by, and hastening to his own room locked the door behind him.

Once more alone, he was so overcome by the agony of his feelings that he dropped into a chair and his strong frame shook with convulsive though tearless sobs. But he promptly recovered himself, pressed his hand to his heart as if to still its throbbings and proceeded to stuff his few possessions into his travelling bag. Only his portfolio he kept back; then he sat down at the table, and mechanically took out the letter to his friend as if to add another postscript, but he vainly sought for words and he finally laid it down, took up another sheet and began to write a short account of the child's illness, with the intention of leaving it to Lucille in case she should find another consultation necessary.

He found a certain satisfaction in clearly wording his statement, and in perceiving how steadily his hand wielded the pen. "At least I have not yet lost my senses," he said aloud.

He had just finished this writing when a man's quick step was heard approaching his room, and then came a knock at the door. He rose with an angry feeling. He could not deny his presence, and yet this meeting was intensely distasteful to him. He unlocked the door with a countenance which was anything but inviting. The moustachied stranger however entered with the most amiable air. Apparently he did not expect a very gracious reception, but seemed fully determined not to let himself be put out by anything.

"My dear doctor," he exclaimed in an engaging manner, and with a friendly shake of the hand. "Pray excuse my intruding on you; Lucille has told me that you refuse to listen to any thanks, but I am not to be daunted; I am a soldier and would think it dishonourable to be afraid of anything; even of the glum face of a benefactor; and so I boldly express my thanks, at the risk of being challenged by you afterwards, and tell you that I shall always feel indebted to you, and that you can command my services at any time as you would those of your oldest friend.—You have worked wonders, you best of doctors! Not only with the little one, whose welfare I have at heart as though it were my own child, but above all with the mother—I can assure you that I hardly recognized her. From the time when her husband my dear brother was buried with his comrades in one common grave on the field of battle, her widowed grief, up to a few weeks ago, had always remained the same. All the efforts of her friends to restore her to her former cheerfulness were vain. Seven years! In truth, I should say that the most legitimate grief might be overcome in that time. Between ourselves, be it said, though I sincerely loved my brother, yet I have found these seven years unconscionably long. Lucille was my lady love as well as my brother's, but then I was only a good for nothing lieutenant, and so I had to yield the precedence to my brother Victor. Now it seems to me that I have every right to assert my claim considering that it is of such long standing. Don't you think so, doctor? But in spite of my perseverance through all these years, not the slightest ray of hope was ever granted to me. I wished to accompany her on this visit to the grave; but no, my request was mercilessly refused. Wait till she has returned, I said to myself; who knows but this visit may be the last stage of her conjugal grief. So I waited for her return, or at least for a letter, but when three weeks had passed without any tidings of her, fearing that some misfortune had happened, I took leave of absence from my regiment, and traced her steps till I found her here at the Dead Lake; not the cold and reserved Lucille of old, but a totally changed being. The gratitude she feels for the preservation of her child, seems to have reconciled her to life, and consequently it will be to you alone that I shall owe my thanks, should I one day be allowed to give her a far dearer name than that of sister. She owns that it is you who have broken the ice, and talks of you with so much enthusiasm that if I did not know that it overflowed from the abundant thankfulness of her maternal heart, I should feel jealous of you."

A short silence followed this artless avowal, during which the young officer paced the room; then walked to the casement, and rapped his fingers against the low ceiling.

"Well," he exclaimed, with his good-humoured laugh, "you doctors are certainly not more fastidious than we soldiers! How did you manage to hold out in this dismal hole? We will now try to make you as comfortable as possible, for of course you are coming with us. Lucille would never reconcile herself to the thought of losing her court physician."

"I much regret," answered Everhard in a calm voice, "that Madam Lucille is mistaken in this case. The child can travel without the least danger; it is even necessary that she should leave this place, where the food is not adapted to her delicate state of health. I had determined to order a travelling carriage for to-morrow, when I perceived your carriage. I could not place the ladies under better protection than yours, so you must pardon me if I leave you to-day."

"Impossible!" cried the young officer in a tone of of the most sincere dismay. "What a desperate clamour the women would set up at your leaving us so suddenly. Lucille, little Fan, even the nurse would cling to your coat tails; I should have to arrest you by barring the way with my sword."

"Possibly they may augment the difficulties of this inevitable and necessary step," remarked the doctor with a grave face, so the best plan will be, not to mention my resolve and at nightfall I can easily depart without any leave taking. Here is a report of the child's illness, take the paper with you, but I trust it will not be required. If you go only short day's journies, the drive at this season will probably be beneficial to the health of the little patient. And so permit me to bid you good-bye. I beg you to present my compliments to your sister-in-law."

"Doctor, this cannot be your final decision; I hope you will yet change your mind; meanwhile I will take this statement and leave you, for I fear I have disturbed you whilst writing. Au revoir."

"Do not betray me." Everhard called after him. The young officer put his finger to his lips, and hastened through the tap-room whistling a merry tune.

Everhard had hardly been alone for ten minutes pacing his room like a prisoner who is meditating how he can escape from his bare and narrow cell, when he suddenly heard the outer door again open, and a step, which sent the blood to his heart, approach his room.

"Is my cup of bitterness not yet full," he murmured to himself.

The door opened and Lucille stood before him with an expression in her eyes which utterly disconcerted him and forced him to cast his down.

"Pardon me my friend," she said in an agitated voice, "if once more I intrude on your solitude, though you so evidently avoid me. You even intend to leave us without a word of farewell. My brother-in-law did not admit this; but I was aware of it from his manner when he left your room, and as I have long suspected this to be your intention, I was not much astonished, though greatly grieved. I owe you so much that it would be useless again to repeat my thanks before we part; but it is not generous in you to deprive me of all opportunity of rendering you any service, or of showing you the deep interest I feel in you. I am per-

suaded that my friendship is not incapable of giving
you relief if you would but return the confidence with
which I have always treated you from the first hour
we met.   A secret grief consumes you.   What would
I not give to be able to aid you in bearing the load
which oppresses you! Now could I leave you, perhaps
never to meet you again, and have to reproach myself
with the thought, that although knowing, that you,
dearest and most devoted of friends, were suffering
deeply, I yet allowed a miserable fear of appearing
curious and importunate to deter me from making any attempt to assuage those sufferings or to learn their cause!"

"No," she continued with heightened colour, "I
know that you are not selfish enough to burden me
with this unbearable grief and remorse, only because it
humbles your pride to acknowledge your sufferings to
a woman."

He did not once interrupt her, but stood with his
eyes fixed on the ground.   When she had ceased
speaking, he made an effort to answer her but he did
not look up.   "Thank you," he said, "I know that
your questions proceed from the kindness and bene-
volence of your heart; and be assured that if the weight
which oppresses me could be lightened by human
means, I would apply to you for help—I was enabled
to come to your aid, why therefore should I not accept
succour from you? But there are certain circumstances
in life which cannot be altered, and in such cases, I
think it is foolish weakness, and even culpable to give
vent to useless complaints, and to importune one's
friends with them.   Let us part. When the health of your
child is completely restored to its former bloom, the sad
impressions connected with the remembrance of the Dead

Lake will vanish from your mind, and with them the image of a man who"— . . . .

Feeling that emotion was overpowering him, he suddenly stopped, and walked to the window to regain his composure. When after a moment he again turned towards Lucille, he saw her leaning against the door post, pale as death and with the same pained expression on her countenance that he had noticed the first day of her arrival.

"Good heavens, what ails you?" exclaimed he; "Know then, if you cannot bear the feeling of being indebted to me, that we are quits. If I have succeeded in saving the life of your child, you have fully acquitted this debt by preserving my own life."

She looked up with surprise.

"Yes," he continued; "on that very table, on the night I first met you, I wrote a farewell letter to life. The letter still lies there, so you see that I have changed my resolution. I do not say that I feel grateful to you for it. Possibly non existence has its dark side too, but it cannot be worse than remaining between life and death neither suited to the one, nor prepared for the other—enough of this! Is it your fault if the life which you saved was not worth the trouble? Do not let us prolong so painful a meeting. Our paths now diverge—You return to your home, I——go where fate leads me. I am driven on by my destiny like a stone which a boy rolls before him. I thank you for the happy days I have spent in this wilderness; they have been the first, for a long time, in which I felt that I lived. It is a pity that they must pass away like every thing else in this perishable world."

"And why must they pass, away?" she asked looking up with anxious and imploring eyes. "Why will you not accompany us?"

"Why? because"—he suddenly stopped. His eyes whilst wandering round the room had fastened on the letter to his friend which lay on the table, beside the travelling bag. A sudden thought flashed through his mind. "You wish to test the value I set on your friendship, and that it is not pride which prevents me from availing myself of your kindness; well then take this letter, but promise not to read it before to-morrow. Will you promise this?"

She only bowed without looking at him.

"This letter contains every explanation which I could not bring myself to utter. When you have read it, you will understand that I can no longer remain here, and that you ought not to detain me. And now give me your hand once more. Let me also thank you again for the happiness of knowing you! He pressed her hand to his lips with much emotion. Embrace your child to-morrow when you have read the letter, and then—but I need not ask you for this; then in spite of all, think kindly of me. I know that you will do so, have you not the heart and soul of an angel!"

He hastened from the room and passed through the empty passage. He heard Fanny's voice in the sitting-room. She talked with the nurse and mentioned his name. This accelerated his steps. He had just presence of mind enough left him to throw a handful of money to the landlady, and to bid her good-bye, then he followed the cart track which led into the valley, and hastily turned round the first corner without looking back. After he had walked for a quarter of an hour unconscious of all around him, only blindly driven on by the dim feeling that if he once looked back his strength would fail him; it suddenly occurred to him that he was walking northward in the direction of Germany, instead of turning towards the lakes of Lombardy as he had at first intended. "What does it matter," he said to himself; "what is home to me, am I not everywhere a stranger?" He descended to the bed of the mountain stream which flowed by the road-side. There he rested for a while, bathed his feverish brow with the cold water., and listened to its gurggle as it flowed over the pebbly bed. The sound reminded him of Fanny's clear voice when she laughed for the first time after her illness. This recollection so over-powered him that the tears streamed from his eyes, and he let his grief take its course without trying to check it.

A cart which passed him in its slow progress up the hill, roused him from his painful thoughts. It occurred to him, that the carter would stop at the inn and there probably see Lucille and her child. That happiness would never be his again! However he re-mained firm to his resolve, and wandered on till he felt, in his trembling knees and exhausted frame, how deeply the last few hours had affected him.

He had now reached a more expanded part of the valley; he sat down beside a small shed which had formerly served as shelter to the workmen of a quarry. His head sank on his chest, and he was soon absorbed in gloomy thoughts and reveries.

An hour passed and found him still sitting there half stupified; neither feeling pain nor wishing for any thing. He only heard the rushing of the water and stared vacantly at the stones and mosses at his feet.

Suddenly he started up, the tread of horses was heard, and the grating sound of the heavy drag as a carriage proceeded slowly down the hill. A secret presentiment thrilled through him, he looked up with a feeling of terror, and to his dismay recognized the carriage of the young officer.

On the box beside the coachman was seated the nurse, her fat good-humoured face shaded by a large straw hat and a blue veil, though the sun had now sunk low, and only a few slanting rays reached the deep glen. His first thought was to spring up, and fly before them. But even if he could have got in advance of them here on this steep road, once in the plain they would speedily overtake him; so he had no chance of escaping. He stealthily rose and approached the door of the hut. "They have not yet seen me," he murmured; "they will drive past, and then this last pain will have been overcome; but why could they not have spared me this?"

He entered the shed half ashamed of slinking away, and hiding like an outlaw.

Through all those days of inward strife he had never felt so thoroughly wretched and unhappy as he did at that moment. Now when his last strength was exhausted, he had to witness the triumphant progress of one to whom he bitterly grudged the prize that was denied him.

Cautiously he pressed against the wooden partition of the hut he could not refrain from looking through the small aperture which stood in lieu of a window, and once more gaze on those dear faces.

They were now so close to him that he could examine the inside of the carriage. On the further side lay the child asleep, wrapped up in blankets, and cloaks. Lucille sat beside her, and held her hand, but her eyes searchingly scanned the road. Where was her young protector? "He will follow on foot," thought Everhard. "Thank heaven they have passed; now all is over!"

Suddenly the carriage stopped. The coachman jumped off his seat, and opened the door. Lucille hastily descended and walked towards the hut. A few moments later and she stood with a bright flush on her cheek before the bewildered young man.

"You see that all your resistance is vain my dear friend," she said in a trembling voice. "You wished to escape, but we follow you; we discover your hiding-place, and now hold you fast in spite of your re-sistance. We cannot do without you, you must . . ."

"For heaven's sake," he cried, greatly agitated, "what has happened. Has the child had another at-tack?"

"Our child sleeps," said the charming woman, and her voice sank low; "but still we want you my dear friend. This time . . . this time, it is the mother who entrusts her life to you."

"Lucille!" he exclaimed, well-nigh distracted, and seizing the hand which she offered him, drew her into the hut. "Can I?—may I hope?—Will you indeed . ."

"I must ask you to pardon me," she replied blush-ing still more deeply: "I could not wait till to-morrow, but read your letter the moment you were gone. Then, I may as well confess all,—I had to sustain a severe conflict within me, but I soon felt that I never could again arrive at a clear understanding of my own heart, if I let you depart. You have broken your vow, and have resolved to bear life for my sake, I can only return this by surrendering myself to you. He to whom I pledged my faith, never had another wish during his life than to see me happy. I am convinced that if I could now explain to him how all this has happened, he would release me from my word. When I had clearly perceived this, I could find no rest. I have confided everything to my brother-in-law. He has remained behind with a heavy heart; but he told me to shake hands with you in his name. 'If he can make you happy Lucille,' these were his last words, 'I will try not to hate him.' Will you make the trial my dear friend?"

Unable to contain himself any longer he fell on his knees at her feet, clung to her hands, and buried his face in the folds of her dress. He could not utter a word except her name, which he stammered out repeatedly in faltering accents.

"How is this?" she whispered. "Overcome this emotion, and be a man. You ought to be my support; I must look up to you. Have I not done so, during all these days?"

He rose slowly. "Pardon me darling," he said, pressing her to his heart, and ratifying on her lips a mute vow. "My knees could no longer support me. This day has brought me too much misery and bliss. Now I am strong again, now my heart can once more sustain hope and happiness. Let us walk to the carriage, I am impatient to embrace our child."

DOOMED.

DOOMED.

Meran, 5th October 1860.

A WEEK has passed since my arrival and I have not written a line! I was too much exhausted and agitated by the long journey. When I sat down to write, gazing on the white blank pages, it seemed to me as if I were looking into a camera obscura. All the scenes which had greeted me on my journey appeared so clearly and vividly before me and chased each other as in a feverish dream till my eyes filled with tears.

More than once during the journey I had felt the tears ready to start, but I was not alone, and I had no desire to be pitied, and questioned by the strangers who occupied the carriage with me.

Here it is different—I am alone and free. Already I have learnt by experience that solitude only can bring freedom. Why am I, even now, ashamed to weep? have I not a full right to do so? Is it not sad that my first glimpse of the beauties of this world should also be my last?

Truly it were better that I closed this book, and left the blank pages as they are. With what can I fill them but with useless complaints. I had imagined that it would be pleasant and consoling to write down every thought that crossed my mind, every event in this my last winter. I wished to bequeath this book to my dear brother, my little Ernest, who is as yet too young to understand life and death; but some day or other he would prize it, when, asking about his sister, he found no one to answer him. Now, however, I see it was a foolish thought. How could I wish to live in the memory of those dear to me, in the image of my last illness. Better that he should forget me, than have impressed on his mind these pale features which frighten even me when I look at them in the mirror.

" Evening.—

—The atmosphere heavy and lowering.—

For several hours I have been sitting at the open casement. From thence one can overlook the beautiful country of the Adige. And far beyond the walls of the town and the wide-spreading* poplars which border the stone-dike beside the rushing Passer, the view extends over the lower pasture-lands, intersected with a hundred rivulets, where the cattle feed, to the distant chain of mountains which bounds the horizon. The air was so still that I could hear the voices of the promenaders on the *Wassermauer***—or was it a fancy of mine?

The children of my landlord, a tailor, peeped in curiously through the door till I at last gave them the remainder of the chocolate in my travelling bag. How joyfully they ran down with it to their mother! Soon I became more calm and cheerful. I found that I had been wrong in dreading my own soliloquies. Why,

---

* Not the Lombardy poplar, but the populus Alba, or Abele tree, which is wide spreading.

** Name of a promènade at Meran.

The Translator.

even considering these leaves as a legacy, should they only contain sorrow? Did I not leave home, where I was tied down by a hundred fetters with the full determination for once, to enjoy life and liberty? And shall I now bear witness against myself that I am unworthy of that freedom?

Certainly it will be but a brief enjoyment, but all the more firmly will I grasp it and not embitter it by weakness and absorbing self-pity.

The landlady told me that this morning a burgher of Meran, who had never suffered from illness in his life, had died suddenly in his prime. They had all expected that he would attain to a good old age, and, probably, he had thought so himself. Comparing my fate with his, is not mine preferable? Probably, like the generality of men, he had spent his days in toil and labour, looking forward to a time when having earned a sufficiency, he would be able to rest, and enjoy the remainder of his life. His end was unexpected, whilst I know mine. And is not this difference all in my favour? Is not spring yet distant, and should I so fully enjoy this reprieve, were its short duration concealed from me? Oh, truly it is a blessing not to be overtaken, and surprised by death; to watch his slow approach, and only then, face to face with him, learn to live. I can never sufficiently express my thanks to our doctor, my dear fatherly friend, for not keeping the truth from me—thus has he fully redeemed the promise he gave to my dying mother, always to stand by me as a friend.

The night has now set in. I can hardly see what I write. In my whole life, I have never felt so thoroughly at peace as here, in this beautiful forecourt to the grave.—Father! that I could but waft one breath of it to your depressed and sorrowful soul. Good night! Good night, my little Ernest. Who has put you to bed to-night? Who shall now tell you fairy tales to send you to sleep?

The 6th Afternoon.

To-day as Frau Meisterin brought up my dinner, she eagerly tried to persuade me to take a walk and not to sit so much at home. It was so fine on the Wassermauer. So many people were to be seen there; she was sure it would divert me. I could not make her understand that all I wished was to collect my thoughts, and not to divert them; and that I did not feel the slightest desire for the company of strangers. At last, I convinced her by declaring that I was still so weak and so tired with the journey that the two steep stairs were as yet too much for me. Then she left me, and I continued to write.

I have been obliged to put aside my embroidery; it now hurts my chest. I had even to send away my landlord's little girls to whom I had intended to give sewing-lessons.

To-day a doubt weighs on my mind. It seized me suddenly for the first time on waking this morning, and came upon me with great force and persistence. I want to solve it now. Strange, that it should not have struck me sooner. I was so fully convinced that I was doing right! I knew that no one would miss me at home, that my father felt pained at every unkind look my step-mother gave me, that I could no longer be of use even to Ernest, since my step-mother had insisted, in spite of his tender age, on sending him to school, only to avoid seeing him, and having to take care of him.

My father shed tears when he clasped me for the last time in his arms; still my departure relieved him. He wished what is best for me, but what can he do?

This morning, however, the question suddenly occurred to me, whether I had not left other duties; whether any human being, not utterly disabled, has a right to sit down idly or go holiday making for a whole winter. Only since I have felt happy; since the littlenesses of the empty commonplace provincial life have ceased to oppress me, have I begun to question myself as to what right I had to enjoyment, more than all those thousands to whom death is not more distant, than it is to me, and who are forced to strive and wrestle to their last breath, and here am I closing a truce with the enemy, and celebrating a festival as if I had been victorious.—

7th October.

That question for which my poor head could find no answer, I have solved to-day when I came home as shattered from my first walk as if I had laboured for a day in chains. No, I am fit for nothing but rest, and if it taste sweeter to me than to many, that cannot be a cause for self-reproach. Am I not more easily contented than others? If I am of no use, am I a burden to any one? Even if I did not avail myself of the small inheritance left me by my mother, but kept it intact for my brother Ernest, would it exempt him from the necessity of supporting himself by his own exertions? Part of it will probably remain for him, for as I experienced to-day, my strength is already scantier than I had imagined. Who can tell how short my winter in the South may be? I shall not frequent the walk under the poplars. To-day I felt uneasy among those poor, coughing, dressed up people, who tottered about with their baskets full of grapes, and seemed eagerly to imbibe new hope with each berry. By those whose faces expressed hopelessness, I felt still less attracted. It may sometimes be soothing to frequent the society of fellow-sufferers; but when the same fate creates totally different feelings, then that which could otherwise unite only separates, and one feels all the more forcibly the difference of character. Not to one of them, would I have ventured to speak of the peaceful and grateful mood I enjoyed. They would either have looked upon me as an eccentric enthusiast, or thought me a hypocrite.

Can they be blamed for it? Possibly I too might have feared death had I loved life more. And why was my life so little loveable?

Only a few can understand the deep feeling of immensity, and peace with which nature fills my soul. For two and twenty years I never set foot beyond the walls of a small uninteresting commonplace town. In these days people travel much. But for the long illness of my mother, and after her death, the care of my little brother, I too would probably have wandered forth from that desolate little place. This beautiful valley already seems to me like the world to come, like a true Garden of God. The first time I inhaled this air, I felt as if I already glided over the earth, borne on the wings of my soul. It was certainly a pity that they did not support me better as I toiled up the steep narrow stairs, but what business had I to descend them, when every glance through my windows is an excursion into Paradise.

The people with whom I lodge are very poor. The man works till late at night, and his wife has enough to do, attending to the wants of her large family. The inside of the house looks dusky and gloomy. When the porter of the hotel who from the simplicity of my dress inferred great meagreness of purse, first took me through the long dark passages, and the gloomy courts, and we scrambled up the delapidated staircase, over the landing where dusty furniture, old spinning-wheels, beds, earthen ware and provisions of maize lay in confused heaps, and the spiders, undisturbed for many years, spun their webs, I felt oppressed and my heart beat so that I had to rest at every third step. But the first glance at my small low room reconciled me quickly to the thought that this was to be my last earthly habitation. That old fashioned writing-table with the brass mountings looks like the twin-brother of the one which stood in my dear mother's room. That arm-chair is just as high and heavy, and as brown with age, as the one she used. A few bad prints on the wall, which disturbed me, I immediately took down, and hung up the portraits of my parents instead. It now seems to me as if I had been at home here for years. In one of the corners on a black wooden console stands a crucifix which though I have not been brought up to it, causes me deep reflection. I have received all my books. My father sent them after me and now I want nothing more. At the same time he wrote me just such a letter as I expected from him. That trait of conforming oneself to what is unalterable without further struggle, I have inherited from him. Six lines from Ernest to tell me that he is very happy at school with his little comrades, and a greeting from my stepmother; at least, the letter contains one, but probably my father has added it without asking. Now I will write home. How much more freely could I do so, if I knew that my letters reached my father's hands only.

The 10th—Evening.

What strange people one meets with! An hour ago I was sitting, quite unsuspicious of any interruption, at my window reading, and enjoying the mild evening breeze—the sun now sets at five o'clock behind the Marlinger mountain, yet the air retains the mildness of a summer evening, and the tips of the high mountains to the East, a ruddy glow, for many hours longer—when there came a knock at the door, and a short stout lady, quite unknown to me, entered coolly, and introduced herself to me, expressing a most cordial desire to make my acquaintance. She had seen me on the Wassermauer the only time I had walked there, and had immediately taken a great interest in me, for I was evidently very ill and very lonely, and she had resolved to speak to me the next time we met, hoping to be of some use to me.

"For you must know, my dear child, that I, as I stand before you, am fifty-nine years old, and have not been ill for one day, except during my confinements. My two sons, and three daughters are also, thank heaven, perfectly healthy, and are all of them married and settled in life. But you see I have always had a passion from my earliest youth for helping those people who were not so well off as I am, for nursing the sick, and for rendering the last offices to the dying. My late husband used to call me the privileged life preserver; you cannot imagine a better nurse than I am, for you see I am of a generation when professional ones were as yet unknown. I can easily do without sleep, and can even assist at any operation without the least show of weakness. I have come here with a friend of mine who cannot last much longer. When the poor thing is released from her sufferings, I shall have more time at my disposal than now; she has always to entreat me to leave her and take some exercise—and so my dear child if you want support, advice, or help, apply to no one but me; you must solemnly promise me this. Of course I will no longer allow you to spend your days all alone. I will often come to see you. I never stand on ceremony with my friends, and so you must take it kindly if I tyrannize over you—it will be all for your good. I understand nervous complaints as well as the best of doctors—amusements, air, excitement, are the remedies I prescribe. *A propos*, which doctor have you consulted here?" I answered that I had not applied to any, neither intended to do so as I knew that my malady was incurable. She shook her head incredulously, so I took from my portfolio a sheet of paper on which our doctor had drawn a sort of representation, to shew how far the disease in my lungs had spread. She examined it with experienced eyes.

"My dear child," she at last said, "this is all nonsense, the doctors are all the same, the more they talk, the less they know. I could lay any wager that your interior has a totally different aspect from this." I told her that she had every prospect of being able to ascertain this, but that I declined the wager, as unfortunately I could not win it whilst alive. She only partly listened to what I said, and she continued in so loud a voice that it pierced to my very marrow, to give me an account of different illnesses which tended to shew how little doctors were to be relied on, accompanying it with so many details, that it would have made me sick, if I had not had courage and presence of mind enough to cry for mercy. At length she rose, and in taking leave she made a movement as if to embrace me, and was evidently surprised when I coldly and stiffly gave her my finger tips. She rustled out of the room in great haste, and with many promises to return soon. I had to sit for half an hour with closed eyes to calm my nerves. A sharp odour of acetic ether which surrounded her and which she strongly recommended to me as a powerful neurotic, is still prevalent in the room, and those sharp peering eyes, and the determined expression of philanthropy in her broad face still haunt me. Only the thought, that for some days at least, I was safe from another invasion, gave me some consolation. But my former *tête-à-tête* with destiny; that which gave a peculiar charm to this place are now lost to me, unless I speak to her yet more intelligibly; and that, even in a case of self-defence, would be most painful to me.

And is this human sympathy! The few who love us pain us by it, because we see that they suffer with us—and those who do not love us—can they please us? "Only beggars know, what beggars feel" I once read in Lessing. But can beggars give alms?—

The next Morning.

I have had a restless night. I am so little in the

habit of speaking, and being spoken to that the shrill voice of the charitable lady still resounds in my ears. In my dreams I had a fierce quarrel with her, till at last she took off her fair front and threw it in my face —I woke up with a shudder and bathed in perspiration. What rude things I had said to her, among others that I would bequeath to her my lungs, preserved in spirits of wine. How exceedingly impolite we are in our dreams!

I dressed myself hastily, but even now I am in terror of another invasion—my humble little corner, where I had hoped to die peacefully—this too has been disturbed. Even here I cannot find quiet! I really must go out and try to find some safer hiding-place.

In the Afternoon.

To-day I have met with great events and have boldly surmounted them—first a high mountain then an adventure with a savage—finally I have revelled in nature, and solitude to intoxication. And although I am so tired that I have to summon all my energy every time. I raise my hand to dip my pen in the ink, yet I have renewed my inward strength, and have got over the effect of last night's encounter. Now I could boldly confront a whole company of coffee drinking sisters with false fronts.

How beautiful is my burial place, how marvellous the light that streams on it. I fancied that I had already remarked the magical effects of this light, but find that only to-day the scales have really dropped from my eyes. Seriously I believe that what we in the north call *sunshine* is only an imitation of it, a cheap mixture of light and air, a sort of gilded bronze in comparison with the real solid priceless gold which is lavished here.

I moved slowly up the cool and gloomy Laubengasse* where a shiver always seizes me and a peculiar oppression stops my breath. Then I reached the small Platz with the fine old church. The Platz appeared all black and red with the costumes of the peasants of the neighbourhood, and of the valley of the Passer. Their trim holiday dress consists of a short dark jacket with red facings, red waistcoats, and broad brimmed hats. Most of the people are fine-looking and stately, the men however, much handsomer than the women. Of the latter, I have only remarked since I came, two pretty faces with regular features.

As it was a peasant's holiday, they stood about in dense groups and none of them took the least notice of the suffering stranger who glided past their clumsy elbows. Over the whole Platz hung a thick cloud of acrid tobacco smoke, which gave me a fit of coughing, so I preferred to go round the church rather than endeavour to push my way through the uncivil crowd.

In the buttresses of the church, old tomb stones were immured. On one of them I read an inscription so full of meek resignation that I was greatty touched by it. One, Ludovica, was buried underneath it in the year 1836. I will write down the inscription, I learnt it by heart:

> "Separate they lived, and lonely,
> "Father, mother, and only child
> "Till death had them together bound.
> "In blessedness themselves they found,
> "For aye and ever now united.
> "So the early fading of the rose,
> "Is to be envied; it is repose."

* Lauben. A provincial term for arcades.

The Translator.

The quiet and fervent tone of these verses accompanied me for many hours. I walked pensively along the narrow streets up to an old gateway which leads through a weather-beaten tower, scarred with French bullets, into the valley of the Passeier. The view which from thence suddenly opened before me filled me with awe, by its strangeness, beauty, and grandeur. I sat down for half an hour on a large stone beside the gateway, from whence a steep path leads to the Küchelberg, and up to an old tower, formerly a powder-magazine, which now peacefully keeps watch over the vineyards like a pensioned veteran.

Just before me on a rock which projects from the Küchelberg, I perceived the ruins of Zenoburg, and considered whether my strength would carry me thus far on the broad and uncared for road, or if I should content myself with crossing the stone bridge from whence I could see the cheerful village of Obermais. A woman approached me with a basket of grapes and peaches on her head. I bought some fruit and after eating it felt invigorated. So I set off, pausing at every step to look down on the Passer whose water now dark blue, now flaked with white foam, flowed through the arch of the bridge. How boldly yet lightly the vines hang from the rugged rocks on the banks of the river; among them grows the wild fig-tree covered with purple fruit. Running water conducted in canals refreshes the leaves, and now and then turns a wheel. Large chesnut-trees rise from the depths. Everywhere luxuriant growth and rejoicing nature meets the eye. Mine rested with especial pleasure on the varied colouring of the rocks; here of a warm brownish tint, there of a silvery grey. How picturesque those peasants, in their bright costumes look, coming down from the Küchelberg, and that cart or rather two wheeled sledge, drawn by strong whitish grey oxen, and laden with vine-leaves, descending the Zenoburg. And above all a sky the colour of which, I had held till now, to be a fiction of poets, and painters. While I so walked on and wondered, I said to myself this is all mine this is my joy and no one can take it from me. Could it be more mine if instead of, for one moment, I had looked on it for centuries? Who can say if the best part of every pleasure does not consist in its transientness; how otherwise could the happy ever grow tired of their bliss . . . . . .

"I had probably walked on too fast while thinking of all this, so that when I reached the top of the hill, I had to rest on a bench which stood before a pretty house. My eyes closed in involuntary slumber. All was still around me, only the Meran church bells which deafened me below sounded softly up here and lulled me to sleep. How pleasantly we dream in the mid-day sunshine, when the light penetrates our closed eyelids, and blends in our fancy with the marvellous colours and rays which have nothing tangible or earthly in them. Sitting quite still for some time, I probably went to sleep, but suddenly I started up as I felt something cold and moist touch my hand; it was nothing worse than the nose of a large dog, who standing beside his master, watched me curiously. But the appearance of the latter was so horrible, that I would willingly have believed it to be a dream, to be got rid of by speaking and moving. It was a tall bearded man whose age I could not define. His hair hung over his forehead, he wore a heavy and enormous hat, covered by a wilderness of cock's feathers, fox tails, and strange

furs, casting a fierce shade over his eyes, which however as I remarked afterwards, had a most innocent
and harmless expression. Probably I plainly showed
my terror, for the mysterious apparition, which seemed
to have risen from one of the old tombs of the Zenoburg, laughed good-naturedly, holding a very small
pipe between his even white teeth, he told me not to
be frightened. He was only a Saltner, who watched
the vineyards, and as I had entered his district he requested a penny for tobacco. In my consternation, I
gave him half a florin in silver, and hastily turned away,
as I did not feel quite secure in the close proximity of
his bright spear. But the piece of silver which is
scarce here, or perhaps a holiday humour made the
giant quite tame and officious. He walked without
ceremony by my side, and noticing that I climbed with
difficulty, he energetically supported my arm with his
great paw. I had to put a good face on the matter,
and indeed; ended by being thankful for his help, as
I could hardly have managed to ascend alone the last
steep bit on which the ruins of the castle stand. It
struck me how reserved he was in his questions, and
how communicative about his own affairs. Comparing
this charitable brother with the uncharitable sister, who
had visited me yesterday, how much more elevated
was the natural feeling of this peasant, than the obtrusive refinement of the so-called higher classes.—
On the top of the hill it was indeed beautiful. With
the exception of a small chapel and a solitary tower
which remain intact, the castle is in ruins; only a few
fragments of walls, thickly covered with ivy, are standing. Luxuriant grass grows beneath them, tribes of
lizards rustle over the sunny stones. Tangled creepers

of every description hang over the walls, and far below, so that a falling stone would dash perpendicularly into the water, the unruly Passer flows underneath the shelving rocks at the foot of the hill.

My armour bearer pointed out to me, on the opposite heights towards the south, many old castles and small villages, where the vine cultivators live, and told me the names of the different mountains, as I comfortably sat on the grass with his dog lying beside me.

At noon the church bells rang; he ceased talking took the three cornered hat off his head and the pipe from his mouth, and crossing himself devoutly, he prayed in silence. When the sounds had died away, he put his hat on again, puffed at his pipe, and asked me if I were hungry.

I answered in the affirmative, but said I was still too much exhausted to undertake my homeward journey. Without a word he descended the hill with stalwart strides, and disappeared.

Ten minutes later a little girl carrying a basin of milk, some bread and a piece of the fête-day roast, hurried up the hill and looked about for me, then silently and timidly placed the very welcome refreshment before me. After many vain attempts, I at last coaxed the child to speak to me. She told me that the Saltner had ordered it all for me in the house below; he himself was busy in the vineyards, and would not come again. The child then ran away and left me alone to feast in this delightful solitude. Never had I eaten a more delicious meal.. I was quite ashamed of having consumed all, and having to carry back the empty dishes.

With difficulty I persuaded the good people to accept some money; probably the Saltner had forbidden them to take any. In vain I looked for him on my back. I do not even know his name.

Is this not quite an adventure? and have I not reason to note this day.

October the 12th—Morning.

This morning on waking, I thought how strange it is, that each different class should envy the supposed freedom of the other, although no true freedom can be found where the sense of this difference of classes exists. Perhaps while I am casting a longing glance at the life of these poor peasants who pass their days among vines, fields of maize, and mulberry-trees, and who know as little of the hundred narrow conventional considerations of propriety which rule the so-called refined classes than the silk worm knows of the glittering misery which may one day be covered by his web; to them the life of a town lady who if she chose might spend her days in waltzing may seem a life of supreme happiness and freedom. They are tied to their labour hour after hour, and when they rest on Sundays they can as little free themselves from the tedious customs which confine their enjoyments, as they can in the heat of a summer-day, exchange the heavy woollen skirt with the hundreds of plaits, for a lighter dress.

The educated classes certainly have this advantage that they *can* emancipate themselves when they will, but still would such a one not be blamed by his equals, just as peasant is blamed when he goes out shooting in the harvest time? Altogether. . . . .

1 *o'clock.*

No I will not bear this any longer, if I had to

challenge the whole world for it. The dying surely need not lie, need not submit to be tormented, and smile complacently all the while. I am so revolted and harassed—my nerves are so bruised, that I wish for a speaking trumpet to be able to declare through it at the open window, my most solemn renunciation of all society; unfortunately my tormentors are dining at this moment, but this must happen sooner or later.

I will have an iron bolt to my door of an hundred pounds weight, and an iron mask for my face when I take a step out of my room.

The landlady has just brought up my dinner; well it may get cold, I have no appetite for it. My heart is beating fast with anger and agitation.

I am sick to death of all the talking that has been buzzing in my ears, and could no more be stopped than the stream which turns that wheel beside the bridge. That at least legitimates its noise by its useful activity.

Among all the good things I had to say of yesterday, I forgot to mention the vain attempt of "the life-preserver" to see me. Now I thought she will have at all events remarked that I do not wait for her permission to breathe the fresh air and for the future will let the light of her charity shine on more grateful beings. I little knew her.

Whilst I was writing I heard her step coming up the stairs, and laying aside my diary, I quickly took a letter which I had begun from my portfolio, and intrenched myself behind it, determined to defend myself to the last drop of ink.

My poor forces were overthrown by her at the first assault. Letter writing! tired! what nonsense; it was for my health I was here, and my nerves required

amusement and rest. No, as I had run up the Küchelberg yesterday like an unreasonable child, she had
come to-day to prevent the repetition of such suicide
and to show me what it was to take the air in a health-
ful way. Oh, yes she had found me out, I was not
pleased to see her again so soon! but a young lady
who lived by herself was on no account to be neglected.
I was only to submit to her authority, and would
certainly be grateful to her afterwards.

I put on my hat silently and resignedly. I could
not even feel angry at her clumsy and good natured
tone, though it made me suffer bodily pain.

Chattering incessantly she dragged me towards
the winter grounds, as the most sheltered part of the
Wassermauer is called, for there an old cloister and
its high garden-wall keep off all cold winds, evergreen
shrubs flourish and the rose-bushes are still covered with
roses. This place is always crowded, the band plays
and the whole society of strangers walk there or sit
basking in the sunshine. My protectress seemed purposely to have brought me here with the intention of
introducing me to this beau monde. I had to run the
gauntlet of a curious, but to me quite indifferent crowd
of ladies and gentlemen. I saw not one face that
pleased me, heard not one word that reached my heart.
Then the heat under those arbours, the noise of the
importunate brass band, and the rebellion which was
chafing within me against this soft tyranny, nearly drove
me distracted.

Still more revolting to me than the dull unfeeling-
ness of the healthy, was the behaviour of many of my
fellow sufferers. There sat a young countess who as I
heard had been parted from her husband, in order to

avoid all excitement, but she was not too ill to notice my simple old-fashioned dress, which she scanned from head to foot, and then with a crushing look, she wrapped herself up in her cashemere burnouss, as I sat on the bench beside her.

And that young girl who treated me as an old acquaintance in the first five minutes, and told me all the scandal of Meran, though death was written in her face, and her cough went to my heart. Are those figures of wax, dressed up automatons, who exhibit all their old minauderies, though when spring comes they will have to lie in their coffins.

It seemed to me quite a deliverance when the dinner-bell of the hôtel de la poste rang, and most of the company departed and my protectress had to go to her sick friend. I hardly bid her good-bye. I could no longer speak, or listen to a word, for I felt quite paralized; so she has at last obtained her object and tried her cure on me, and the result is, that both in mind and body I am more dead than alive. Certainly that is a sort of recovery.

The 13th—Evening.

I have at last succeeded, and cannot sufficiently express my joy at this achievement. I reflected that it was only just, that if I wished for freedom, I should purchase it by the exertion of some courage and determination. Armed with a book, I calmly walked through the winter grounds without recognizing any one, sat down in the midst of the whole society and read for several hours without once looking up.

Of course the life-preserver made her appearance and at once approached my bench, but I coolly told her that talking hurt me; she looked astonished, shrugged her shoulders, and left me to myself.

I saw very well that she was offended. So much the better! If I find no better occupation I will do this every day; I feel a certain satisfaction in it. Whilst I sat surrounded by all those tiresome people, I triumphed in my courage and the victory I had gained in not having allowed myself to be daunted. Certainly the conflict had made my heart beat faster, but even courage is not to be learnt in a day. And then is it not doubly refreshing to read the grave and beautiful words of our greatest poets, when from the different conversations around, one picks up words which show what inferior spiritual nourishment society puts up with.

Possibly this may be a proud and over vain thought. But some pride surely is pardonable in one so isolated. Is it not most presumptuous to retire within oneself, and be contented with one's own society? Surely he who prepares for death has a right to think of his soul above all things, and how is this possible, in the midst of the thoughtless, soulless noise, commonly called conversation?

Already they show me plainly that I am not to their taste. To-day when I appeared on the Wassermauer, with my book, all the benches were occupied except one, on which sat only a pale and melancholy looking young man, who is daily partly led, partly followed by a servant to a sunny corner of the winter-garden and there sits covered up with costly furs. Had the ladies, who were talking, and embroidering in the arbours deigned to move, they certainly could have made room for my slight person, whose crinoline never molested any one.

I saw however that they had resolved to cause me embarrassment. Oh, how sharp, unamiable, cold, and even inhuman our faces become, when we are determined to show our dislike to some one of our fellow creatures! I felt quite frightened at the stony features, dark looks, and drawn down lips of the company. But soon I was ashamed of my cowardice, and of having allowed it to be perceived. So I looked as if I saw no hostility in their countenances and quietly sat down beside the young man, leaving space enough between us, even for the wide robes of the countess. I was deeply absorbed in my book, but though I never looked up, I knew exactly what were the glances they cast at me, and could have written down the benevolent remarks that were whispered beneath those arbours. The sick young man hardly moved, only from time to time he sighed—I pitied him; he appears to be one of the most suffering of the invalids here, and to bear his illness with difficulty. He must be rich for I saw a costly ring glittering on his finger.

We sat side by side for several hours, and I was on the point of making some observation to him about the book I was reading merely for the sake of rousing him from the melancholy thoughts which seemed to oppress him. Where would have been the harm? But now a days, care is taken to make us feel ashamed of every natural impulse. So I remained silent and read on. Suddenly he let a silver pencil-case fall from his hands, as he was going to write down something in his pocket-book; he made an effort to stoop, breathing with difficulty and I, without much hesitation, anticipated him,

and picked up the neat little pencil-case. He thanked
me with rather a surprised look: I myself blushed
deeply, and hearing a derisive titter from the ladies'
bower, I lost my composure for a few minutes. I
thought with most tormenting perspicacity of all that
would be said of the crime committed by a young lady
in being of use to a young man. What would he
think of me? I had slightly glanced at him and remarked no smile on his melancholy face. If after this
proof of how little worldly knowledge I possess, he
thinks me very countrified, why should that annoy me?
If I am contented to be so, why should I be angry
with him for perceiving it? He bowed very politely,
as half an hour later I rose to go. By this time I had
come to an understanding with myself, and felt so
composed, that I returned his salutation without the
least embarrassment. Even the black looks of my protectress, who had been immediately taken possession
of, by the other ladies, could not spoil my appetite for
dinner.

Here comes the soup unfortunately, it is of a
lighter colour even than the fair curls of the charitable
lady. What a pity it is, that with the dying, taste is
not the first thing to depart. How I wish for one
good home cooked dish.—

Evening. The first autumnal winds
carrying with it some poplar leaves.

A letter from our dear old doctor, my best friend.
He wants to hear how I am getting on, how I feel,
and how the climate agrees with me. He reproaches
himself for not having hidden the hopeless truth from
me; at the same time he praises my courage and firm-

7*

ness; he does not try to change or put another con-
struction on his former words; he knows it would be
useless. "Remember, dear Mary," he adds, "that
miracles still happen every day, and that all our science
and knowledge only teach us to marvel at everything
or nothing. He is aware that my best comfort is to
know the truth, and to live in the truth as long as life
is granted me."

Several days later. I have lost the date.
Beautiful autumnal evening.

Here was so much wind in the forenoon that I
had to remain in-doors. I was busy altering my dresses
for my chest becomes more and more delicate and
they oppress me. In the afternoon the wind subsided,
and I walked out, down the broad street called Renn-
weg. Numbers of cows and goats were driven through
it—not a pleasant circumstance attending the walks
here. I tremble every time I see one of those clumsy
horned heads approach me though I know that they
are not so stupid as they appear, and have not such
strong prejudices against a lonely female, as my wise
fellow-creatures. It is my bodily weakness which in
case of need could not find shelter behind a stout
heart, which leaves me defenceless. So I kept close
to the houses, and arrived safely at the Western gate
of the town from whence the road leads on to the
beautiful and sunny Vintschgau. A path which passes
at the foot of the Küchelberg and then winds through
the vineyards tempted me and I slowly walked in that
direction. It pleased me to see the heavy bunches of
purple grapes hanging from the trellis above me, the
huge yellow pumpkins, the ripe maize in short all the

riches of a southern autumn. Now and then I met peasants at work; tubs filled with grapes and carts laden with vine-leaves passed me. It seemed strange to me that the work was done so quietly, without music or singing, for I had always fancied the vintage to be one of the most noisy and brilliant of festivals. The people of the country are of a lazy pensive disposition and never sing at their work. If one now and then hears a song it is owing to there being many Italians here, who are easily recognized by their fiery and lively gestures.

A hundred paces distant from the gate, close under the mountain, lies a solitary farm. My landlady had told me that there one could get milk fresh from the cow. As I am not a good walker, I entered the little garden and ordered some milk and bread. Only a few strangers occupied the benches, but just beside the door underneath a large orange-tree, sat the pale young man, whilst his servant further, off, was refreshing himself with a glass of wine. He had not touched the glass of milk which stood before him, and as I was going to pass, he rose, bowed, and offered me a seat at his table, saying that it was the most sheltered spot. It was the first time I had heard him speak several sentences together without stopping. His deep sad voice was very pleasing. I gladly accepted his offer and when he begged me to take his untouched glass, as he was not thirsty, I could not refuse without giving offence. Finally we began a conversation, though much broken by pauses, during which he relapsed into his melancholy dreaming. Only once he smiled slightly, but it made him look still more sad when his pale lips parted over the bluish white teeth. We had been talking of the dull monotony in the life of the patients here; of the tiresome sitting about in the winter garden. I said it reminded me of the caterpillars and cocoons which my little brother keeps in glass boxes. These also crawled about indolent and depressed amongst their food, satisfying their gaoler by feeding greedily, and eyeing each other curiously when they accidentally met; then they proceeded to their winter sleep, if by chance they did not find the air too oppressive for them, and died. He laughed, and said: "your comparison is much too flattering; do you think that our fellow-worms ever feel as light and free as *they* become, unless in a purer atmosphere than this terrestrial one?" "That depends," replied I, "on whether, when they proceed safe and sound from their cocoons, they find their glass cage open. Otherwise they may be reserved for a still more cruel fate. Few enjoy the liberty of their wings; they are generally caught again, and struggle on a pin till their bright colours turn to dust."

He remained silent, and I was half sorry for having led the conversation to so strange a theme; to divert his thoughts, I spoke to him of the stiff, foolish narrow minded views of my native town, where in the style of the so-called good old times, every one embitters the life of his neighbour in the most amicable and ceremonious way. I then told him how free and released I felt since I knew I was doomed to die. My fetters had been loosened like the fetters of those who are sentenced to death. He listened with interest but looked incredulous. When I had done speaking....

The next day.

Yesterday I could not have been interrupted **in a**

more unwelcome manner. My door suddenly opened and the life-preserver, the sister of charity, the lady without nerves, rushed into the room with a particularly stern and solemn countenance which boded no good. Without taking breath after running up the stairs, she sat down, spread her skirts over my sofa, and without any circumlocution began to lecture me. Possibly she may be of use where bodily nursing is required, but for spiritual care she certainly has no vocation. A more clumsy way of touching on delicate subjects I have not yet met with, and I have certainly not been spoiled in that respect. I was informed that I had been guilty of great sins, and could only make atonement for them by deep contrition. The unaccountable whims of a sick person might, perhaps, excuse the highflown manner with which I had received the friendly advances of many estimable ladies, and the way in which I had withdrawn from their company. But I had dared too in the face of all society to make advances to a young man, and yesterday had gone so far as to accept his glass of milk, and his company on my way home. She had never heard of such a thing. A girl without the least education but with a sense of decency and a proper regard for her reputation would never have thought of doing so. After these occurrences she would certainly never have set foot over my threshold again, had not conscience, and her good nature bidden her warn me. I was alone here, and had no one to look after me if I went astray. That young man did not enjoy a good reputation; his illness was the consequence of a dissipated and reckless life which he had now to expiate by an early death. If so near to the grave, he was still so unscrupulous as to compromise a young creature like myself, then all persons who had any regard for morality must condemn his outrageous conduct, and endeavour to save his victim.

During this speech I remained petrified, and my heart beat so violently that I could not utter a word; but when she stopped and cast a severe look at me, the convicted sinner, I rallied all my remaining spirit and answered that I thanked her for her solicitude, and did not at all doubt her good intentions, but that I did not think I had committed any impropriety—still less had gone astray—that I did not believe my reputation to be in any danger. I knew what I could, or could not do, and would be responsible for it. I did not see why the fact of having one foot in the grave obliged one to give an account to the world of every free but innocent action, particularly as even that would not protect one against its malignant judgments. I had not come to Meran, I continued, in order to ingratiate myself with a society entirely strange to me, but to spend my last days in the manner most agreeable to me, and most in accordance with my nature. You must allow me, my dear Madam, I concluded, not to be led by considerations which, perhaps, may be useful to others. When I had delivered this speech I felt quite startled at my own boldness yet I was pleased with myself. This I thought will at all events make an end of it; and so it was; at least, I hope so, for my protectress rose with a dignified look which sat oddly on, her round face adorned with the little ringlets and said: "Good-bye, Mademoiselle, you are so independent that it would be indiscreet in me to prolong my visit," and with these words she sailed out of the room. So I had at last got rid of her, but not of her sayings, nor of my thoughts. Oh, the sad cold littleness of the world! Is there no spot on earth where a poor human being may be permitted to die after its own fashion? Is one to go tightly laced even to one's last breath? No, they shall not get the better of me; I do not love them, then why should I not despise them; or at least not notice them when they cross my path? Possibly I may have been thoughtless, but thoughtfulness requires time, and I have not much to spare. Certainly if I had to live with these people for an immeasurable time, it might be prudent not to exasperate them, and to bow before them—prudent, but annoying, and in my opinion, hardly worth the while. What harm could they do to me; at the worst they would leave me alone, and could they do me a greater favour? She said that he had caused his own sufferings. Is he for that less worthy of compassion? Perhaps, the remorse he feels is the cause of his melancholy, as the consciousness of my undeserved fate is the cause of my gaiety. Each of us has lived a different life, and has now to resign it. I have nothing to repent of, and nothing to regret; he does both, and so each of us dies a different death.

Why should it be a crime to exchange a few unconstrained words? Do not people who have set out together on a long journey fraternize, and become friends at the first station? Are they then to be blamed if they exchange a few words before starting.

Monday, the 21st October.

I spent my Sunday at home in writing, and reading the letters of Mendelssohn's youth, which in my opinion show his character to much greater advantage than his other writings. They convince me still more that even a complete and free man of genius can work earnestly at his own improvement. If I were a man, I should only care to be an artist. This seems an extravagant idea; for those not endowed with talents perceive only the outward freedom of the existence of a genius, and not the anxieties and labours of his vocation. But in some of the attributes of an artist's nature, in the power of desiring freedom, and of maintaining it, in enthusiasm for noble deeds, and in admiration for all that is beautiful, I should not be found wanting, and armed with these weapons could pass a lifetime in waging war against petty formalists and pedants.

But of what use are all these to me, a girl, with death before me. Well, at all events they will teach me to die calmly.

Mendelssohn's letters have awakened in me a longing for music. I hope I have not been extravagant in hiring a small piano. This morning it was brought to me, and now stands in my room. I have not played for a long time, and after reading Mendelssohn's letters felt quite ashamed of stumbling through his songs without words. I must purchase some sonatas and study them. I confess that at the first notes of music I burst into tears. The last conversation has left in me a wound which bled afresh, as the first sound of music reached my heart after so many weeks privation. I let my tears flow freely, and played on till I grew calm again.

"The 22nd."

I have seen him again. I had avoided him these last days. Though I am quite determined to go my own way; still they have succeeded in robbing me of my first unconstraint. But to-day I met him at the bookseller's shop, where I was looking out some music. He asked me if I had felt unwell, as I had not appeared on the Wassermauer. I blushed and replied, "no, but I had not felt inclined to walk there." Then we talked about music which he greatly likes. "Once I was in possession of a voice," he said, smiling; "but it has departed this life before me." As we came out of the shop I at first wished to bid him adieu, and walk home alone. Then I felt ashamed of my cowardice, and walked on with him to the gate which leads on to the Wassermauer. The day was lovely, and the promenaders walked about with their cloaks on their arms. Only a few yellow leaves reminded one of October. As we followed the course of the Passer and passed the benches occupied by the so-called good society, I was pleased, and happy to feel so much at ease. I tried to cheer him up and when I had succeeded in making him laugh I applauded my own spirit which was not to be daunted. I said to myself, "Does it please you my good people to put on disdainful looks, and to wrap yourselves up in your own virtue, as much as it does me to see this pale face, on which death has already cast its shadow, light up with the serenity of an evening sky. We walked up and down for a whole hour, and I did not feel in the least tired. This time I closely examined his countenance. Whatever lies behind him, it can be nothing base or mean. His features are neither regular nor can they be called expressive, but when he speaks there is something refined and thoughtful about his face which becomes him well. He cannot be more than twenty-six years old. His manners are easy, and natural, and plainly show that he has mixed in the best society. I, with my provincial style of dress, and little knowledge of the world, must contrast strangely with him.

I have looked over the book of strangers trying to find out his name; *before*, I only knew where he lived; I have now discovered that he can be none other than a Mr. Morrik *Particulier* from Vienna. What an odd position! probably it means independent. Then I am a *Particulière* with more right to be so than he has. He is dependent on many things; on his fortune, on his melancholy thoughts—on his servant, who carries his cloak and furs for him.

The 23rd.

Last night I dreamt much, and very reflective dreams. In one of them, I again met Halding, who for years has never troubled my thoughts. I spoke to him as indifferently as ever, and asked after his wife and children. I was glad to hear that they were very well. Then still in my dream, I considered what would have been my lot, had I accepted his hand. I should now be established in America, in a fine house, and have riches and health, for I should not have passed through the sufferings of the last years, in my father's house—I should not be thinking of dying. I thought over all this, as I saw the red cheeked wife, who had so soon consoled him after my refusal—I shuddered at the idea of such happiness. This may appear foolish, full of pretension, and ingratitude.

What fault could I find in him except that I did not love him. Many people found him most amiable, and I thought him even too much so, for a man. As a woman he would have made the best, most docile, and virtuous of wives, but just for that reason would, as a husband have made me most wretched. More than once I have been given to understand that my character was too determined and energetic for a girl. Did not the long lecture of the life preserver tend to show me how deficient I was in feminine timidity and reserve. If this be true the fault lies with my destiny, which threw me early in life on my own resources, and made me independent. One to whom the world and life makes advances may well await its approach but one who must confront its struggles, cannot do without reliance on God, and on himself. If I required any proof that no unwomanly boldness, no desire of dominating lies in my character, I would find it in my dislike to womanish men, who must lean for support on a wife; and towards manly women who only find their happiness in ruling.

The 26th.

A few quiet and uniform days have passed. I felt very languid and disinclined to everything and I remained at home, as the change from the hot sunshine to the dark arcades always hurts me. I read, and played a few sonatas, and felt that even solitude brings many heavy hours with it.

To-day I walked out and the first person I met was Mr. Morrik, as he really is called—I heard an acquaintance address him by that name. We sat for a long time together on a bench amidst the evergreen shrubs in the winter garden for underneath the poplars the air is now getting too sharp. Society seems to have reconciled itself to the unpardonable and unheard of crime, committed by two candidates for death, in talking to each other, and no longer disturbs us. So to-day we had a remarkable conversation. It began, instead of ending, as such conversations when they are earnest and agitated are apt to do, by the utterance of the most hidden thoughts which are usually kept back, till, after having turned over different questions, they suddenly break forth in the ardour of the contest. It was not the first time that I experienced in myself a habit of thinking aloud. To my own great astonishment I, this time suddenly took heart, and poured forth my most hidden and unavowed thoughts and feelings; so that when the words, I was uttering struck my ear I felt quite frightened at my audacity in harbouring such strange ideas, and still more in delivering them to a stranger. It sometimes really appears to me as if I had two characters within me—the one spirited, out spoken, and clever, and this one seldom shews itself—the other, silly and girlishly shy, which sits by in fear and trembling when the other speaks, and cannot muster courage to interrupt it. I forget what gave rise to this conversation. I only remember that before I knew what I was saying I found myself in the midst of an eager, and passionate sermon. The subject I treated was "the fear of death," which is so plainly written in many faces around us, and also in his pale quiet features. I have now forgotten the greatest part of my lecture, though as the words flowed from my tongue it pleased me much and seemed to me impossible to be refuted. I only remember that the text of my sermon were the words of Goethe: "For I was made man, and that means, that I have striven" —etc. "Why then if we are all combatants," I began, "Who sooner or later must perish beside their colours, why should it be a disgrace to those only who bear arms by profession to meet death with cowardice; why should it not also be considered repugnant to the esprit de corps, and the honour of humanity in general, to cling to life with groanings and lamentations when danger approaches. Soldiers who slink away on the eve of a battle are brought back dishonoured and disgraced, and are thought too despicable to be allowed to fight in the ranks of the brave. Why should a dying man who prays for a respite of days, and hours, and even minutes, not forfeit our sympathy and obtain only a little pity for his weakness? "So it was I spoke. I felt like an old trooper who exhorts his men before they commence the assault on an entrenchment. I believe that at that moment, if the whole of the society had gathered around me to listen, my ardour would only have increased. In the midst of my harangue, I cast a look over the beautiful landscape which lay bathed in sunshine and it seemed to inquire of me whether it were so very contemptible not to close ones' eyes readily on all we have learnt to love, when we do not know, when and how they will open again or whether they will like the change. But this mute interrogation did not disconcert me; I had an answer all ready; so I continued: "What you have once enjoyed is yours for ever. What has time to do with our immortal soul? and if the soul be immortal, will not the best part of our life, our love, all that we have striven, and yearned for be purified and increased, and remain ours for ever. And how few really happy sensations do we owe to that which we shall leave here below. How many delusions cling to our dearest friendships, *must* cling to them for in the midst of our enjoyment we feel restless, and dissatisfied! Then why not leave with a serene countenance this dreary world, where the brightest light throws the darkest shade?"—I could have talked on for ever, had not a vehement fit of coughing cut short my power of speech. Then only did I consider what effect all this might have on my silent and melancholy companion and whether it would not have been better to wait till our acquaintance had ripened somewhat, before I displayed my small knowledge of life and death. That which was a specific for me, his nature might not be strong enough to bear, and then what good would it do him? Should I not appear to him as hard and obtrusive as the lady without nerves had appeared to me. Had I the least right to force my aid and advice on him? However the words had been said and could not be recalled. He remained buried in thought for full ten minutes, and left me time to reproach myself bitterly. Then he began in a grave and affectionate tone to dispel my fears. He said that he agreed to every word I had spoken, and that as he took a great interest in me, it pleased him to see me meet my fate so well armed, and with so much fortitude; but that human destinies were different. "It is unjust, "he continued," to expect from the sick the same strength and courage, which we justly demand in a troop of active and healthy men. Do you not believe that in a soldier who camps in the snow and marches twelve hours a day, the body and blood which he stakes when he hazards his life, and limbs must be of a more vigorous nature than those of the poor wounded man who from the hospital hears the report of the cannon and shudders. And is he for that to be despised? But there is another difference which a girl cannot well understand. A man who has any knowledge of life must perceive that his destiny is not merely to enjoy himself, but that he has a task to perform, duties to fulfil. Do not you think that it must be painful to have to leave the world without having even begun this task? You must not forget this difference Mademoiselle: The soldier fulfils his duty in dying: every other man in living except his death be a sacrifice or an example to others. How can he who has hitherto only lived to neglect his duty die without feeling his death to be a new fault, a new faithlessness. We have exchanged so many confessions," he went on, "that it would be foolish to keep back, one, which to be sure is wholly personal and may not interest you. To judge from the opinions you have expressed you seem to think that my gloomy and unhappy humour is the consequence of an unmanly despair at the prospect of certain death. Perhaps you will be inclined to think more favourably of me when I tell you that my illness has taught me to look upon a life of vain amusements, caring and cared for by nobody, a life of pure selfishness as unworthy of the exercise of great medical skill, and of the benefit of this much lauded climate. The past would not hinder me from dying calmly—it was an empty life nothing worse. It is the future which I had hoped to conquer just when it was too late; wisdom came but strength left me. It is that gnaws at my heart and makes it impossible for me to leave life with the same cheerfulness that you do. Believe me I was not worse than the best of my equals. I spent my youth in idleness, gambling, travelling and such trifles and fancied as long as my father lived that it was a life suitable to my station, and this was also his opinion. I took great pleasure in the intellectual amusements as they are called. I was present at the début of every actor singer and musical composer. I collected fine pictures, cultivated music and took a part in any amateur quartett, and that not badly either. Suddenly my father died and his property, his fortune, his political obligations, and connections were left without a head. Nobody had dreamt of so sudden an end. Now it was my turn, now I had to advance to the front and to take an oar, and just at that time strength, and power to act were taken from me. How this happened and how much or how little the fault lies with me is not to the purpose. Let us suppose that this misfortune was not caused by any fault of mine, but that it came upon me as the stone falls from the roof. Do you not allow that my feelings on looking at the past may well be different from yours? and so are the feelings with which I view the future." I was on the point of answering, *what*, I hardly know, probably it was to ask his pardon for my hasty condemnation, when I was prevented by an old woman who offered roses for sale. He took a bunch and gave her a florin in silver which she held in her hand, and looked at with astonishment, as here one only meets with dirty torn paper money. He made a sign to her, that it was all right and laid the bouquet on the bench between us. A gentleman then approached, and spoke to him. He rose without taking leave, but did not return to me. Soon after I walked away leaving the bouquet on the bench. Now I regret it. What crime have these poor roses committed that I should grudge them even a short reprieve in a glass of water.

Evening.

I went out again, and as I must confess, only to fetch the roses. It seemed to me like a wrong towards living beings, to leave them to wither on the bench. I found them untouched, and now they stand fresh and flagrant outside my window. I had to place them there, for the nights are now so cool, that I dare not leave the window open. I will now read to quiet my agitated thoughts. The roses have brought back to my mind the epitaph on the tombstone:

> So the early fading of the rose
> Is to be envied : it is repose?

This sign of interrogation has slipped from my pen and I cannot make up my mind to strike it out. Truly, it is a question, whether a poor human creature has a right to envy his fellow men for anything, even for death.

The 29th

To-day is my birthday; I formerly never took any notice of it, and did not expect others to do so. This one however as it is my last one on earth, I resolved to honour and solemnize as much as I could. Quite early in the morning I summoned the little girls of my landlord and gave each of them a dress I had made for them, a cake and a kiss. Then I walked out though the day was chilly and without sunshine.

On the stairs I met Mr. Morrik's servant, who came to ask if I were unwell, as I had not appeared on the

8 *

Wassermauer for several days. I felt pleased that some one inquired for me. After the recent conversation in the wintergarden I appeared to myself so unamiable, that I did not think it possible that any one should care whether I lived or died.

I walked up and down for some time underneath the arcades, for the rain swept through the narrow streets, and it was disagreeable to be out there, as a piercing wind which they call here the Jaufenwind had arisen, and though the Küchelberg kept it off in some degree still it now and then blew in gusts round the corner. I felt so dull and unemployed, so dreary, that by way of pastime, I bought some figs and peaches and ate them. I soon felt, that in this cold weather, I had not done wisely, but made bad worse by sitting down beside a woman who was roasting chesnuts, and eating some of these to warm me, and thereby only succeeded in nearly making myself ill.

So this is my holiday! It serves me quite right; How can an unemployed person think of holiday making. "Sour workdays, sweet holidays," that is a different thing. More and more clearly I see that he was right, and that I was not only wrong, but have wronged him. It is only the heartless and selfish who would not feel regret at being called away from this life without having done any good in it. He was very kind and forbearing in trying to find a difference between his position and mine. Have we not all of us duties? Did not my mother fulfil hers till her last breath? And here am I happy in my unprofitable solitude, and joyful as a child who has shirked school.

Here are letters from my father, and little Ernest. Birthday congratulations. I will read them out of doors.

The Jaufenwind has cleared the sky, and the sun shines so warmly that I can no longer stand the heat of the stove, and have to open both windows.

In the Afternoon.

This day has after all been celebrated; by a reconciliation which consisted in a second dispute. As the unexpected sunshine brought every living creature out into the wintergrounds, I walked on from the Wassermauer towards the west, till I reached the spot where the Passer flows into the Adige. There I saw at a distance Mr. Morrik sitting on the trunk of a tree in the sunshine, with his servant at his side. He observed me also, and rose to meet me. I was much embarrassed, for it seemed as if I had come in search of him; however it was too late to turn back; and why should I have done so? Was it not true that I was pleased to see him, and wished to speak to him. I owed him the satisfaction of telling him that he had converted me, and that all my death defying wisdom appeared to me now like the delirium of fever. I could hardly wait till an opportunity presented itself of confessing this to him, and so I almost started when he anticipated me by calling out: "How happy I am to see you! You will wonder at the miracle you have performed on me. During your heartfelt speech I felt what a deep impression it made on me; but like the rest of the world though I saw I was wrong I did not like to acknowledge it, and so I supported my cause as well as I could. We have not met since then, and in the meanwhile I had time to recall it to my thoughts, and after a few hours consideration, I felt I was completely changed and could have sworn never to desert the colours you carried so valiantly before me."

"What will you say," I replied despondingly, "when you hear that I myself have turned traitor?" "Impossible," he exclaimed, laughing—and it was the first time I had seen him, not only smile, but laugh heartily—"and so even you are affected by human weaknesses; but beware of me, for I will bring back the deserter, willing or unwilling; not to pass sentence on him, but to entrust to him again the standard under which I will conquer or die."

There now arose an absurd contest between us, each defending the very point he had vehemently disputed a few days ago, and trying to depreciate his former opinion as much as possible. "You must confess," he at last exclaimed, "that in whichever way the wisdom of a Daniel might theoretically settle our dispute, *my* opinion, I mean your former one, is by far the most advantageous. Since my conversion to it, I feel reconciled to Providence, to the world, and even to myself, as—yes, as you were before you were led astray by me. Now, although my position, my sufferings and the few pleasures left to me are the same, they appear to me tinged with fresh and glowing hues, instead of the dull grey which shrouded them before. I look on the past as I did then; but can I win back what I have lost by losing also that which remains to me? You were so right in saying: in every minute, we can live a whole life. How many minutes, nay days, weeks, perhaps months still lie before me, and shall I not employ them? That which I had intended to do is not of such great importance after all. Humnanity will not be much affected by its failure;

but even had it been of the utmost importance, nothing can now be altered. I cannot go back. I can only advance and should there be some task for me to perform in the next world, I shall be better prepared for it by courage and confidence than by the useless despair of which I now feel heartily ashamed, before you, and should be still more so if you had not left your position, high above the rest of mankind, and had shown no human weakness."

I can only write down dryly all that I remember of what he said; but when he himself utters his thoughts there is so much cleverness, originality and wit in them that they refresh the mind, like the inhaling of vivifying salt, and never leave a bitter taste behind.

It was a delightful hour. Had we been two men, or two women, we would have shaken hands at parting and have fraternized on the spot. We have now agreed to meet daily on the Wassermauer; we still think differently on several points and have not much time to decide them.

The letters from home have also pleased me. Ernest is quite impatient at not seeing me for so long. The poor little fellow does not know how long it will be before we meet. Meanwhile it has grown dark. I will have some music and so close the day harmoniously.

The 3rd November.

Pleasant days are rare guests in this world. Since I last wrote we have only met twice. The day before yesterday the weather was damp and foggy. I walked in the wintergarden, but he was nowhere to be seen. I only perceived the malicious inquisitive face of the young lady who always takes a seat close to Mr. Morrik and me, hoping to hear some of our conversation. The life preserver also arrived, and looked at me severely from head to foot, as I passed before and I heard her say to a lady who sat beside her, intending it for me: "That poor young man; how he has to suffer for talking so much." I shuddered and was very nearly going up to the uncharitable sister, in spite of what had passed between us, to ask her for news of him. Fortunately he sent his servant in the afternoon, to tell me that he was confined to his room by the cold weather —it had snowed during the night—and that I ought to take great care of myself as the transition from autumn to winter was very dangerous. In spite of this I went out both yesterday and to-day with the hope of seeing him, but in vain. When two people are isolated among the rest, how soon they grow accustomed to each other's society! He has no acpuaintances here except the doctor, whom he greatly likes. I sometimes feel inclined to consult this doctor—not to hear anything about myself, I know enough of that; but to hear if he really is doomed or only fancies himself so."

The 5th—Evening.

The wind has changed and now a scirocco is blowing. The whole country of the Adige is covered with fog, a warm soft rain drizzles against the window panes. The poplars have lost so much of their foliage that I can easily trace the outline of the beautiful peak of the Mendola. The vineyards are autumnally bare, the cattle are now sheltered in the stables, everything is prepared for winter, and I am heartily glad of a warm nook. My father writes of much snow and cold, whilst here the southern wind still brings an Italian warmth with it, and in the little garden below my windows, the roses bloom as gaily as if they were quite certain that the snow would never descend from the top of the Muth to the village of Tirol — still less reside on the Wassermauer.

The 6th—Morning.

The roses really seem to be right. The most beautiful sunshine awoke me; the stove shall enjoy a holiday. The green meadows in the lower part of the country are as bright as in May. Half an hour ago I received a note from Morrik saying that he wished to take advantage of the fine day, and enjoy a ride over the nearest hills as walking was forbidden him and he asked me if I would accept his company, and join him. In that case he would fetch me at ten o'clock with the mules. I wrote to him without much deliberation that I would be very happy to do so. Now when I think of it . . . . . .

In the Evening.

Fortunately I had no time to think over it, or I should probably have thought many foolish and superfluous things. My landlady came to announce that the gentleman was waiting for me below, and at the same moment his servant entered to carry down my plaid and bag, so I had to hurry away. He had dismounted when I came down, and the pleasure of seeing him again, after so long a time, looking tolerably well and cheerful, the mild clear day, the view, and the prospect of a pleasant ride helped me to overcome my childish embarrassment. Society had at last got accustomed to see us talk together whilst walking, why should we not also do so on mules. So we rode gaily through the Laubengasse, and over the bridge, where to be sure the whole company of strangers rushed to the railings of the wintergarden, and followed us with their kind looks and remarks. On the other side of the bridge, the road turns to the left and ascends the hilly streets of the cheerful village of Obermais. We soon found ourselves among the leafless vineyards, and in trotting past the houses, saw the grapes pressed in large tubs, and barrels filled with their juice, and under the bare trellises, preparations for next year's harvest. One can hardly imagine anything more picturesque looking than one of those tall fine looking young peasants ploughing underneath these bowers with their strong grey oxen, or as in that beautiful picture of Robert's, resting his cattle while he leans on the pole between them. The whole surrounded by a frame of trellis work, which here supports the vine in the form of a vaulted arcade. They all left their work when we passed—I rode in front on a very quiet animal, led by the guide; Morrik just behind me, so that we could exchange the expressions of our delight at all these beauties of nature, and his servant brought up the rear.

When we had mounted somewhat higher, I involuntarily stopped; the view was so wonderfully beautiful. The entire valley of the Adige lay far beneath us, the river glittered between meadows and sands, and the more distant mountains encircled the whole with their clear and beautiful outline. But how can words describe a scene which the brush of the most able painter could not do justice to. Neither of us spoke, we remained in silent awe, and could only marvel. Had not the mules become impatient, who can say whether we should not be on the same spot still. My docile bay who was more sagacious than he looked, pondered, and shook his head with the conspicuous ears, over the folly of mankind in stopping where no fodder was to be seen: so he moved on slowly to supply our want of judgement, and the others followed. We left to our right a beautiful castle belonging to Count Trautmannsdorf, and the little church of St. Valentine, which stands quite isolated in a sheltered valley. Our way then again turned to the north over a hill which rises at the foot of the Ifinger, whose snowy summit towered in the clear autumnal sky. The whole ridge of the hill is covered with solitary farms, intermingled with old castles that are now chiefly inhabited by rich wine growing peasants who, during the summer months, lodge invalid strangers. I have forgotten the names of most of them, only one of them I remember, the castle of Rubein. There in front of the old battlements stand tall slender cypresses, like guardians round an old sarcophagus and contrast by their sombre hue with the green and yellow foliage of the vine. We took a hasty survey of the courtyard. The small open gallery supported by pillars, the steep stairs, which lead up to it, and in the corner the old, and now nearly bare walnut-tree round which myriads of birds were fluttering and singing, so that it seemed as if they had enjoyed too much of their grape harvest and were now intoxicated and overmerry. I could fill pages with a description of the beauties of these heights. Further on, towards the valley of Passeir, the road gently ascends underneath noble chesnut and walnut-trees, and the view opens out to the Küchelberg, and my dear old

Zenoburg, till it rests on the high projecting village of Schönna with its old castle.

When we arrived it was just noon. We were both tired by our long ride, hungry and silent. The sights in which we had revelled still occupied our thoughts, and here again our eyes hardly sufficed to enjoy the view which extended far and near from every window. I entered the tap-room, whilst Morrik talked to the landlord outside, and sat quietly in the dusk for a while with closed eyes endeavouring to recover my calmness.

The room had a projecting bay window which formed a sort of recess, where sat, as a hasty glance when I entered had shown me, a young peasant, and a girl with their dinner and wine before them. They seemed to notice me as little as I did them. Morrik then came in, and sat down at a table beside me. He appeared more cheerful than usual, but also looked paler, as if the air had fatigued him. We talked about indifferent subjects. Suddenly the young peasant rose from his seat in the window, and with a full glass of wine in his hand, approached our table. "With your permission," he said, "the gentleman won't object to my drinking the health of this lady, as we are old acquaintances." Then he took a sip, looked at me over the edge of his glass, and gave it to me to drink from. I took the glass, but looked at him rather puzzled. He seemed quite unknown to me, and appeared to be flushed with wine, and in a waggish humour, so that I was really frightened.

"Well, well," he said, as I was silent, and Morrik gave him no encouragement; the hat of a Saltner, and a beard of three months' standing certainly give a fellow somewhat more of a diabolical look than his holiday clothes. But if I did not seem appalling to her then, there is still less danger of it now, particularly as her brother, or her sweetheart. . . . .

"Natz," the girl interrupted, "what nonsense you are talking. The young lady does not look as if she felt a great horror of you, but to drink wine is forbidden to those who are ill; is it not so your honour? Ignatzius has a notion that no one can live without wine. Oh what a wild fellow he is! I have been begging and entreating him for a whole hour to come away. We are going down to Meran for our pledge, you understand, our betrothal; but there he will sit, sit till night comes on, and when the wine is well up, forsooth, a pretty figure we shall make before the deacon. Do persuade him to come away my lady——"

"Heigh-ho what's this!" exclaimed the young fellow, whom I at last recognized as my friend of the Zenoburg, "don't you see Liesi that this gentleman and lady are in no hurry either? What do you say to that, sir? she already takes the reins; the women are always in a hurry to get the men into their power. A smart fellow often pauses on this road and drinks his last bachelor's bottle with all the more relish. In other respects," he continued, casting a proud and merry glance at her, "I cannot complain; she is a tightly built lass, and has her senses about her; and certainly she has not been picked up on the highways—Only this setting down, and domineering, that is an affliction to be sure; but even the strongest and most determined fellow must submit to it—How have you fared?" turning to Morrik, the lady here is very nice, and I would not mind changing with you, but then there would be an end of playing the master of the house, "well every one has some burden to carry."

"Ignatz," I said, for Morrik still continued silent, and I feared he would set the young fellow down, whose tongue the wine had loosened, somewhat ungently, "this gentleman is neither my sweetheart nor my brother. We are both of us strangers here; who only had agreed to make this excursion together. You talk about commanding but that demands strength. A poor woman who will be buried before the spring arrives, neither has spirit nor inclination for it. And now go with your Liesi to Meran to the priest, and don't let it be said of you that you did not know what you were doing when you gave her your promise."

The girl who was fresh and blooming, and had a frank and intelligent countenance, now also rose and took the young man by the arm.

"Thank you, young lady," she said, "for helping me to get off with this fellow. Say God speed, to the gentleman and lady, Natzi, and then come along; and I hope ma'am that you will change your mind about dying. I was a servant girl in one of the lodging-houses down at Meran during two winters, and know many a one who quite recovered after having ordered his coffin, and many a one who thought he was breathing his last breath, afterwards climbed to the top of the Muth. The air of Meran is so fine that I should not wonder if it woke up the dead. But now good-bye your honours, or this one here, will go to sleep on the spot where he is standing."

There really seemed some danger of this for he stood leaning against the table, and vacantly stared at the floor. He nodded dreamily towards us, and willingly let himself be led out.

I cannot deny that the whole scene had made a painful impression on me. It did not exactly show the young fellow to disadvantage, but his talk of which I have given the main part without his strong expressions had vexed me. Morrik did not seem much edified either by this encounter. The landlady who brought in our dinner, also asked importunate questions, and so did not improve our humour. Moreover the air was heavy in the low room and the smoke from the kitchen penetrated into it. The cooking too was bad, so we were glad to have done with it and to breathe again the fresh air. We walked slowly along the narrow paths among the picturesque farms, talking little. My cheerfulness however soon returned. "Are you not well?" I asked, as he pensively walked beside me. "I cannot complain," he said, "I should feel neither care nor grief if thoughts did not oppress me."

"Perhaps it would relieve you, if you could express your thoughts."

"Perhaps it would make it worse. My thoughts would hardly please you."

"Your confidence at least would please me."

"Even if I should confide to you, that after all, I fear you have too much confidence in me?" I looked at him enquiringly.

"Look here," he continued, "the little you know of me, is perhaps the best part of me; thence I am persuaded that you think much too highly of me, and would be disappointed if you heard the judgement which other people, who to be sure know me still less than you do, have passed upon me."

"Is it not the same with every one of us," I replied, "either we are judged too heighly or undervalued by our fellow creatures. Even our nearest friends do not always see us in our true light. But shall I for that lose my faith in the durability of our friendly intercourse, the term of which is so very short."

He smiled sadly. "I have a sure presentiment that you will outlive me; perhaps for many years. Since I have known you, your health has visibly improved, and who can tell whether the sentence pronounced on you by your doctor may not one day be laid aside with the rest of the sayings which false prophets have recklessly uttered. You shake your head. Well we will leave the future to decide this question. I carry the sure tokens of death too plainly within me to mistake them. So it causes me much deliberation whether I am not wronging you, in enjoying your society, your conversation, may I say your friendship? without heeding the injury your kindness may do you. You are so far above many things, which, in spite of their meaness, are all powerful in this world; how strong and cruel that power is, I myself have painfully experienced. Lest you should feel hurt at a man's reminding you of the prejudices and opinions which usually have more influence with women, and which hitherto, in our friendly intercourse, we have despised, you must know that I should not be here, not be ill, not be dying if I had been more careful of the judgement of others and of the light, or rather shade which I throw on all with whom I associate."

We had seated ourselves on a stone, close by the roadside, and covered with moss and ivy from whence we could see the beautiful mountain peaks and the sloping heights of the Passer through the branches of the chesnut-trees.

Children on their way to school surrounded us at some distance, peasants passed, and cows were led to the fountain. He did not heed them, but continued in a low voice: "Perhaps you do not know, dear Marie, how much an independent position influences our nature for good or for evil. It is now useless to moralize on the subject, but one thing to be observed, is, that a man who is not restrained by any tie is very apt to despise those who are bound by considerations, or prejudices. I have already told you that I was better than my reputation. As I could easily dispense with the assistance, protection, and good-will of my fellow-creatures, I thought I could also dispense with their good opinion, and only laughed when the *home-made* people, as I used to call them, painted my character in darker colours than it really deserved. They envy me my freedom, I often said. As I am not dependent on them for anything, they want me at least to bow down before their moral tribunal. What would freedom be worth if it did not teach us to depend on ourselves and the voice of our conscience alone? So I went my way, and let them talk. Every path in life leads past human habitations, and whoever seeks admission into these must steady his steps that he may not be suspected of being a vagabond or a drunkard, and no peaceful citizen will let such a one cross his threshold. I will not give you a long history—to be brief; I made the acquaintance of a most amiable girl —perhaps, it was for the first time, that I felt warm friendship, and inspired it. The young lady had been engaged for several months to an officer whom I had formerly met in rather light society. At that time he was absent on duty. I am convinced that I would never have entered the house again, had I felt anything like love for his betrothed. But as matters stood, I gave myself up to the charm of this harmless and cordial intercourse, the more so, that her brother saw no objection to it. The family was wealthy and much esteemed. Small parties were given in the house, where dancing, comedies and tableaux-vivants went on, so that many young men were always assembled there even during the absence of the betrothed, and his future bride gaily joined in every amusement. Suddenly I remarked that her brother treated me with coldness and reserve; I was on the point of asking him the reason of this, when he anticipated me by writing a polite letter in which he expressed his positive desire that I should never again enter his parents' house. Of course, we had an explanation in which I was informed that the officer to whom his sister was engaged had charged her to break off all intercourse with me, as I was a man of no principle. Several other circumstances added to the irritation caused by this unfortunate affair, and though I did my best to spare my fair friend every sorrow, yet the affair took a serious turn. The conversation ended in a duel. I shot into a tree, but the brother whose blood was hotter than mine, grazed my side with his bullet. It was not much to speak of, but the agitation which I with difficulty repressed, the cold of the winter morning in which I drove for several hours in my carriage back to town, and the pain and rage I felt at seeing this pure and charming tie so foolishly rent asunder, all this laid me prostrate. I only rose from an inflammatory fever to be sent here as incurable. And now, dear Marie, you will understand why I can no longer make light of your innocently walking by the side of a man supposed to be without principles. I who, at least, have always adhered firmly to one thing, and that is not to seek my own happiness at the cost of another's."

I had long made up my mind how I should answer him. "If you have confided all this to me, with the hope of changing my opinion," I said, "you little know me. It can only confirm me in the belief that I do well in availing myself of the right of speaking the truth to you. A right which is only granted to the dying.

"All the good I have enjoyed in this life I have had to struggle for. I so truly prize our mutual friendship that I will not renounce it so easily. What would friendship be worth, if one had not the courage to acknowledge, and defend it when attacked. How mean and false, should I not appear in my own eyes, and in yours, if I changed in my conduct towards you because bad or silly people accuse you of things which I know to be untrue. I too depend on no one, in consideration of whom, I being a girl should subject my feelings against my convictions.

"If my father should ever hear that in my last days I had formed a firm friendship with a stranger, he will only think highly of the stranger in whom his daughter confided.

"So no more of these reflections which ought never to have troubled you, and we will remain what we were before, good comrades. Is it not so, my friend?"

"Till death, he said, and pressed my hand,

greatly agitated. I soon succeeded in cheering him again, and this happy day would have closed harmoniously, but for an event which to be sure troubled only me. We rode home early, as the sun so soon sets behind the mountains. Morrik was very merry, and talked to his mule, jestingly giving it credit for a sense of the beautiful; he stopped at the farms, and spoke to the children and their mothers, and as we rode past a white bearded old man whom we met panting up the hill, he stuck a paper florin in the old peasant's hat, and was delighted with the thought of what he would say when a passing acquaintance told him of the strange ornament. So we reached the bridge by a shorter road, there I saw on a bench a young Pole whom I had several times noticed, and not in the favourable sense of the word. I had now and then met him alone, and then he had stared at me with such a fierce look in his dark eyes that I always hurried past him. He is evidently one of the most suffering of the strangers here, and his passionate temper seems constantly to be in revolt against his fate, and this inward conflict distorts his otherwise handsome and attractive features. His strange costume, all black, with high boots, and a fur-cap with white feathers in it, gives him a striking appearance, which sometimes has haunted me in troubled dreams, always menacing me with terrible looks. To-day he sat quite quietly, and did not appear to see me. Morrik was in front as the bridge is so narrow that two riders cannot cross it side by side, and I had to pass close to the bench on which he was reclining apparently asleep. Suddenly he jumped up seized the bridle of my mule, and looked at me fixedly with piercing eyes; he wanted to speak, but only burst out in a frantic laugh, so that my mule shied and gave such a start that it nearly sent me flying over the parapet of the bridge. Before I had recovered from my astonishment, he had disappeared round a turning of the road. The guide in a fury sent a curse after him, and I had hardly time to enforce silence on him, before we reached Morrik, to whom I would on no account mention this singular adventure until I ascertain whether there is any mystery concealed under it. I have written too much, and my pulse is beating feverishly. This night I shall have to pay for the pleasures of the day. Good night.

The 8th Nevember—rain and sirocco.

This the second day we have had of this unwholesome air in which no patient dares to go out. It is a pity. I had anticipated the pleasure of discussing different subjects with my newly acquired friend, which I had refrained from doing before we had so cordially shaken hands as comrades. Now, I must wait patiently. Strange that the solitude which formerly seemed to me as life itself becomes only the resort of necessity now that I have associated with a genial and intellectual mind. I must content myself with my books and music. Every morning he sends his servant to enquire how I feel. The ride seems to have done him good, I still feel it in my limbs. I will write home and tell my father of my new friend; I know it will please him.

The 11th November.

Now, at last, the southern winter has commenced its mild reign, and people say that this will continue. Yesterday I again remained out of doors from two o'clock till sunset with Morrik on the Wassermauer, not always conversing, as he in compliance with my request brought a book with him. The poems of Edgar Allen Poe, he showed them to me with a smile, saying that these were the true expositors of his own feelings before his regeneration, as he called it. I have taken the book away with me and have lent him instead "The wisdom of the Brahmins" by my dear Rückert, of which, however, one can only take in finger-tips at a time, but every pinch of this snuff, to continue the clumsy simile, freshens the mind and dispels congestions.

"You really have given me a spiritual medicine," Morrik jestingly said, "I must beg of you to go on prescribing for me, for that desperate American had quite unsettled me."

He told me that people had talked a great deal about our excursion to Schönna, and looked at me to see if that annoyed me. "Do not let us please them by noticing it," I answered, "just as we enjoyed the sunshine without allowing the gnats and flies that buzzed about us, to spoil our pleasure." We have tacitly agreed never to talk about our illness, as most people here do, and either make themselves unhappy by it or find consolation in it, according to the warmth or coldness of their hearts. But I often perceive that he fancies erroneously that my health is improving, instead of which I distinctly feel the contrary. The momentary relief which I experience is just what characterises the approaching end in this disease. I fancy that I breathe more easily and move with less effort. I also eat more and sleep well, probably owing to exhaustion, which increases, though I have the illusive feeling of more vigour and ease. As I walked home to-day—I dine at three o'clock—I really felt hungry, but I know how it is with me.

To-day there is at Meran besides the usual market one of those large meat ones that take place in the autumn when the Lauben are transformed into long rows of butcher's stalls, and butchering goes on in all the court-yards. On every peg, there hangs the half of a pig or a calf which is sold to the peasants, who come in great multitudes from the Vintschgau, Passeier, and Ultner valleys, and from the different farms in the neighbourhood. Other booths are filled with various merchandize: iron-ware, clothes images of saints and numberless trifles. Between these boothes the people push, press, and jostle, so that if one is not in danger of one's life, one is at all events nearly suffocated as the smell of the meat mingles with the fumes of bad tobacco. I have even seen boys of ten years old walk about with short pipes in their mouths, and the smoke hangs over the market-place like a heavy fog; the lungs that can stand it must really be strong as healthy. I nearly fainted. Those great strong fellows would not stir a step out of my way. Fortunately my friend of the Küchelberg and his Liese came to my rescue, just when I most needed it. By plenty of vigorous elbowing he at last got me safely through those human walls. He was again somewhat flushed with wine, but he nevertheless appeared to me like a guardian angel and I easily forgave him the question he jokingly asked me about my brother or sweetheart. I could not make him understand that the gentleman was neither the one or the other, though very dear to me.

My landlady has just brought me in my afternoon meal. My hunger has grown so morbid that I cannot wait till supper time. Probably these are the last figs of this year. Thank heaven that ham and bread are not restricted to any particular season. What if I played our old doctor the trick of dying before the spring, and that of starvation!

The 19th November.

I can hardly hold my pen, I tremble so with the agitation of this last honr. How rashly I hoped that the weeks would glide on peaceful, and full of sunshine like the last one; one day resembling the other. In the forenoon, those happy hours on the Wassermauer with Morrik; the remainder of the day, my books, and letters, or my work and my piano, which I fancy sounds more and more melodious every time I play on it. And now this occurrence! Moreover I cannot speak of it to any one, and above all before my friend, before Morrik, I must appear as if nothing had happened. Is it not all some fearful dream! Has that poor man, I may say that madman, though he vehemently protested against the suspicion, really spoken words to me that I could not understand, accompanied by looks that I shudder to think of, for they seem to me to have been more expressive than his words. I ought to have listened to the secret misgivings which warned me against the solitary road on the Küchelberg, since that scene on the bridge. But I knew that Morrik was not on the Wassermauer, and did not like to be there without him, particularly as the band was to play on that day.

I had walked on so totally absorbed in my own thoughts that I had passed through the gate towards

Vintschgau before I knew what I was doing: it is still as warm there as summer is at home, and one may saunter on through the leafless vineyards and find every now and then a bench inviting to rest. Where my thoughts were I know not, when suddenly he seemed to emerge from the ground, and stood by my side holding my hand. My fright was so great that I could not utter a sound but I fixed my eyes firmly on his face and saw that he opened his lips with an effort. He began first in broken German, and then fluently and vehemently in French, to excuse himself for the scene on the bridge. He had been blinded by pain and jealousy, and would willingly cut off the hand that had seized the bridle of my mule, if by so doing he could obtain my forgiveness. While he spoke I vainly tried to free my hand from his grasp. I looked around but no one was to be seen, the road was deserted. This roused my pride, and my courage; I drew back my hand, and could at last ask him what authorized him to speak in that way to a stranger. He was silent for some time, and a violent conflict seemed to rage within him. Every nerve of his face twitched convulsively. What he at last said I *will* forget, I listened to it as if it were not addressed to me. *Could* it be addressed to *me*, whom he did not know, with whom he had never exchanged a word? Is a passion that is roused by a figure gliding past like a shadow, by one who is inwardly dead, and only outwardly has a semblance of life; is not that passion but a freak of madness; and is a madman responsible for the words he utters? Only when he threatened Morrik, I began to think such an insanity dangerous, and not merely to be pitied. I do not know what I said to him, but I

saw that it made a deep impression on him. Suddenly
he took off his high black cap with the feathers in it,
and stood humbly before me; "Vous avez raison,
Madame," he said in a deep thrilling voice which before had had a harsh hoarse tone in it. "Pardonnez-moi,
j'ai perdu la tête." Then he bowed and walked across
the fields towards the level part of the country, where
I could for some time distinguish his dark figure moving among the willows.

After having written all this, it seems to me that I
look upon what has passed with more calmness; and
compassion gets the better of my indignation. I looked
at myself in the glass and could still less understand
it.   It will also always remain a mystery to me how
such a scene could take place between two natures one
of whom did not feel the slightest inclination for the
other, who on his part made impetuous attempts to
draw near.   I know that not only affinities draw characters towards each other but also contraries; but can
indifference also have that power? The longer I think
of it the more clearly I perceive that his mind must
be deranged.   I will, after all, mention it to Morrik, for who can say to what I may not expose myself if I should a second time encounter this madman,
defenceless, and fright should paralyze the self-pos-
session which I need to subdue him.

Several days later.

The pain of mentioning this dreadful encounter
to my friend has been spared me. It would certainly
have agitated him, the more so, that he has been
much less cheerful lately, and often walks quite absently beside me.

The poor young man whom I dreaded will never again cross my path. His clouded mind is now brightened by the light of heaven. This morning when my landlady came to me, she told me that a young Pole had died in the night. The description she gave me of his person is exactly that of the poor madman. A hemorrage had carried him off in the night and he was found dead in the morning. I now reproach myself with having spoken too harshly to him, but I had no other weapon than my words. If they were too sharp and wounded him more deeply than the offence demanded, the alarm of that moment may excuse me, and the fact that I did not immediately perceive the state of his mind.

Evening.

Tired, agitated, and in conflict with myself.

To-day when I met Morrik, I welcomed my dear friend with particular pleasure, after these last painful days. He told me without laying much stress on it—for here one is accustomed to the disappearance of some known face—of the sudden death, and asked me if I remembered the handsome young man. I said: no, and then felt heavy at heart as though I had committed some crime. In vain I tried to persuade myself that by this untruth, I had cut short any further conversation on the subject, and perhaps the necessity of telling other falsehoods, I cannot get rid of the painful feeling that I have wronged my friend who has so much right to hear the truth. I shall again have a bad night, and shall not be able to rest till I have confessed all to him, and begged his pardon.

The next day—I believe it to be the 23rd,
cold and foggy.—

I am severely punished. The cold prevents his walking out. Now I must wait patiently till to-morrow comes, or perhaps till the day after. It has become quite a necessity with me, not to let the least breath of untruth, or misunderstanding come between us.

Edgar Allan Poe with his morbid discontents; his bitter and hopeless sarcasms, is now congenial to me. There is a frame of mind when wisdom is repugnant to us, as a bowl of sweet milk is to a man in a fever. Only that . . . .

Two hours later.

Are calm and peace really only words void of meaning in this troubled world? Cannot even those retain them inwardly who had won them. I begin to think that I should not be secure from the events, and storms, which harass my last moments, even were I shut up in a walled in tower, where the ravens brought me my food through the barred windows. If no other catastrophe were possible, an earthquake would root up my place of concealment, and break through the walls, and I should be again cast out into the world among strangers, whose affection would distress me, when I had ceased to care for their aversion.

A visitor disturbed me this morning; the last person in Meran whom I should have expected to see in my room! No less a personage than the Burghermeister of the town. He came to spare me the disagreeable surprise of a solemn summons, and disclosed to me that he had been entrusted with a letter for me, and with the testament of the writer, who names me his sole heiress.

I looked helplessly at the Burghermeister. The thought of my father's death did not occur to me. If this dreadful event were to happen; if I should lose him before my hour had arrived, at least the pain of inheriting from him would be spared me. But who in the whole world—?

I glanced at the letter which the Burghermeister had with some hesitation laid on the table, and saw a handwriting that was quite unknown to me. "I don't know this handwriting," I said wonderingly, though a sudden misgiving seized me, as I remarked that the direction was in French. My evident astonishment seemed to relieve him. He probably had supposed that a more intimate acquaintance had existed between me, and the writer of the letter, and was prepared for a painful scene. "Do you wish to read the letter now or later?" he asked. I opened it at once, and read it with a beating heart but without any outward show of emotion, at least I believe so. The letter was filled with the rhapsodies which I had before spurned from me with horror. They were hardly subdued by the approach of death, though the unfortunate man must have felt it coming. I have not as yet deciphered much of it. The indistinct French hand seems to have trembled at every stroke with violent emotion.

But not a word of the legacy; only wretchedness and accusations against fate which had rent asunder the fetters of passion, instead of loosening them; confused tumultuous words, and ideas, written in order to lighten the burden of one heart, and to weigh down the other with it.

When I had laid down the letter, the kindly old gentleman turned to me, and seemed to ask for an explanation which I could not give. When I had told him that I was just as much astonished as he was, he departed, leaving me a copy of the will for further consideration, but he seriously advised me not to refuse so considerable a property in the first moment of excitement, though I was of age, and need not consult the wishes of my father. He would call again in a few days.

I will take a walk, I feel as if I could no longer remain in the room with those papers; as if they impregnated the air with the fever heat from whence they proceeded. I did not even require to read them a second time to come to a decision; I——, or the poor of Meran—can there be a doubt which of us will outlive the other, and will need the fortune most.

In the Afternoon.

Truly this is a disastrous day. I wish it were past. Who can tell what the evening may bring!

I went out with the foolish hope of meeting Morrik, instead of whom, I encountered all the strange though well known faces in the winter garden. I can generally now pass them with indifference, but they were this day again to wound me deeply.

I perceived that they laid their heads together and whispered as I went by. On one of the benches sat the young *chronique scandaleuse* whom I have long ceased to bow to, as she tosses her head whenever I come near her. The place beside her was the only unoccupied one, but hardly had I sat down, when up she started and moved towards another bench, begging two ladies to make room for her. The blood rushed to my face but I was not conquered. At last the life preserver, who had not deigned to address a word to me for weeks past, rustled into the arbour. This time her heart was too full; she came up to me and said, so loudly that every one could hear her, "Well my dear, I suppose we are to congratulate you. The young Pole has bequeathed to you, his large fortune. Poor young man! To be sure you always kept *him* at a great distance. It is no wonder that he soon died. It is really quite touching that even after his death he offered his broken heart to you."

"You are mistaken," I said. "I have not accepted the legacy which was only left to me by the error of an unsound mind. But even if it had been clearly the intention of the deceased to appoint me his heiress, I would not have accepted it. I am not moved, either by the kindness, or the malevolence of strangers, but generally turn my back on both." Then I quietly read on. There was a great silence in the arbour, and I could hear the quicker breathing of the fat old lady without nerves, as well as that of the little lady who hates me. I did not take any further notice of what they whispered and tittered around me, only I several times distinguished the name of Morrik, purposely pronounced very distinctly. Even that cannot hurt me. But as I walked home, shivering in the damp foggy air, and feeling inwardly as sunless and gloomy as the sky was outwardly. I should have liked a good hearty cry. I feel so weary, that not even tears will flow. Life, happiness, sorrow, everything, seems stagnant within me.

The 25th November.

And now this! this verily is the last drop in the cup of bitterness. This blow strikes at the very roots,

and no storm is needed to level to the ground the
falling tree a child could overturn it. And that this
blow should come from the hand, from which I least
expected it. That just where I had hoped to ease
my heart, I have brought it back more heavy still.
To-day I at last found him on the Wassermauer. The
sun shone brightly; I felt revived and hoped to gain
peace and relief from the conversation I had so long
wished for. I thought I could easily explain to him
this last occurrence, and I was not disappointed; he
smiled when I told him how sorry I was for my want
of truth towards him. He took my hand and before
releasing it he pressed it to his lips. I felt strangely
moved. He had heard of the legacy of the young Pole
but had never doubted that I would refuse it. Everything now I thought was smoothed and settled, and I
cast a grateful look at the sun as if his kindly beams
had cleared it all.

How came it that we again turned to that unlucky
theme? Alas it was my fault. I wished to convince
him more fully still that my feelings for the poor madman had always been cool, and indifferent; so I began
again by saying, how the bare thought of that meeting
filled me with horror; how inexcusable it was to let
people who were so evidently deranged walk about un-
watched. He looked straight before him, and said: "You
are mistaken dear Marie, he was not more deranged
than I am who sit beside you, and I hope I do not in-
spire you with fear. He even has the advantage over
me, for he has eased his heart of the burden which
still oppresses mine."

"I do not understand you," I replied, and I spoke
the truth.

"Then I will continue silent;" what good could speaking do me?

After a pause: "But no, why should I remain silent you might then only fancy something worse. Is it so contemptible, if a few steps from the grave we once more look back on life, and there perceive a happiness which would render it loveable and worth having if only it were not too late, and if then one grows distracted with misery and longing, and with rage against fate? If though dying one longs to press to one's heart the dear one who is denied to us, and breathe our last breath on her lips? That is what happened to the poor lad who now sleeps a dreamless sleep—and so...." He paused and looked at me. There was not a soul to be seen underneath the poplars and he again took my hand. "You tremble! before me too," he said. "Forget my words."

I could not speak. I felt that my last and best happiness was destroyed; the harmless confidence, the warm cheerful intercourse to which my heart clung. Again I was alone, I felt it must be so, if I would not add remorse to my other sufferings. "I will go home," I said, "I feel unwell; you must remain here, and enjoy the sunshine which makes my head ache to-day. I will write a few lines to you in the afternoon to tell you, if I feel better." Then I rose, gave him my hand for the last time; entreated him by a look to say no more, and left him.

I will see if I can collect my thoughts sufficiently to write to him.

In the Evening.

I lay the copy of my letter to him between these leaves, and feel relieved now that it is over; physically relieved, but the weight on my heart still oppresses me. This is the letter:

"Meran, the 25th November.

"MY DEAR FRIEND!

"Let me to-day, bid you farewell for the last time in this world, and express my hope of a happy meeting in the next, towards which we are tending. It will be easier for both of us to take leave of each other now, while we are still under the impression of a pure and friendly intercourse, than it would be later when we should have felt that we do not agree in higher matters, and this I fear would sooner, or later have been the case, for your last words still sadden and dishearten me, as I never thought words spoken by my dear friend could have done.

"How I wish we still lived in the past; then I was happy and hoped that you were so. Why did you speak, why could we not calmly have awaited our destiny, and stood firmly by each other as true comrades till the end came.

"I hope that this calm and premature farewell, though it may cause you a momentary pain, will in time soften your thoughts, and give you back the clear-sightedness with which we a short time ago looked on the past, and hoped for the future. We cannot avoid meeting now and then; let us pass one another with a silent bow, as if already we were shadows moving in a higher sphere.

"I need not tell you that I shall always retain the warmest friendship for you, and I beg you to keep yours for me, though at one time it seemed over-shadowed by darker passions.

"Farewell my dear friend; show me that these

words, which come from the heart, are understood, by not answering them."

"MARIE."

The last of November.

I long for snow and ice for the cold winter air of my home. This sun that shines day after day in the clear blue November sky makes my eyes and my heart ache. This morning I woke with a pleasant surprise; it had snowed in the night and the soft snow still lay unsullied, and pure on the roofs and on the road. Now it has melted away, and only a few traces of it are left. People again walk about in light cloaks, and with dry feet under the leafless poplars.

My father wrote yesterday that he fully approves of my descision regarding the legacy. I immediately informed the Burghermeister of this, and have already received a vote of thanks from the administration of the poorhouse funds, which I would willingly have dispensed with. I now write rarely in this journal. One day resembles the other; they are like the leaves of a tree in the late autumn; all of them are brown, only one falls to the earth sooner than another.

The 1st of December—at Night.

A shooting festival has taken place and enlivened the quiet town of Meran. Early in the morning I was awakened by the band of music which accompanied the shooters from the Sandplatz in front of the Post to the targets. Then the whole day long the report of the rifles was heard and made me feel quite nervous, and later the shouts and jodles of the peasants who arrived rather the worse for wine. In the evening fireworks were displayed on the left bank of the Passer, and it was very pretty to see the population of the town, and the strangers walking up and down, and enjoying the mild air by the light of torches which were placed along the Wassermauer. Then a strong sirocco arose, and wildly swept the rockets across the water, made the torches flicker, and drove the spectators into their houses by bringing on the rain. I saw the spectacle from my window, and remained there till the last spark had died out in the dark starless night.

How long it is now since I have spoken to any one except to the people of the house where I lodge. The wish that my lips might be closed for ever grows stronger every day. Oh for an hour of the cheerful, confidential talk I once enjoyed with Morrik, and then to go to sleep and dream that same dream on to Eternity! But I must endure till my time comes.

The 4th December

When my time has come, shall I find courage to resist my longing to see him once more, and in spite of my resolve, bid adieu to life with my eyes fixed on his. I think he too would wish it, whatever his present thoughts may be regarding my sudden rupture with him. Sometimes the idea torments me that he may have possibly misunderstood my letter and think that I drew back because I feared gossip. I should like to tell him once more that this is not the case; that I only did it for his sake, for his peace of mind, and indeed for mine also.

How is he now? Can he walk out? Who will help him to bear the long solitude of the day. I am truly grateful to him for having granted my wish in not having answered my letter. Still something seems missing in my life, now that I no longer see him, and cannot judge for myself whether he is cheerful or melancholy; how he bears his sufferings, what he reads, what he thinks—his thoughts even, I could once read in his face, his countenance is so clear and open.

Yesterday I met his servant. The faithful creature bowed to me; I should have liked to ask him how his master was; however it is better not.

The 11th.

Took a walk to the Zenoburg; that dear walk of former days, but not with my former spirits. As I passed by the house where he lodges, he was just coming out; he perceived me and stood still and motionless to let me pass. I dared not look at him, but the first glance told me that he had become pale and grave—nearly as much so as when I first saw him. He did not bow, but remained in the shade of the doorway as if fearing to frighten me; so I passed him with my eyes fixed on the pavement.

The hill seemed much steeper to me than when I walked up the first time—probably I have grown weaker—and *then* I was happy. What is it that hinders me from being so again, in spite of all my efforts and self-command. Is it merely compassion for him, and the want of that intercourse which had become a necessity to me. No, it is not that alone; it is as if I had been infringing on some duty. But how could I have acted differently? Can one trifle with the hopes and happiness of this life, when death is so near.

The 16th December—Evening.

A trying but pleasant day has passed. I have

packed a small Christmasbox which I intend to send home. When all the trifles I had worked for my father, Ernest, and my step-mother were laid together; the pretty wood carvings, the picture of Meran, and the figure of a Saltner which I had dressed up for Ernest as like the real ones as possible, I was as happy as a child with its own Christmas presents. And then the packing of it all; as the box was not quite filled, I crammed in all I could get hold of; some pomegranates, a box filled with dried figs, another one with chesnuts, and one of those sweet Christmas-cakes made of honey and raisins. The box will tell its own tale of Meran.

My landlord's apprentice carried the box to the post. Then for the first time for several weeks, I walked on the Wassermauer. The strangers sat on the benches as they had always done, only foot-rugs had become more general. Morrik arrived soon after me. This time we silently exchanged salutations as had been agreed between us. He looked kindly and calmly at me probably to see whether I appeared well and cheerful. I was much heated by my Christmas packing. When I got home I looked at myself in the glass and perceived that it was only a transient flush of agitation, perhaps of pleasure. Now that we have again met so unconstrainedly I fancy that the future will seem easier to me. I need only imagine that I never exchanged a word with him but that I have simply read a story in which one of the characters had attracted me—that I now meet a stranger whose face recalls my idea of this character, and therefore that I take great interest in him. We did not sit down beside each other. I walked several times up and down the Wassermauer with a lady who was very kind to me, inquired why I had so persistently remained at home, and then told me all about herself and her children, from whom she had been separated for the sake of tranquillity. Tears started to her eyes as she said. "To be separated from those dear to us in order to enjoy quiet and peace of mind!" Oh you good doctors! what bad physicians for the soul you are.

Christmas Eve.

What am I to think of this! An hour ago a Christmas-tree beautifully decorated with oranges, pomegranites, and sweet meats, and covered with wax-lights was brought into the room by my landlady. The tree is so high that I was obliged to place it on the floor and yet it nearly reaches the ceiling. A strange maid-servant brought it, my landlady tells me, and would on no account say from whom it came. I have now lit all the tapers and am writing by their light, after having given my landlady's children some Christmas-presents, for the people here never have Christmas-trees.

Now that I am again alone, I ransack my brain to find out who could have sent the tree. The kind lady who may also feel the want of Christmas joys, and Christmas lights? But surely she would have written a letter to say so, and then our acquaintance is so short. Many other kind faces have passed by me in my daily walks, but to whom of these would it have occurred to brighten my Christmas eve. I must confess that in my first irritation, I wronged many of them, and might certainly have found some pleasing acquaintances among them, if my first longing for solitude had not expressed itself so repellantly. Now no one would willingly speak to me.

Can the tree have come from *him?* but that would

be contrary to our agreement. One who must and will keep silence cannot offer presents. It is easier to give than to receive silently, and yet how is it possible to express one's thanks after having already bid farewell.

The more I think of it the more uneasy I become. It is not all as it should be; something unnatural and indefinable seems to have come between us; something pernicious that would revenge itself on us.

Here come letters from my dear ones, from home! But I must first put out the tapers and light my little lamp. Some of the twigs are already crackling and glimmering. The last spark has died out on my last Christmas-tree. The church bells are ringing while I am writing these lines by the light of the moon which is now keeping me company, my lamp having died out.

December the 28th.

We have met again, our hands have touched, and our eyes have encountered each other; but what a sorrowful meeting. The vengeance I expected has come.

The program of a concert was brought to my lodgings. A player on the cither was going to perform in the Assembly rooms at the Post. I am no longer displeased at being roused from my own thoughts; so I went, as I very much like the cither, and have always wished to hear a virtuoso perform on it. When I arrived the first piece had begun, and only three seats in the front row were unoccupied; they seemed to have been kept for some expected personage of distinction: I found myself compelled to take one of these seats of honour, and did not do so, unwillingly for the tone of the instrument was rather low, and there too, I could observe the movement of the performer's hands. The air soon became oppressive; the heat of the stove, the crowded room and its low ceiling all combined to make it so. I was much flurried at first, but I soon grew calm, and listened with delight to the charming and touching sounds. Suddenly the door was opened softly and quietly, and Morrik entered. He stopped when he saw the room filled, but did not like to turn back. Some gentlemen near the door pointed out to him the empty seat beside me. He slowly moved up the room, and arriving at my side, sat down with a slight inclination of the head. My breath stopped and I feared he would perceive the trembling which seized me, as the arm of his chair touched mine; however he appeared to be much calmer than I was, and to listen to the music with more attention; so after a time I mastered my agitation, and listened too, absorbed in an exquisite and sweet reverie. I felt as if the melody were a celestial atmosphere in which our mutual thoughts and feelings rose and intermingled; a harmonious communion of soul with soul banishing all that had hitherto divided estranged and tormented us. I cannot describe how this sort of visionary dream comforted me. I felt persuaded that the same thoughts touched him also. Our eyes were fixed on the cither, and yet it seemed as if they met in one long book.

Even the applause and shouts of bravo! hardly roused us from this ecstasy. The pauses between the pieces only lasted for a few minutes, and at the end of one of them the cither-player put by his cither, and brought out an enormous instrument which he called the divine Kikilira, explaining in a few words that it was an instrument peculiar to the Tyrol, ·and had been constructed by a simple peasant. It is a sort of wooden harmonium—the notes are formed of very hard wood, and the tones are produced from them, by the sharp and rapid blows of two small hammers. It has a harsh shrill sound, and one could hardly have found an instrument more opposite to the cither. It rudely put to flight all my exalted thoughts and feelings, and seemed to outrage my very soul. I would willingly have left the room, had I not been afraid of offending the performer. I feared for Morrik, for I knew how exceedingly sensitive he was with regard to every noise. I slightly glanced at him. He sat with closed eyes his head reclining on his right arm, as if trying to shield himself from this sudden attack.

All at once I perceived that his lips grew still paler, his eyes opened partially and lost all expression; then his head sank heavily against the back of his chair.

Several of the audience also observed this, yet no one moved to assist the fainting man. I fancied, judging by the scornful expression on their faces, that they with malicious pleasure, purposely left this benevolent charge to me. I got up and begged the performer to stop, as a gentleman was unwell. I sprinkled his forehead with eau de cologne, which I always carry with me, and let him inhale the vivifying perfume. Part of the company had risen, but none of them left their places: it was only to observe the spectacle more at their case. Only the cither-player came to me, and helped me to support Morrik, when his senses had returned; and to lead him the few steps to the door. Once out of the room, where the fresh December-wind blew across his face, he recovered completely. He looked inquiringly at me, then remembered what had occurred and leant slightly on my arm as I led him down stairs. "I thank you;" was all he said, and we walked on together as his servant was nowhere to be found. I accompanied him up the *kleine* Lauben, as the street leading past the Post is called, and as far as the church from whence we could see his lodgings. "Do you feel better?" I asked. He bowed his head and made a movement as though he now wished to walk alone. Ere we parted he pressed my hand endeavoured to repress a sigh, and silently turned towards the house. I watched him till he had reached the door; he walked with firm slow steps, and did not once look back. When he had disappeared, I too went home.

I feel so overcome by this event that I must lie down; my head is nearly bursting with pain, and when I close my eyes the harsh hammering sound of that wooden instrument, which surely has received the name of "divine" in derision, rushes wildly into my ears, and I feel feverish and exhausted from the heat and oppressive air of the room.

The 11th January.

A fortnight of sickness and suffering, during which I did not open a book or play a note on the piano— It was only a slight influenza, sleep and diet have pulled me through—though one night when the fever tormented me with horrible visions, I was on the point of calling in a doctor, as my landlady constantly urged me to do. The people here have great faith in medicines. I am glad that I can now again stand on my feet, and owe it to no one but myself. I will venture on my first walk to-day. The air is cold, but still, and the sun is so powerful that I can boldly open my casement. I long to hear something about Morrik; but whom can I ask.

The same day.

My presentiment was right; the visions in my feverish dreams spoke the truth. He is seriously ill with typhus fever. He has been laid up ever since that concert and sometimes the fever is so bad that he lies unconscious for hours. I met his doctor just at the gate of the town, and mustered courage to ask him for news of Morrik; and what good would restraint do me; it would only be ridiculous for does not everyone already know that I led him out of the concert-room, and across the streets and is not my show of interest very innocent, though unfortunately it may seem improper. The doctor looked very grave and I should have liked to detain him, and extract from him a decided answer to my question as to whether there was any immediate danger, but just then one of his patients accosted him, and our conversation was broken off. With what feelings I sat down on the sunny bench, and gazed at the water, watching the logs of wood floating down the stream, and swept away by the force of the current every time they tried to cling to a stone. And is it not so with us poor human creatures; do we not float down the stream of life! and are the happy moments we enjoy anything better than a short rest on a cliff from which we are severed by the first passing wave.—Oh, come peace, come! My heart will break with its stormy throbbing. How shall I be able every morning to endure the pain of imagining him dying, and of not being able to watch for his every breath! Oh heavens! and has it come to this, that I must see him leave this world before me; I who never dreamt of such a possibility.

January, the 12th—Evening.

At last I have gained my point; and the calm I now feel amply compensates me for the struggle I have had to endure. I have just come from his lodgings where I have passed the day with him, and shall do so again to-morrow, and all the days that are yet granted to him.

How I passed this night, God to whom I prayed in my calmer moments alone knows. In those dark hours, when sorrow and hopelessness took away all feeling of *His* presence, and of my own strength, life, time, eternity whirled about in my giddy brain just like the helpless logs of wood tossed by the waves.

In the morning I begged the landlady to go to his lodgings and enquire how he bad passed the night. She told me that a stout elderly lady with fair ringlets had opened the door of Mr. Morrik's sitting-room—He lay in the adjoining room and talked so loud in his fever that one could hear him distinctly from the outside. The lady asked who had sent her, and on hearing who it was, had made a wry face, and sent her away with the information that there was no change.

This was a terrible blow to me. I knew what he thought of the professional philanthropy of the life preserver, and that he had always purposely avoided her. And now there was she listening to his feverish talk, and plaguing him with her officiousness in his lucid intervals. I could not bear the thought.

It was early in the morning when I ascended the stairs of his lodgings, fully determined not to let any consideration, except what was necessary for his wel-

fare and tranquillity, prevail over me.   My courage
only deserted me for a moment when on knocking at
the door a shrill hard voice called out, "Come in."
All my coolness and presence of mind returned however, when I felt the cold lustreless eyes resting on me,
with a severe rebuking expression; and with a quiet
voice I said that I had come myself to have news of
him, as the information of my landlady did not suffice
me.   Before she had time to answer Morrik called out
my name from the inner room.   "I will go myself," I
said, "and ask the sufferer how he feels.   He seems
to have recovered his senses."

"Mr. Morrik receives no one," she said, "and your
visit would be against all propriety, a reason, to be
sure, which is of little importance to you?"   "At the
death-bed of a friend, certainly not," I replied.   He
called à second time "Marie;" so opening the folding
that led to his bedroom, I entered without a moment's
hesitation.

The small room looked dark, as the only window
opened on the narrow, gloomy street, and was partly
covered by a curtain; still it was light enough for me
to see that his pale face was brightened by a ray of
pleasure when I entered.   He stretched out his hot
hand, and tried to lift his head.   "You have come!"
he whispered, "I cannot tell you how your presence
relieves me.   Do not go away again, Marie, I cannot
spare you, my time is so short.   The lady out there,
you know whom I mean, her very voice pains me; her
presence seems like a nightmare to me, but I cannot
bring myself to tell her so.   I tried to hint to her that
I preferred remaining alone, but she answered that:
patients were not allowed to have a will of their own.

Please remain with me, when you are here I shall see and hear no one but you, and I promise never to annoy you again."

He talked on in this strain in so low and hurried a voice, that the tears sprang to my eyes. I pressed his hand warmly and promised to do all he wished. His face brightened in a moment. Then he lay quite still and closed his eyes, so that I believed him to be asleep but when I tried to draw away my hand, he glanced at me with a sad and pleading look. At the end of half an hour, he really slept. I returned again to the sitting-room where the lady sat on the sofa. She was knitting in great wrath, and the poor meshes had to suffer for my offence. I perceived that there was no time to be lost, so I told her with as much consideration for her feelings as I could, that the patient was very grateful to her for her kindness, but that he would not trouble her any longer as I was going to nurse him with the help of his servant and of the people who lodged him. "*You*, my dear?" she slowly asked, casting an annihilating look at me.

"Certainly," I replied quietly; "among all the visitors here I am the nearest acquaintance Mr. Morrik has, and so we should both think it strange if I left the duty of nursing him to an entire stranger, who moreover has so many other charitable duties to fulfil."

She stared at me as though my mind were wandering.

"Is it possible," she at last said, "that you do not feel, that by this step you will for ever ruin your already so much damaged reputation. Are you related to him? Are you an old woman. who is above suspicion; or are you in need of a nurse for yourself, my dear?"

"I am perfectly aware of what I can do, and what I can answer for," I said, "I regret that our opinions on the subject differ, but I cannot change mine. I shall remain here; and certainly I cannot hinder you from doing the same. Do not be uneasy about my reputation; I believe I told you once before that I have closed with this world, and submitting the case to a higher judge, I hope to be acquitted." She arose, took her bonnet and said: "You will not expect me to remain in the same room with a young lady whose moral principles so widely differ from mine, and to sanction by my presence an intimacy which in every respect I hold to be most reprehensible. Nothing remains for me but to hear from the patient's own lips whether he desires my departure. If the doctor should sanction this continual emotion for a patient suffering from typhus fever, it is no business of mine."

With these words, she moved towards the folding doors, but I quietly stopped her and said: "Mr. Morrik sleeps, so I beg of you not to disturb him; and from this sleep you may gain the tranquillizing assurance, that my presence is rather beneficial to him than otherwise."

After these words we only exchanged a silent and formal curtsey, the door closed on the deeply offended lady and a load fell from my heart. I opened the door of the balcony which also leads into the garden, to let out the odour of acetic ether which the lady without nerves had brought here too. Then I looked round my new domain, and it pleased me much. What a difference between this elegant, handsomely furnished, and lofty apartment, and my own small room with its scanty furniture. Here, his writing-table loaded with all the luxury of portfolios, inkstands, and different trinkets; there, the shelves with his finely bound books; the comfortable arm-chair, and above all the pleasure of breathing the fresh air merely by stepping out on the balcony shaded by awnings from whence a few steps lead into the garden. How sunny, sheltered, and secluded it looked down there; only the splash of the fountain was heard, and the lullaby song of a nurse who sat on a bench with a pretty baby in her arms.

I was so charmed with the peace of this abode that I actually forgot who was lying in the next room in a feverish slumber. I was shocked at having been led for a moment into this obliviousness. I stepped to the door and listened. He called "Marie" in a low voice. When I looked in, he said: "I heard all; you are my guardian angel; I owe you the first refreshing slumber I have had for a fortnight."—"Sleep on," I replied, "you are not to speak. Cheer up, and dream pleasantly." He nodded faintly, and again closed his eyes.

In the afternoon the doctor came. Him, at least, I must exempt from the accusation I recently brought against all doctors; that of being bad physicians for the soul. When I told him why I had remained, he smiled. Has Morrik spoken to him of me? I do not think so. But what pleased him more even than the departure of the life preserver, whose beneficial influence on the nerves, he evidently doubts, was the fact that Morrik had slept for three hours and that his pulse was calmer.

When I accompanied him to the door, and ventured to ask him what he thought would be the end of this illness, he shrugged his shoulders. "The danger has not yet passed," was all he said. I had thought so.

At seven o'clock I walked home; the servant watches by him during the night. He slept when I went away, and did not even feel my hand when I touched his before leaving. I will sleep now; I want to be at my post early in the morning. For a long time I have not felt so peaceful and calm as this evening. Now nothing can again estrange us.

The 13th.

He woke in the night, and immediately asked for me. The servant could hardly quiet him with the assurance that I would certainly return in the morning. I found him much agitated; only after a long explanation, in which he followed me with difficulty, did I succeed in convincing him, that it must be so, that it was necessary that the day and night watches should be relieved. "But if I should die in the night?" he asked. "Then you will send for me, and I will come to you instantly." When I had promised this, he went to sleep again. He does not eat a morsel and his hands are fearfully thin.

I am more convinced than ever that my presence tranquillizes him. The afternoon passed very quietly. We did not speak to each other, but the door between the two rooms was left open, so that he could see the light of my lamp, and watch my shadow on the wall; he had expressly desired this.

I read for a long time, and listened to his breathing. No other sound reached me. Only when I had to give him his medicines I went to him. Then he always had some gay and affectionate words to say to me, but without any tone of passion in them.

"She is a fairy," he said to the doctor, "she makes even death appear a festival to me. Formerly, doctor, I always felt inclined to say to you: 'That thou doest, do quickly.' But now it is of great moment to me that you should prolong my life for a few days. I can never have enough, even of your horrid potions, now that a good spirit gives them to me."

The 15th.

Yesterday I could not write. He was much worse. To-day he is, at least, not worse still; what a sad consolation! The hard frost continues. The fountain in the garden is covered with ice, and not a flake of snow to soften the piercing air, and to relieve the chest. I long for snow, for I am convinced that he will not be better till the air softens. To-day I stood for hours at his bedside, and he did not recognize me. In his delirium, he talked of people and countries unknown to me, and then I saw how little we really know of each other; and yet a moment later when he called me by name, I felt how near and dear I was to him, and that we do know of each other our best feelings and thoughts. All that is really worth knowing.

The 19th January, 5 o'clock in the morning.

I have just come home after four and twenty sleepless hours, and yet I feel that no sleep is possible for me till my feelings are more calm and collected, and I have expressed them in these leaves. I feel like one

11 *

who has been blind, and who struck by the first ray of light, is made aware of his happiness by a dazzling pain. I will try to speak connectedly, though what is the meaning of beginning, middle, end—what is the significance of these words, when eternity has mingled with time; when dying, one awakens to a new life, which is subject to time, yet still bears the impress of eternity.

These are but weak and unconnected words, and I wished to speak clearly.

The days which have passed since I last wrote have been so sad that I could not speak of them. Yesterday evening when the doctor came quite late, I had sent for him as my anxiety increased every hour, he did not conceal his fears. "We must bring on a crisis," he said, "or he is lost." They put him in a tepid bath and dashed cold water over him. This excited him to such a degree that even through the closed doors, I heard his groans and his loud and un-intelligible exclamations. When he had been again laid in his bed the doctor came to me. "I will re-main with him during the night," said the excellent man; "any blunder about applications of ice might be of fatal consequence. You must go home and rest, the day has been too fatiguing for you." I told him that even at home I should find no rest, and would rather remain and watch with him. He did not press me further as he saw that I was quite decided. Had I not given my promise to Morrik that I would not be absent when his end was approaching. So I sat down in an arm-chair at his writing-table and took up a book only for the sake of holding on to something— to read was impossible; for that a clear mind is re-

quired, and mine was clouded over with a dark shadow,
and all my attention was rivetted on the sick-room
where the doctor sat by his bed changing the compresses himself, and only now and then giving the
servant some order in a low voice. The moans and
the rambling indistinct words which broke from those
feverish lips cut me to the heart; this is still his voice
I thought, and these are, perhaps, the last words that
he will ever speak to me. I cannot nnderstand their
meaning, nor does he himself. Oh, what a leave
taking!

I will not dwell on this scene; the remembrance,
even, of that dreadful time makes me shudder. We
heard the hours strike from the church-tower; ten,
eleven o'clock, midnight.—In the next room stillness
now prevailed. I kept in my breath and listened
anxiously, questioning myself if this were a good or a
bad sign. I tried to rise and creep to the door to
hear if he yet breathed, but I found that the agony of
the last hours had nearly paralyzed me, and I could
not move. Or was it only that I could not muster
courage and nerve myself sufficiently to face the dreadful certainty.

Strange! I had thought myself quite familiarized
with death, even if it should approach the bedside of
my dearest friend. And now, instead of calmly facing
it, I shivered with fear like a child in the dark.

I know not if I could have endured these feelings
much longer without fainting, especially as I had not
swallowed a morsel the whole of that day. At last,
just as my strength was giving way the bedroom door
opened, and the doctor came out quietly. "He is
saved."

The shock these words gave me was so great that I burst into a fit of hysterical tears. The doctor sat down opposite me and said: "You weep, Mademoiselle, and perhaps the word 'saved,' seems to you only as a bitter mockery, when coupled with the name of a patient whose life was despaired of before this last illness seized him. But it is just on this illness that I found my hope of saving him. Nature has risked a bold experiment and has succeeded. It is not the first time that I have observed her employ this admirable device by which she first kindles a conflict in the nervous and blood systems; and then summoning the last vital powers, she combines all her forces to drive away the enemy who had taken entire possession of the citadel. Now you will see that our friend, if his convalescence after this fever proceeds without any disturbance, will make rapid progress towards the full recovery of his former health, which was once with reason despaired of. Now I can safely send him to Venice in March, without any fear of his catching the typhus there, as this fever seldom seizes the same person twice. The soft sea air will be most beneficial to his lungs; and though I never meddle with prophecies, I can say, almost with certainty, that in this case— taking it for granted that no outward disturbance occurs —our patient will in less than a year be as strong and healthy as ever."

A slight noise in the inner room, called the doctor again to his post.

He stayed away only a few minutes, but at least I had time to become more collected before he returned. Can I acknowledge even to myself that this great revolution in all my ideas startled me more than it pleased me? So he was to live, and I firmly believing that he was to follow me into another world had as fully taken possession of his soul as if it were written that we should only be separated for a short time, and would part with the mutual wish of: A happy death to you! instead of a happy life to you!

Fortunately this selfish regret only lasted till the doctor returned, and I could say with a heart full of pure joy and gratitude, Thank God, he will live! He will once more enjoy his youth, his strength, his plans, and his hopes! When the doctor was again beside me he said, "They are both asleep: both master and servant. I settled the poor fellow, who certainly has been greatly fatigued, more comfortably in his arm-chair and he did not awake. It seems as if he knew that he is no longer wanted, now that the crisis has passed, and nature herself has taken charge of nursing the patient. I advise you to follow his example Mademoiselle and to lie down on the sofa and go to sleep. I have kept a cup of tea for myself and do not mind in the least remaining here till morning, and will feast meantime on our friend's looks. I cannot let you walk home in this cold winter night, you would by so doing risk all the benefit you have obtained by your stay here." "Benefit!" I exclaimed; "you must know that I have no illusions whatever with regard to the state of my health. I am perfectly aware how little I have to risk. If I have gained anything by my stay here it is only a reprieve of a few days or weeks."

"Pardon me," he said with a smile, "if I do not share your opinion. To be sure we professional men are often worse prophets than the uninitiated. At least we are less confident."

As during the last few days I had written some letters at Morrik's writing-table, I had brought with me the portfolio, in which I keep our old doctor's drawing, I drew it from the portfolio, and handed it to him. "Now you can convince yourself that I am only repeating the prediction of one of your colleagues," and I told him how I had come to Meran.

The drawing appeared to make some impression on him. He shook his head after looking at it, and then said, "I generally examine the patient by auscultation myself before I give any opinion. You say that you have spent the winter without any medical assistance or advice, and perhaps you were right in doing so, for truly our power is very limited. Far be it from me to force my opinion on you, but it would interest me greatly to discover whether your looks, your movements, your voice, and your pulse are only deceiving, or whether this drawing is to be relied on. Would you let me ascertain this?"

"I have no objection to it," I replied, "but you must permit me, whatever the result may be, to have more faith in our old doctor than in you."

After auscultating me, he sat down for about ten minutes in front of me, and after taking a long draught of tea, he answered my question as to whether the drawing was not right after all. "I will not venture any opinion on that subject; all I can say is, that if your lungs really were in that state, then the Meran climate has worked wonders. We have had several cases here, in which the patients sent to us had been given up and were supposed to be in a hopeless state, yet those very patients are enjoying life to this day, to their own and their doctor's astonishment. The time you have staid here is however much too short to have operated such a marvellous recovery, and so I have my doubts about this drawing. I would even venture to say, if the assertion be not too bold, that you have never had any inclination to disease of the luñgs, but that your illness is simply caused by great exhaustion of the nervous system. You say that your doctor is an old practitioner, but auscultation is a recent discovery and if Hippocrates and Galen had to speak on the subject they would certainly commit themselves deeply. You look incredulous dear Mademoiselle. Next year we will again speak of this, for it will be most beneficial to your nervous system, which is in a very irritable state, if you spend another winter here and only visit your relations during the summer."

Could he have assured me positively of all this and proved it by a hundred scientific arguments it would have been in vain. I feel only too well that it is impossible. We had a long dispute about it, and his smilingly sarcastic tone, and confident manner made me at last lose all patience, and I uttered all the invectives I had ever heard against his profession, only exempting our dear old doctor from this sweeping condemnation. It was rather curious to hear a patient quarreling with his doctor for awarding life to him. But if life were again given back to me, could I receive it thankfully as a blessing, would it not appear only as a renewal of bondage after this short dream of freedom?

I could not rest till I had then and there in the presence of the doctor written to my old friend and besought him to come to my rescue; and save me from this return to life into which they wished to delude me.

The day had not yet dawned, when the doctor and I left the house. Morrik's servant was now awake, and his master slept, to awaken to a renewed life. The doctor insisted on my ordering a sedan chair; but I refused decidedly, and went to post my letter myself. I then begged the doctor not to mention what had passed between us to any one, and above all not to Morrik till I had received an answer. He promised it, and smilingly took leave of me, after seeing me to the door of my lodgings. As I toiled up the steep stairs, I again felt convinced that ere long I should ascend them for the last time.

The mountain tops are not yet red with the rising sun, the air is foggy, and flakes of snow begin to fall. My room is comfortable and warm, as the small stove does its duty. If I could but find sleep. This mounting guard has been too heavy a service for the poor invalid. A great battle has been won without him, and he himself has been deluded with the hope of a victory the fruit of which he would not care to enjoy.

January 30th.

Yesterday, I remained at home, as I had rashly promised the doctor not to leave my room till he gave his consent. He said that the honour of science was at stake, if I brought to naught the opinion he had pronounced, by my reckless enterprizes. It is also necessary for our friend he added.

This morning he came to see me. God be praised Morrik it seems, improves rapidly. I dared not ask him if he had inquired for me, had missed me. It appears that he eats and sleeps a good deal.

Rain and snow help me to endure my imprisonment. I shall probably remain at home for the whole of this week. I do not wish to meet anyone. I feel a strange uncertainty and anxiety till the answer from my friend arrives.

I shall not know what face to put on when I meet my fellow creatures. Shall I appear to them as one who after a short rest among them will suddenly take up his staff again, or as one who has changed his mind and is determined to remain. I feel restless and un-settled since that conversation with Morrik's doctor. My home is neither in this world, nor in the next; my mind is uneasy. I fancy that every one looks at me suspiciously, as the police looks on a vagabond whose passport is not in proper order, and who cannot state from whence he comes nor whither he is going. And I shall have to pass another week in this disagreeable state of bewilderment before I can receive an answer, even if he wrote by return of post.

To-day I ought to write to my father but I cannot bring myself to touch a pen—my feelings are in such a sad state of confusion, often it appears to me that my body and soul cry out to me "you *cannot* live;" then suddenly the blood flows again so warmly and vigorously through my veins, that it seems to mock my aching heart, and worn out nerves. In those moments I take out my drawing as if it were a sure bill of exchange for a better world, but the doctor treated it with so little respect, that even this paper has lost its tran-quillizing power. Formerly I was so sure that Death like grim Shylck would insist on the acquittance of his bond, but now I begin to fear that favour, instead of justice, will be shown me, but is it a favour to be restored to captivity?

The 15th.

Still no decision! This cold foggy weather continues. The only ray of light in my gloomy existence
are the daily tidings my landlady brings me that Morrik's nights are good, and that he is gaining strength
rapidly.

I must here confess a foolish action I have been
guilty of. I have bought a new dress, and a silk
neckerchief, just as any other girl might do. To be
sure they were brought up to my room by a grey haired,
half blind pedlar; who came in with his packages
dripping with the cold damp fog. I pitied him when
he resignedly tied them up again, after I had told him
that I should hardly wear out the dress I had on. But
could I not have given him some money, as a com-
pensation for his useless trouble. It is a very pretty
summer dress. I wonder who will enjoy all the blessings and riches of summer in it?

The 1st February.

I have slept on it, and yet have not gained more
composure. When the letter arrived yesterday, I
trembled so with excitement that I could hardly open
it, and then at first all the lines danced before my
eyes. When I had perused it all my ideas were in
such a state of tumultuous confusion that I thought I
was going mad. Was it pleasure? was it dread? was
it self pity? No it was the certainty that we poor
mortals can have no firm and steadfast support in this
unstable world. I believed that I had at least one faithful, honest, intrepid friend; and he too has deceived
me. I fancied that at least my own unbiassed in-
stincts, and presentiments could not mislead me, and
I find that they too had conspired against me.

But the more I read this letter the less angry I feel with him. I will destroy he answer I had begun in the first impulse of my disappointment. He meant it well, and has done his duty as a doctor but I always come back to my old maxim, that all of them are bad physicians for the soul. Did he consider before trying this energetic cure whether, though it might succeed with the body, it might not do irreparable mischief to the soul; or had he kept some "heroic remedy" as he calls it, also for that case. He knows me well—could he not have known me somewhat better? He is right in saying that without this deception I never would have consented to leave my home, my family; and never would have freed myself from those depressing bonds which wore out my life, never have allowed myself the rest which was so necessary for my recovery.

Was it not principally to spare my dear father, who already has so many cares, the additional one of seeing me die without the possibility of saving me, that induced me to leave him.

I would certainly have forced myself to look happy, and to submit to my destiny till I had made myself ill beyond human aid. He knew what suited my character when he deceived me in this cruel way. I have ever preferred the most dreadful certainty to a hopeful uncertainty. If peace and quiet were the only remedies which could strengthen my suffering nerves, and ward off the menacing disease from my oppressed chest, then I could only be saved by the firm belief that I was doomed. And the undecided wavering hope of life would only have aggravated my illness.

How artfully the crafty, malicious, cruel friend brought about what he thought good for me. This drawing, with what seeming reluctance he put it in my hands, in order that I might have impressed on my mind a fixed tangible vision of my danger, that I might be well armed against all rising hopes, all glimmering wishes. Then his exhortation not on any account to consult a doctor who would certainly only seek to delude me, to spare my feelings, in the way all medical men treated their patients. His emotion when I left, his praise of my firmness and self-command—Still I cannot bear him ill-will. He does not know what sort of life it was, he sought to give back to me, by this stratagem. After having resigned it, it appears so paltry and valueless; how painful it is to me to begin anew with all the trifles of this world to which I had already become dead, and to bear what now seems doubly odious to me after having lived in a higher and nobler sphere; to fall back into the dreary drudgery of a girl's life; to be once more tied down to the narrow, commonplace customs and prejudices of a small town; to be observed, judged and pitied by one's so-called friends, who know so little of the characters of their acquaintances, that they invariably mistake their good qualities for their bad ones.

I must cease! my thoughts are lost in the deep gloom of a sunless future, in which the dear faces of my father and Ernest are the only bright spots.

What radiance streamed from the open gate, the entrance of which was guarded by the angel of death.

February the 3rd.

The doctor has just left me. He has taken the letter with him, as he thinks it very remarkable, and says he has not yet met with such a thorough physiologist as my old friend. Perhaps he wishes to show the letter to Morrik. From *him* not a word; I did not like to question the doctor, as I had heard in the morning, that he was getting on well, and yesterday for the first time, enjoyed the warm sunshine on his balcony.

To-day I fancied the doctor was very absent hurried, and mysterious; I had to ask him if he permitted me to walk out. He nodded, and said; "Mind you do not agitate yourself by any exciting conversation." With whom should I speak?

So I must begin life again, where, and under what circumstances? I should like to keep a school; but here the people are all Roman Catholics.

Leave these dear mountains, and return to that dull town to look again on the monotonous faces of its inhabitants with their air of self importance, the obtrusiveness of which disturbs my very dreams. However I cannot leave my father. Fortunately he has not been duped as I have been. He agreed to the stratagem of our malicious friend.

It appears strange that Morrik should not have made the slightest inquiry, or sent any friendly greeting to me. He probably feels that there must be some change in our relations to each other, as it is decided that we are both to live. But some acknowledgement of our former friendship . . . . . or does he not feel the pain and bitterness of having found each other, only to lose one another again for ever.

The doctor says that so severe a crisis often changes the whole nature, and so his soul which has arisen renewed, and invigorated from the paroxysm of fever,

has probably kept no remembrance of his companion
on the road to death.   Well I must submit to it.

Let him forget me; I will always remain to him
what I have been.

The 5th—Morning.

Received a letter from my father congratulating me.
I shed tears over it.   Whilst every one was condoling
with me I felt happy, and now that I am again given
back to life, and ought to rejoice I feel wretched.

These desolate winter-days, the sun shining with
the heat of spring, make me feel miserable in body
and soul; it is but a sterile. . . . .

February the 6th.

Yesterday amidst all my hopelessness, a spark of
courage kindled within me.   I left my writing and
walked to the window.   I felt heartily ashamed of my
cowardice, my grief, and my ingratitude towards God.

What had become of the sentence which I had
once so valiantly used as the theme for a sermon?
"For I was made man; and that means that I have
striven."

The wings of angels which I had expected are not
to be mine yet.   I must still be up and doing, and if
necessary, must work my way through the world with
these mortal arms of mine, and be thankful if some
day I should be able to twine them round a dear friend
and there find rest.

The remembrance that I had once approached a
higher sphere and had learnt to know it, or at least to
anticipate it, will always remain with me for good and
for evil.   For good, as I carry away with me an everlasting treasure of golden thoughts; for evil, as many
things which formerly I should have deemed riches,

will now appear insufficient to me. Yet I would not spare the past.

I have written to my old friend this morning and have reconciled myself with him; and now I will try to be reconciled to myself, for I was justly angry with my own weakness. Must I not be at peace with myself, before I can once again engage in the battle of life.

The 8th February.

And where is the free and happy mortal who is permitted to glide through life as on wings, whose forehead reaches the clouds, who can say that the dust on the road of life has not touched his soul, no barrier hemmed in his steps, or obstructed his sight, that every hour he feels within him an eternal bliss and freedom. To few mortals has fate awarded such a lot as awaits Morrik after his heavy trials. My heart beats with joy when I think of the brilliant future that lies before him. How little I grudge him his happiness; I rejoice in it. It seems strange to me, that only a fortnight has passed since I stood beside his bed. How much has occurred since then! When he hears my name, he will perhaps look up wonderingly, and try to recollect where he met me.

Here I sit thinking and planning for his future, like an old woman who after many long years is told that a friend of her youth has thriven and prospered in life, and who says: " He has well deserved it; his character was noble and generous; I knew him well when I was young!"

The 12th February.

The wisest thing I now can do is honestly to confess my folly and then have a good laugh at myself. How long is it since I again resolved to be a true combattant? And now? What a heroic achievement to lay down my arms and run away without having even the courage to desert, but to lose heart when half way, and turn back again. Well done brave warrior! If I did not look on the whole thing from a ludicrous point of view, I should feel deeply ashamed of myself.

Well this afternoon the air was so warm and spring-like that the sun drove me from my customary lonely walk on the Küchelberg. Not a breeze stirred, the lizards whisked about as gaily as in summer, and there is no foliage to afford shade; the tendrils which were formerly trained into cooling bowers have probably a good reason of their own for not budding as yet.

I turned back, and for the first time for many days ventured on the Wassermauer, which was not much frequented.

My heart beat as though everyone already knew that I had slipped into the society of the doomed, under false colours, and had been sent back with a protest.

I tried to find a ready answer in case anybody should ask me; "and so you have changed your mind, and are not going to die?" All the small sins I had committed in the belief that it was pardonable to gratify every wish, as the wish of one dying, rose in array against me. How impolite, how regardless of giving offence I had been to every one for whose good opinion I did not care. There is that stout old gentleman with a small thermometer in his button-hole, who fastens or unfastens one of the buttons of his overcoat at every degree more or less of cold. At first he had lectured me about my health, and I had not only continued my imprudent courses but even, when I once met the fat philanthropist, unconsciously let down my veil, to his great astonishment. There is that young girl, with whom I never exchanged another word, because after the first quarter of an hour of our acquaintance she kissed me, and read aloud a poem which her brother had composed. There is that lady with her two big mustachioed sons, who with great foresight, had cautioned me against any flirtation with them, and after all was much offended when I followed her advice and turned my back on them; and above all the poor little chronicler of scandal, who can now only come out by means of an arm-chair, but still has strength enough left to rejoice over the weaknesses of her fellow creatures. What a character she will give me, when she arrives in the next world before me! Well I hope He who judges up yonder will be more lenient than the good people here below. I was thinking over all this, and feeling very much provoked at my own paltry cowardice which seemed to flourish again and prevented me from attaining the indifference and disdain with which I had formerly looked down on the life here, when I reached the Winter garden, and glancing along the benches and arbours, what I saw there put the finishing stroke on my remaining courage. There sat bolt upright, and expanding around her the skirts of a dazzling toilette, the lady without nerves, and beside her, silently looking on the ground, and perfectly restored—Morrik! She was eagerly talking to him, and he listened patiently, a kind smile even brightening his face. I grudged her that smile, as I would have done to no one else. I cannot express the misery I felt, the

longing to be away, never to see, or be seen of them
again; never to be forced to speak indifferently to those
with whom, in the presence of death, I had exchanged
words full of weal or woe.

I fled across the bridge, and along the highroad
which leads through the beautiful valley of the Adige,
and after passing several villages reaches Botzen sixteen
miles off. I soon left the first village of Untermais
behind me, and then sat down on a bench, and there
collected my thoughts sufficiently to devize a plan,
which though wiser than the rest was still exceedingly
foolish. If I walk on for several hours, I thought, I
shall reach Botzen to-day, and probably some carriage
or omnibus may overtake me, and give me a lift. Once
at Botzen, I can write to the people with whom I lodged,
and apprize them that I was forced to leave suddenly,
send them some money, and beg them to pack my
things and forward them to me. By so doing, I should
never again see them all, and should avoid the trials
and pain of leave taking in case anyone should care
about my departure—at least it will not trouble *my*
rest. And who will care? Perhaps the doctor, and I
can write to him. I need not be uneasy about *him*
whom I once called my friend. He must have *quite*
recovered, if he can sit beside the lady without nerves,
and smile when she speaks to him in her shrill voice.
When I had taken this resolution, I felt quite satisfied,
at least I fancied that I was so; so I walked bravely
on towards the south, and tried to enjoy the fine scen-
ery around me; the green meadows, the bare rugged
mountains with the snow glittering on their summits,
the picturesque houses of the peasants, the vineyards,
the rushing streams which I passed on my way, and

above all, I tried to rejoice in the thought that I had now put an end to all my doubts and cares, and had depended on no one but myself. It seemed quite a relief to return home, and to hide my broken wings. They had been too weak to soar aloft, and had not borne the test of freedom. Is not that a common misfortune among caged birds?

The sun had now set. I had passed a village the name of which I did not know, and had there drunk a small glass of wine as, I was shivering in my light cloak. The air was sharper than was agreeable to a patient spoiled by the warm sun of Meran. I became more and more uneasy as I wandered alone, along the highroad, in the twilight. I often looked back to see if nothing was coming that might give me a lift. An omnibus passed me, but it was crowded with smoking peasants, and did not look inviting.

After having walked on for another hour, nearly famished, and with no shelter in view, the brave heroine who had formed such daring projects, sat down on a stone by the way-side, and had a good cry, like any other baby which had strayed from its home. Truly death is easy, and life is hard!

Heaven knows what would have become of me had not a lucky chance, no, it was kind Providence, taken compassion on me. Suddenly I heard the rolling of a light cart, and the crack of a whip, and looking up I recognized in the charioteer, my friend of the Küchelberg, Ignatius.

After scanning the lonely figure, with sharp eyes he pulled up. A touching scene of recognition took place, which ended by Ignatius lifting me into his cart, and driving me homewards. He had concluded some wine business in Vilpian and was in high spirits. He was quite satisfied with my declaration, that lost in thought, I had walked on and so strayed far from Meran. There I sat wrapped up in coverings, and conveyed home as speedily as possible. Fortunately we did not approach Meran before dark, and did not meet anyone except the doctor, who came out of a house just as we were passing through Untermais, and who little suspected who was hiding from him in that cloak and veil. During the drive, kind Ignatius gave me a detailed description of his conjugal felicity, with a freedom of expression which I had to pardon on account of the wine of Vilpian which had loosened his tongue. "Certainly," he remarked, "Liesi still had her old propensity for setting down and knowing better; but he had at last come to the conclusion that she really *did* know better. A single person did so many foolish things, but when two kept house together all was quite different. Where one was at fault, the other succeeded, and two pair of eyes saw just twice as sharp as a single pair could do. Then his Liese was so handy and clever in every respect, just as he had always wished his wife to be. She always had a kind word for him, in short, life seemed a paradise to him since his marriage." Once he asked after the gentleman who had been with me at Schönna. When I told him that he had quite recovered his former health, he hummed a song, and nodded and winked at me so mischievously that I got quite angry.

The good people with whom I lodge, stared in astonishment when I told them how far I had wandered. I then informed them that I would leave after another week. I have been told that the passage over the Brenner is now free from snow and the cold is not very keen. I must take advantage of this early, and probably transient, spring for my passage over the Alps. . . . . .

I now make a solemn vow that to-morrow I will do public penance for my childish flight of to-day. I will walk on the Wassermauer, speak to my few acquaintances and tell them how marvellously I have recovered my health. I will confront even the lady without nerves, and see if I cannot be restored to her favour. It would have been really too disgraceful if I had reached Botzen. To run away like a rogue who dares not look an honest man in the face. Then I quite forgot too that this diary would have remained here, and who knows into whose hands it might have fallen.

The next day—Spring has burst forth.

Can one write down what the heart can neither seize, nor comprehend? I will try.

When I rose in the morning I did not in the least fear all the trials which this day would bring me, all the test of courage I should have to undergo in front of the enemy. Had I known what bliss was awaiting me, I would have perhaps run away overpowered by its greatness. Yesterday I wrote that life was hard to bear; but hardest of all for a poor weak heart to bear, is great happiness when it has never before tasted it from youth upwards, and is then suddenly crushed and overpowered by its weight. It cannot cease to ask itself, "Will it not be taken from me before my strength is equal to it?" There is one comfort however in this, that no true happiness has to be borne alone. This deep and heartfelt bliss can only be given us by a fellow creature, who in bestowing it on us, shares it with us. There lie the first violets they too bear witness to the spring which has this day come to me. I had a refreshing rest after my long wandering of yesterday; softly rocked to sleep by a conscience which had grown quite easy since I had firmly resolved not to be ashamed before the world of the crime I had committed in returning to life.

When I rose the day was far advanced. While dressing my hair before the glass I perceived that my colour was returning, and when I put on my dress, I remarked that I could no longer wear my funereal clothes; they have become much too tight for me and confine my chest. The old hoary headed pedlar came in good time! It is long since I have had a fit of vanity. But if one is to live, why not do like other women? When I had done plaiting my hair, I came to the conclusion that after all, I did not look so very old. I do not know how it happened, but my thoughts then suddenly turned to the young Pole, and I began to consider what charm was attached to me, that any-one could fall in love with, at ten paces distance. Probably it is all a matter of taste.

For the first time I was ashamed of my old-fashioned clothes, and when putting on my hat, determined to have a new ribbon for it, before I ventured out on my thorny walk among the strangers. And so it came to pass that as I was going to leave my room, my head filled with finery like that of a silly Miss in her teens, the door opened and in walked Morrik. I very believe that he had forgotten to knock. I was somewhat startled, but he did not seem to notice it. He was quite absent and shy.

He did not even sit down, but walked at once to the window, and admired the view; then examined the writing-table, and talked about rococo furniture with the air of a connoisseur. All at once he burst forth, and begged my pardon for the liberty he had taken in calling on me, but that he was starting for Venice to-morrow morning, and wished to take leave of me. He wanted also to excuse himself to me and to thank me.

I sat down on the little sofa, and could find no word in reply but: "Won't you sit down." I still had my hat on which did not appear very hospitable but he seemed to think of nothing but how to express in words, what weighed on his mind.

"What must you have thought of me," he at last said, "when you neither saw nor heard anything of me, after that night when you, and the doctor watched by my bedside. But I am not quite so bad, so heartless, so ungrateful, as you must have supposed me. The truth is that I can recollect no more of what happened during my illness than I can remember of an uneasy dream. I certainly fancied that I had seen you at my bedside, that I had received the medicines from your hands, and that it was you who had arranged my pillows. I had also a vague impression of some strange scene between you and my bête noire, the lady without nerves. But when I had considered it all, it appeared to me, so strange that I quickly banished it from my mind. Had I not received the letter from you, in which you so seriously and decidedly bade me farewell. To be sure your landlady came daily to inquire for me, but then many other persons did the same. Why should you not have been civil, though everything was at an end between us. So I feared to act against your stringent orders, by trying once more to approach you. I even doubted whether you would not consider it as an offence if I were to write a line to you before leaving, and send you a bouquet as is customary in this country. You will now understand my astonishment when having accidentally met the life preserver, I heard from her that all that had seemed to me a dream, had actually taken place; that you had really been my deliverer and faithful guardian, and with noble generosity, had taken pity on my sufferings and not resented all that had estranged us, and had so suddenly put an end to the bright and happy days of yore. Now I can hardly thank you sufficiently. I feel quite unhappy, and bewildered when I think of the past. I wished to tell you so yesterday, and to clear up all that must have seemed incomprehensible to you, but you were out when I called. Were you not told that I had been here twice? Perhaps you would rather leave everything unexplained, as it was before; quite without my knowledge and will. Your interest was only for the dying man. Now that it is decided that I am to live, I am perhaps quite as much estranged from you as when I rashly uttered the words that pained you so much. Well, I am to leave Meran to-morrow, and you will be freed from the constraint which my presence has caused you."

What I answered; what he said, when he spoke again; how it came that his hand held mine, and that he again called me "Marie," as he formerly had done, how can I tell?

The air seemed suddenly filled with intoxicating music, my eyes were dazzled with the rays of heavenly light which appeared to stream through the room.

How long this ecstasy lasted I know not; all I know is that Eternity opened before me. I had died happy and without agony, and now I was awakened to a new life, in heaven and yet in this world; dead to all the small cares and faintedheartedness of human life, and arisen to the full glory of peace, everlasting trust, and the eternal knowledge of the truth.

"Come," he said at last, "you are ready for a walk; let us make our bridal visits."

I took his arm, and he first led me across the passage into the workshop of my landlord, where the good old Meister and his apprentices stared at us, and the Frau Meisterin hearing the news, rushed into the room, with a frying pan, which she was just going to put on the fire, still in her hand; she loudly sang my praises, and congratulated Morrik on having secured such a treasure as a wife, till I at last burst out laughing through my tears. Then we walked through the town, and he now and then entered a shop, and bought most useless things only for the pleasure of saying. "Send it to the lodgings of my betrothed, you know the house of the tailor, three stairs high, next door to heaven," and he said it all with perfect gravity.

When we arrived on the Wassermauer, all the strangers were assembled as if by appointment. The band was playing, and for the first time, it seemed to me, that the instruments were in tune, and the musicians keeping time.

At first I felt rather embarrassed, as all eyes were upon me, but that soon passed off, and I was infinitely amused to see how amiable and friendly every one had suddenly become, and how pleased I was with them. We first turned to the life preserver, and actually something like a tear glistened in her small unmeaning eyes when Morrik kissed her hand and told her she was as yet the only woman who had made me jealous. This speech procured me a gracious kiss on the forehead and the assurance that my behaviour was to be overlooked in consideration of my jealousy, and weak nerves. Then came the lady with her two smart sons, the sister with her brother the poet and even the fat gentleman with the thermometer at his button-hole. From them all we received congratulations, and they all assured us that they had known it long ago; to which Morrik answered that in that case they had known more than we ourselves had done; he even joked with the little *chronique scandaleuse*, who alone persisted in treating me with icy coldness. To a child who offered me a bunch of violets he gave his whole purse. The sun shone, the trumpets seemed to call the spring from its winter sleep. And yonder in the churchyard where I had chosen a sunny little corner for my grave, the flowers were blooming, as if after having taught us to live, death had disappeared for ever.

After that, we sat together for a long time and only took leave of each other when the sun was setting.

"Darling," he said, "I have solemnly promised our tyrant the doctor, not to see you again before next spring. Nothing he says is so pernicious to the health of convalescents as a long betrothal between two solitary young people. That was the reason he would never speak out about your nursing me in my fever; although I several times very plainly alluded to it. But you have learned how to write as I know to my own cost, and so we shall still be united. How I shall rejoice at the first letter from you which does not speak of leave taking but of meeting, never to be parted again; not of death, but of a life full of happiness."

We were standing on the stairs in the twilight. We clasped each other's hands and promised to bear this last trial cheerfully. I pressed him once more to my heart before I had to surrender him again; but we both firmly trusted that He who had granted us this happiness would also grant us a future to enjoy it. We shall not in vain have passed from death to life . . . .

I now close this journal: I will send it to you to-day, my dearest friend, perhaps it may amuse you to peruse it on your lonely journey when your thoughts are with me. Is not all I possess, are not all my thoughts yours for ever? The pages contain your name more than once. May it be a clear mirror in which our united images are reflected. I lay this poem between the leaves, I have copied it for you, and have placed beside it one of the violets you gave me to-day. When they bloom again, we shall be once more united, if God permits it—and He *will* permit it.—

> Thou shall't not weep but gladdened be
> And bless thyself at noon, at night,
> When free thy soul with wond'ring glee
> Shall joyful taste love's deep delight.
>
> Of life, the tumult all is o'er;
> No sounds to us from earth can soar,
> As heav'nward now our eyes we raise,
> And on the glorious stars we gaze.
>
> Softly the waves of peace shall flow
> O'erwhelming every grief at last;
> And to our senses the bright glow
> Of endless love o'er all is cast.

BEATRICE.

BEATRICE.

NIGHT was far advanced and yet we three sat together in the cool summer-house, conversing over some bottles of wine from Asti, which we had discovered by a lucky chance, and were now emptying to the health of our friend who had just returned from Italy. He was, by several years, our senior, and had reached man's estate, when we first met him twelve years ago, on our southern journey. His manly appearance, the nobility of his demeanour, and a certain pensive charm in his smile had attracted us from the first. His conversation, his universal knowledge, and the unassuming way in which he displayed it, confirmed us in our first impressions, and at the end of the three weeks, which we passed together in Rome, we were united in as firm a friendship as ever existed between men of such different ages. Then he suddenly left us; he was summoned back to Geneva, where he was at the head of a large commercial establishment.

During the succeeding years we never missed an opportunity of meeting again, so he had not hesitated this time to take the longer route through our town for the sake of spending twenty-four hours in our company.

We found him unchanged in his outward appearance; he was still a handsome man, his hair was hardly sprinkled with grey; his high forehead was white and smooth, but he was more silent than formerly. Sometimes he was so absent that he did not hear our questions, but apparently absorbed in his own thoughts gazed at the wine-bubbles in his glass, or holding a lump of ice to the candle watched it slowly melting. We hoped to render him more communicative by making some inquiries respecting his last journey, but finding that even this favourite theme could not arouse him we left him to himself, and kept up the conversation between us, happy to have him at least in the body with us, and patiently waiting for the time when his spirit also should return.

In the meantime I poured forth all the ideas which had lately occupied my mind. They were crude and superficial and would at any other time have provoked a contradiction from our friend who was a sharp and keen logician. The condition of the Italian theatre had given occasion to this discussion. I maintained that it was not in any way surprising if the Italians, in spite of all their pathos and passion, could not equal the dramatic literature of Greece, England, and Germany; nor does it stand higher in France and Spain, formerly so renowned for dramatic glory. The temperament of the Latin races, their nature and cultivation, are so restrained by conventionalities that the tragic element which consists in concentrating all our interest in one single individual is quite unintelligible to them. Nor do they venture to liberate themselves from the trammels of form and give free course to the spontaneous accents of nature which can alone awaken a tragic awe in our hearts.

Like every conversation on elevated subjects which

does not blindly grope on the surface of a question, so the present one soon led us to the discussion of the most mysterious depths of human nature.

Whilst Amadeus drew figures with his silver pencil in the spilt wine, Otto warmly defended the conventionalism I had condemned, and maintained that even fiction should be subjected to strict moral laws. My proposition that the drama should deal with individual, and exceptional cases, rather than with generalities, and exalt natural laws above social ones, seemed to him pernicious and full of danger, for, he said, the conception of a dramatic crime would then be like the harbouring of a demon in our bosom, instigating to the contempt and intolerance of every thing that clashed with our individual feelings and passions. You would thereby destroy the whole social system, which after all must have some reason for existing, in favour of the boundless liberty of the individual. The only merit you appear to recognize in poetry is that which is beyond the pale of every law. I tried to make him understand that the point in question did not only apply to the collision of the drama with outward forms; in a word that heroic and noble souls were wont to solve the problems of duty, otherwise than those timorous and commonplace formalists who are always restrained by petty customs and considerations. Highly gifted natures, who set an example proportionate to their inward strength and greatness, extend by their actions the limits of the moral sphere; and just so, the artist of genius breaks through, or at least extends the limits that confine his art.

If those noble souls are often actuated by pride and excessive self-reliance, do they not atone for it by their tragical end? at least in the eyes of those formalists who regard life as the most precious of gifts, and who for that reason will never engage in any action, or be led away by any opinion, which according to the laws of society must end in death. Such, however, as are capable of understanding the thoughts and feelings by which those noble natures are impelled, will never resign the right of exalting them, for they cannot be meted with the common measure of morality. They who condemn as immoral, what in our wretched and deficient social organisation ought only to be considered as the sacred self-defence of free and strong characters, will never be sensible of the beautiful, or sympathize with what is generous, they will only discern what is profitable.

Thus had I spoken when suddenly Amadeus looked up from his reverie and stretched out his hand to me across the table.

"Thank you," he said, "for these true and noble words you have spoken; they have pleased me much. Amongst us there can be no difference of opinion as to the fact that custom is not the true standard of morality, and that the mission which poetry fulfils lies beyond the pale of human ordinances. I only protest against your assertion that the deficiency of great tragical poets in Italy is to be accounted for by the conventional fetters which restrain the character of the nation. As if capacity of mind, fancy, morality, and the sense of the beautiful must necessarily be equally developed; as if the one did not often outstrip the other.

"If a great tragic genius, such as they once possessed in Alfieri were to be born again to the Italians, the

pirit of the nation would not be slow to welcome
him, and academic prejudices of style, could no more
keep their ground, than enforced conformity to the
law can oppose the rights and duties of a free born
soul.

"No," he continued, visibly moved, and the tears
glistening in his eyes, "the hollow pathos of their
tragedies is not the touchstone by which we can judge
the soul of that noble nation. I cannot hear you say
this without protesting against it, for if ever there
existed a self-dependent character, in feelings, and
actions; that character was my wife's, and she was an
Italian."

He paused, while we sat mute and breathless with
surprise. Though we had always presumed ourselves
to be well acquainted with him, and all related to him,
we now heard for the first time that he had been
married to a woman he so highly esteemed, and yet
whose existence he had concealed as one conceals a
wrong. He rose and paced the narrow and now dusky
room, and we did not disturb him either by questions
or inquiring looks.

At last he stood still, and began in his deep and
mellow voice: "I never told you this because the
remembrance of it has always overpowered me, and
the mere recalling of these events caused me a fever
which laid me prostrate for a week. Still it always
seemed to me as if I were wronging you, when I used
jestingly to evade your railleries on my bachelorhood.
Believe me, it was principally to redress this wrong,
that I sought your society when I this time returned
from my yearly visit to her grave. Let me therefore
simply tell you all that my heart dictates to me; but

first I must open this casement; the air here is so
oppressive that I breathe with difficulty. So, now, go
on with your cigars and your wine, while I walk up
and down.

"A quarter of a century has passed since those
events, yet they are as present to my memory as if
they had happened only yesterday; they will not let
me rest."

What he confessed to us in that night, till the day
dawned—and even then we could not part—I wrote
down the following day, keeping as much as possible
to his own words. Then I little thought that they
were to be his last ones, his last bequest. He had
rightly judged of the power these recollections still
exercised over him; they brought on a fever, which
clung to him during his homeward journey, and was
aggravated by his exertions during a night conflagration, and a few weeks after our meeting the news
reached us that we had then seen him for the last
time.

The following record is now doubly precious to
me, and I can with difficulty bring myself to allow
indifferent eyes to peruse his secret. Then again I
feel it a duty to bring to light the strange fate of those
two hearts. Are not the expressions of noble and
generous souls the rightful property of humanity? . . . . .

*   *   *   *   *

I had reached my twenty-fifth year when my father
died. Standing at his death-bed, after witnessing his
painful agony, it seemed to me that ten years had
passed over my head. My only sister who was very
dear to me, had shortly before married a young agent
of our establishment, a Frenchman, whose family had

long ago settled at Geneva, and who now entered into partnership with our firm.

He was like a brother to me, and so when he and my sister urged me to travel for several months with the hope of rallying my depressed spirits, I took their advice in this, as in all things, and set out on my journey, the more readily that I felt how necessary to me was some outward diversion to my thoughts.

The change of scene soon realized the hopes of my relations. Youth and vitality were restored. I was again able to enjoy the beauties of nature, and my taste for the fine arts, which had been awakened by my former journeys through France and Germany and now found ample food in Venice and Milan, whither I at first directed my steps, intending to proceed southwards by slow journies.

Above all I was impatient to reach Florence. The marvels I expected to find there caused me to look with indifference on the many beauties of art which I met with on my way thither. Thus I reserved only one day for Bologna, where I took a hasty survey of the churches and galleries in the morning, and in the afternoon I drove out to the old convent of St. Michele at Bosco, in order to quiet my conscience by obtaining a complete view of the wonderful old town from the summit of the hill.

It was one of the hottest days in midsummer, and though I am generally little affected by any temperature, yet the suffocating air on that occasion completely overpowered and exhausted me. The road which leads from St. Michele back to the town was entirely deserted. Above the walls of the gardens the trees and bushes projected their dusty boughs. The wheels of the carriage sank deeply into the burning sand. The coachman drowsily nodded on his seat, and with difficulty kept his balance. The tired horse crawled with drooping head and ears along the edge of the road, in the hope of enjoying the scanty shade which now and then was cast across it by a villa, or a garden-wall. I had stretched out my weary limbs along the back seat of the carriage, and after forming a tent above my head by means of my umbrella I fell into a dose.

Suddenly I was roused from my repose by a rough blow on my face, as if some overhanging bough had grazed me as I passed. I started up, and looking around, discovered a blooming spray of pomegranate lying beside me. Evidently it had been thrown at me over the neighbouring wall. The movement I had made seemed to be a signal to the horse to stop. The coachman quietly slept on, so I had ample leisure to examine the spot from whence the branch had been thrown at me. I did so all the more carefully that I had heard from behind the high garden wall a suppressed girlish titter at the success of the merry trick. I was not deceived; after waiting a few moments, standing upright in the carriage, and stedfastly gazing at the wall, I perceived a curly head shaded by a large florentine straw hat, arise from behind it. A pair of dark eyes, sparkling with fun underneath the solemn eyebrows, turned towards me, and seemed to regard me as some strange animal. But when I raised the sprig of pomegranate, and pressing it to my lips, waved it towards the young waylayer, a deep blush suffused her face, and in the next moment the fair vision had disappeared, so that without the branch in my hand I should probably have believed it to be a dream. I left the carriage and pensively walked along the side of the wall, till I reached a high trellised gate which closed the entrance to the garden. Between the old iron bars of massive mediæval workmanship, I could perceive a part of the grounds of the house which stood with closed Venetian blinds among groups of elm-trees and acacias. I shook the lock of the gate, but it would not open; my hand had already grasped the bell rope, when I was seized with sudden shyness at the thought of entering these strange premises. What a figure I should cut were I asked the reason of my intrusion. So I contented myself with patiently waiting for several minutes in the hope of once more seeing the youthful thrower of sprigs. In the meantime I scanned the house, which was in no way remarkable, as attentively as if I had intended to draw it from memory. At last the heat of the sun became unbearable, and I returned to my umbrella tent. This roused the coachman, he jerked the reins and away we crawled; I with my head still turned bakwards, though no trace of the fair one was to be discovered.

When I reached the hotel of the three pilgrims, a heavy shower freshened the oppressive air, and during the night the streets were so deliciously cool and damp, that I never wearied of sauntering through the long arcades, now stopping to drink a glass of iced water at some coffee house; now admiring the portal of some church in the dim light of the lamps. But in spite of the fatigue caused by this continual walking and standing, I could find no rest till the morning dawned. I would not believe that it was the fair young face that kept me awake, though it continually rose before my eyes. I had always considered it a fable that the spark from a single glance could set fire to the heart, so I believed my restlessness to be caused by overstrained nerves.

The next morning however when my hotel bill which I had ordered the evening before was brought to me, I perceived, now that departure was at hand, how painful it was to tear myself, away. I became pensive; then I suddenly recollected that a friend of our firm lived in Bologna whom I ought to visit. Generally my conscience was not over sensitive in these matters, but now it seemed to me that this civility was of great importance. I also reproached myself for the superficial way in which I had looked at Raphael's St. Cecilia, not to mention several other sins of omission. I discovered that Bologna was a most remarkable town, and that after all Florence would always remain within reach.

I finally succeeded in persuading myself that the pretty thrower of flowers had not the slightest share in this sudden change in my plans. Strange to say the outlines of her face, when I tried to recall them vanished more, and more from my mind, and at last I could only remember the expression of her eyes. During the day time while I fulfilled my duties as a tourist, I did not feel any particular agitation, but when the intense heat had subsided, and I directed my steps towards the villa, as though it were a matter of course, I felt a strange uneasiness, and I can even now recollect the songs which I sang to raise my spirits.

I soon reached the spot and found everything just as I had seen it yesterday. The house looked more cheerful, now that the Venetian blinds were drawn up, and on the balcony stood a little dog, who when he saw me stop at the gate, barked furiously. I could not muster courage to ring the bell. It seemed as if a secret presentiment warned me, and I almost wished never to see that fair face again, and to depart early next morning with an unscathed heart. Nevertheless I once more walked round the boundary wall which extended for some distance, and was bordered on the further side by some peasants' huts, and a few fields of maize, nowhere a living creature was to be seen. I had now reached a point where a low hedge touched the garden wall; I could easily climb upon it, and from thence overlook the garden. As nobody appeared. I boldly ventured. The boughs of a large evergreen oak-tree projected beyond the wall, and I hastily scrambled up and clung to the lowest branch for support. I could not have chosen a better place; at a distance of hardly fifty paces I saw on the parched up lawn which now lay in the shade, two young girls who were playing at battle door and shuttle cock quite unconscious of being watched. One of them wore a white dress and the broad brimmed straw hat which I had remarked the day before. She was of middle height with a figure as straight and slender as a young poplar tree. She moved like a bird with a graceful agility such as I fancied that I had never before seen. Her black hair loosened by her lively movements, flowed freely over her shoulders. The face was very pale, only lighted up by the eyes and teeth. Suddenly the shuttlecock was thrown awkwardly, and she burst into a merry laugh which made my heart throb violently, and the hedge appeared to tremble under my feet. Her play fellow was dressed like her; only with less elegance; she seemed to be of an inferior rank.

I hardly noticed her, I was wholly engrossed by her charming companion. The way in which she lifted her arm to throw the shuttlecock, the eager look in her eyes when she raised them to await the coming one, her delight when the shuttlecock described a circuit in the air, the shake of her head at any failure, every gesture was in itself a picture of youthful charm and vigour.

I clearly felt that my fate was sealed, and for the first time in my life I surrendered myself to the sensations which overpowered and ensnared me. In the midst of this rapture, I considered how I could draw nearer to her without startling her, when chance—no auspicious fate—came to my aid. The shuttlecock, which had been sent up high into the air, flew over the top of the oak-tree under which I was concealed, and fell at some distance into the neighbouring fields. She looked anxiously after it. I do not know whether she then perceived me, but when I instantly sprang after it and re-appeared on the wall with it, I noticed that her dark eyes turned towards the place where I had stood with an astonished and displeased expression. The other girl shrieked, and ran up to her, whispering something which I did not understand, but I could see by her gestures that she urged her to immediate flight The fair creature however did not listen to her, but waited quietly till it should please the stranger to restore her property. When I delayed, quite absorbed in my admiration, her face assumed a haughty and defiant look, and she turned coldly from me. I held up the shuttlecock and with a hasty gesture entreated her to remain. Then I took from my neck a velvet ribbon, to which was attached a gold locket in the shape of a heart containing my sister's hair, fastened them carefully to the feathered ball, and threw it towards her. Fortunately it fell just at her feet, and lay on the light gravel of the walk.

She took a few steps with a most stately air, and picked up the shuttlecock; and noticing the locket she darted a quick and flashing glance at me which pierced me to the very narrow.

Her companion approached her, and seemed to make some inquiry. She did not answer, but silently put the shuttlecock and the trinket into her pocket, and then with inimitable dignity, waved the shuttlecock which she held in her hand towards me thanking me, as a princess might, for an homage due to her.

Then she turned and walked slowly towards the house without once looking back.

I now had no further pretext for remaining perched on the wall, and I dared not make another attempt to see her again on that day; and then what would have been the use of it, had I not gained my point for the present. She had evidently recognized me. My reappearance sufficiently expressed my feelings. I had laid my heart at her feet; she had accepted it, and it was now in her possession. Ought I not to leave her time to think over all this. I was so agitated that had I met her then, I should only have been able to stammer out some confused words like a person in a fever.

That night I slept but little, but in the course of my life I never again lay awake and counted the hours with so much pleasure.

At day break I rose, entered the picture gallery as

soon as it was open and remained sitting before the
St. Cecilia for full two hours. There I searched my
inmost soul as before a clear mirror. I felt that the
spark which had reached my heart was of the true
heavenly fire, and not a transitory illusion of the senses.
Those two hours were wonderfully sweet. It was an
anticipation of future bliss and at the same time an
exceeding happiness as if she were sitting close to me,
and I felt her heart beating against mine. The St.
Cecilia before me, her eyes calmly turned heavenwards,
could not have had a purer foretaste of the celestial
joys than I had that morning. Again I waited till the
time for the siesta had passed, before I turned my steps
towards the villa. But this time I did not content myself with merely looking through the bars of the gate.
I boldly pulled the bell and was not even startled by
the endless jingle it produced. The little dog rushed,
barking furiously, on the balcony, and out of a small
side door, which was next a larger glass one, issued
a little man with enormous grey moustachios which
gave him a ridiculously martial appearance. He approached the gate with evident astonishment at the
unexpected visit. I repeated the sentence without
faltering which I had rehearsed previously: I was a
stranger and intended to publish a book about Italy,
and amongst the rest I wished to introduce a chapter
on the country houses of Bologna. So it was of great
importance to me to be allowed to examine this house.
Particularly as it was built in the old style, and was in
many respects remarkable.

The old man did not seem to understand this. "I
am very sorry sir," he replied, "but I cannot admit
you. The villa belongs to General Alessandro T. . .

under whose command I served. I know your country
well, sir, I marched through Switzerland under Bona-
parte. Afterwards when all was at an end and my
wounds became troublesome, my general transferred
me to this quiet post; and when he married for the
second time, he entrusted his daughter to my care, for
you well know sir, how it is when the daughter is
handsomer than the young step-mother. So we live
here in great retirement, but the Signorina wants for
nothing, for her papa sends her some handsome
present nearly every week; the best masters come to
teach her singing and languages, and my own daughter
is an excellent companion for her. Only she never
goes up to town, her step-mother does not care to have
her there, but that does not distress her, so long as her
father is allowed to come and see her, once a month.
Every time he comes, he enjoins me over and over
again to keep his child as the apple of my eye. And
on the Sundays when she goes to hear mass, Nina
and I accompany her and never lose sight of her.
What do you expect to see in this old house? I assure
you it does not differ in any respect from other villas,
and nothing remarkable grows in the garden. There
is no need to put us in some book; what would my
master say to it. Possibly I might lose my situation
notwithstanding my old age.

I tried to appease him, and succeeded if not with
words, at least by pressing a gold piece into his hand.

"I see," he resumed, "you are an honest young
man, and would not be the ruin of an old soldier. If
you persist in your wish, I will lead you through the
house, so that you may satisfy your curiosity. I can
do so the more easily, that the Signorina is just now

at her singing lesson, so she will not know that I have admitted a stranger."

He unlocked the gate with a heavy key and pre-ceeded me towards the house. The ground floor partly consisted of a large cool hall, from which the sun was shut out by closed Venetian blinds, and heavy curtains. True to my assumed character, I begged him to let in some light so that I might see the different paintings which hung on the walls. They were all family portraits of little value; only one of them which hung above the chimney piece engrossed my attention. "This is the mother of the Signorina," said the old man, "I mean the real mother, who has been dead these fifteen years. She was a handsome woman; the people here called her the beautiful saint. Her daughter is very like her, only she is more cheerful. She resembles a bird, who always merry, hops up and down in its cage."

"She seems to possess the voice of a bird, as well," I remarked, with all the indifference I could assume, "if that is hers which we now hear above us."

"You are right," said the old man. "The director of the Opera in town comes here twice a week. When her papa (*il babbo* he called him) pays her his monthly visit, he always stays many hours, and she sings all her new songs to him, and then the poor old gentleman feels as happy as if he were in Paradise. He has not many joys, and without that child he were better in another world."

"What is the matter with him," I asked, "is he ill?"

"As you take it;" replied the old man, with a shrug of his shoulders; "I for my part would prefer death to such a life. For those who knew him when he was still in the army—the giant of Giovanni de Bologna on the market-place, does not look more high spirited, and chivalrous, than did my general—And now! it breaks my heart to think of it. The whole day long he sits in his arm-chair by the window, and cuts out pictures or plays at dominoes—It seems as if he neither heard nor saw, but when his wife speaks to him, he looks up timidly and nods acquiescence to everything she says. Only with regard to the Signorina he has remained the same, and is not easily to be deceived. Those who attempted it would soon perceive that the old lion's paws have still some strength left in them although his claws have been cut."

"But how came he to sink into that melancholy condition?"

"No one knows. Many things have occurred in this house but the outer world only whispers them. My belief is, that, that woman; I mean to say her Excellency, the young Signora struck his heart a deadly blow and he has never recovered from it. So he drags on the burden with which he has loaded himself, as a resolute old soldier bears hunger and thirst though he should dwindle to a shadow. Well, well, these are old stories now, and cannot be altered."

During this conversation we had ascended the stair, and were approaching the room from which the singing proceeded. The voice had a crude inflexible sound; it was a high youthful even boyish soprano. It seemed as if she sang only to give utterance to her thoughts perfectly careless of the sound.

"What is the Signorina's name?" I asked, when we had reached the top of the stairs.

"Beatrice. We call her 'Bicetta.' Oh what a priceless heart is hers! My Nina often says to me,

'Father,' she says, 'if the Signorina is to wait for a husband worthy of her she will remain unmarried.' See here, Sir; this is her sitting-room. There are her books. She often sits up half the night, Nina says, and reads them in many languages. Adjoining is the little bed-room where the two girls sleep. That picture there, above her bed, represents my poor master in his General's uniform as he used to lead us into action. That small figure in the background who brandishes his musket is me, says the Signorina, and she has lately added the grey moustachioes to give it more resemblance. But come away Sir, there is nothing re-markable in here, the furniture is old. The General once wanted to furnish it anew, but the child would not hear of it because everything had been left just as it was when her deceased mother passed the first summer of her married life in this house. There on the balcony she used of an evening to sit rocking her child's cradle, and waiting for the return of her husband when he had gone to town on business."

I stept out strangely moved and stooped to caress the little dog who wagged his tail and licked my hand. Every word which the faithful old man spoke added fuel to the fire which burnt in my breast, and the voice in the adjoining room fanned the flame with its breath.

Fearing to betray myself, I talked of the way in which the grounds were laid out, about the inlaid table of mosaic work, which stood in the middle of the room; of the faded fresco painting on the ceiling. I could not tear myself away though my guide grew impatient.

Suddenly the singing ceased; the door was thrown

open, and she appeared on the threshold, holding a sheet of music in her hand. She had never been so near me, yet I did not discern her features more distinctly than I had done before.

Everything seemed to dance before my eyes I only remarked at the first glance that she wore my locket round her neck.

The old man started back at her appearance and stammered out some clumsy excuse, at the same time stealthily pulling at my coat.

"Never mind, Fabio," she said, "you can shew the gentleman all over the house, and through the grounds, if he cares to see them." Then turning to her companion, who sat on a low chair with some embroidery in her hand; "You can go with them, Nina. But stay I will first tell you something." She whispered some words to her, her eyes always fixed on me, and then bowed gracefully, to me, who could not utter a word. In so doing she pressed her right hand as if involuntarily on her locket, then returned to her singing-master, who had watched this interlude with curious eyes, and the lesson was quietly resumed whilst we three ascended the next flight of stairs. The old man's daughter walked before us and at every turn of the steps, she examined me with a pensive look but did not speak a word. Only when we had entered the garden, she said to her father: "Bicetta charged me to pluck two oranges for the gentleman. She thought he might be thirsty after his long walk. We will pass by the fountain where they are ripest." I followed them as if in a trance, and looked up at the house towards the window from whence we could still hear her voice. The blind was partially drawn up, so I could perceive her standing in the apartment. I fancied that she turned, and followed me with her eyes. Nina also looked up, and then at me. I did not care to hide my feelings from her, I even wished to make them known to her. But as her father was present I could only whisper to her, when we reached the gate and she gave me the oranges: "Express my thanks to the Signorina, and tell her that she will hear more of me. Give back one of these oranges to her, and tell her when she eats it. . . . ."

But before I could finish the sentence the old man came close to us. He took leave of me with much less amiability than he had admitted me.

I repeated my promise not to betray him, but another suspicion seemed to weigh on his mind, for his honest face remained gloomy.

I passed the night in writing a long letter in which I disclosed to her the state of my feelings and placed my future happiness in her hands. Even in those moments of absorbing passion the step which I was blindly taking appeared to me somewhat wild and romantic, but I took up the orange which lay beside me on the table, pressed it to my lips, and closing my eyes represented her to my imagination as she stood on the threshold, gave me that long and loving look, and bowed laying her hand on the locket.

After having written the letter I slept very quietly, and only awoke when it was broad daylight. I again waited for the approach of evening before I took the decisive walk as my own letter carrier.

Fortune smiled on me. I had composed a most impressive speech, with which I hoped to persuade the old man in case he refused to deliver the letter. But this time Nina came to open the gate. The intelligent

girl did not seem the least astonished at my reappearance. She took the letter unhesitatingly, but
when I asked her if she thought the Signorina would
send an answer, she assumed a diplomatic tone, and
said: "Who can tell?" I told her that I would return
to-morrow at the same hour, and begged her to await
me at the gate, so that I need not ring the bell and
let her father into the secret.

"My father!" she exclaimed laughingly. "We are
not afraid of him. Bicetta need only smile on him
and then she can twist him round her little finger in
spite of his savage air—Come somewhat later to-morrow;
we have our drawing lesson just at this hour, and cannot send away the master for your sake. Will you
do so?"

A carriage now rapidly approached the gate. I had
just time to whisper "yes" to the girl before she silently
vanished. Then I hastened away for I did not wish
to be seen before that gate.

The carriage drew up before the house and my
greybearded friend, the steward, jumped from his seat
beside the coachman and assisted a tall white haired
old gentleman to descend from the carriage. I recognized him at once to be Beatrice's father from the
resemblance of their features. He walked with un-
steady steps, stooping forward, and rubbing his hands,
while a delighted smile overspread his countenance.
A footman took a basket of flowers, and several parcels
from the carriage, and carried them after him. I
pressed close to the wall so that I escaped notice, and
at the same time could watch the whole scene. Before
the bell had been rung, the door flew open, and the
slender white figure of Bicetta clung to her father, who

threw his arms round her neck with a touching tenderness, and partly walking partly carried by him she disappeared into the house with the old gentleman. The others followed, and with a pang of envy I saw the gate close behind them. How the remaining hours of that day, and the following night passed I know not. It seemed to me that a constant twilight surrounded me, a sweet lethargy overpowered me, and a celestial harmony filled my soul. Strange to say though I generally felt little assurance in my intercourse with women notwithstanding my reputation as a good looking young fellow, this time I confidently awaited the decision of my fate, no more doubting that I possessed her heart than I doubted that the sun would rise on the morrow. Only the hours that must pass before I could hear it from her own lips, appeared endless to me. I must here mention an adventure which I had next day in one of the churches. As I roved about the streets hoping by continual movement to restrain my impatience, almost unconsciously I entered a church. Neither paintings, nor pillars, nor the people who knelt before the altars could awaken any interest in me at that moment. My thoughts were far away, and I even forgot to tread softly though mass was going on, till the angry mutterings of an old woman made me aware of my unseemly behaviour. So I stood still behind a pillar, and listened to the music of the organ and the tinkling of the bells, and inhaled the smoke of the incense.

As I absently surveyed the kneeling multitude— I, the son of a rigid calvinist, of course abstained from that devout practice.—I remarked on one of the more retired chairs, just in front of me, a pair of dark blue eyes, underneath a white brow, surrounded by auburn curls. Those eyes were fastened on me, and never changed their direction during the whole service.

I confess that at any other time I would have replied to that mute appeal, but on that morning I was perfectly insensible to any allurement, and should probably have left the church if I had not feared to cause a second disturbance. When mass was ended, the handsome woman hastily rose, drew her lace veil over her head, and walked straight up to me. Her figure was faultless, perhaps somewhat too plump, but the agile grace of her movements gave her a very youthful appearance. In the white ungloved hand which held her veil together, she carried a small fan with a mother of pearl handle. When she was close to me, she partly opened this fan, and moved it carelessly, whilst her eyes were fixed on mine with a quiet but significant gaze. When I appeared not to understand her, she tossed up her head, smiled haughtily, so that her white even teeth glittered, and rustled past me. A moment later I had forgotten this interlude; yet all my joy had suddenly vanished. As the evening approached, I felt more and more uneasy, and when the appointed hour struck I dragged myself towards the villa like a criminal who is to appear before his judge. I started back when instead of Nina, whom I had expected I found her father waiting for me at the gate. But the old man though he looked very morose, nodded when I appeared and beckoned to me to approach. "You have written to the Signorina," he said, with a shake of his head, "why have you done so? If I had thought you would do such a thing, you should never with my consent have entered the house. Oh, my poor dear Master—after all my promises to him—and who knows what will be the end of it. I dare not think of it all."

"Dear old friend," I replied, "nothing shall be done behind your back. Had you been at home yesterday, I would certainly have given you the letter, and as for that, you could have read it and convinced yourself that my intentions are most honourable. But tell me, for heaven's sake?"....

"Come now," he interrupted, "do not let us waste our time. You are an honourable young man, and besides, how can such a poor old fool as I am, prevent these things, even if I tried it. Believe me, sir, she is the mistress, in spite of her youth. When she says: 'I will!' no one can resist her. Now, she will see you; she wishes to speak to you herself."

All my senses reeled at these words; I had hardly dared to hope for a letter and now this!—

The old man himself seemed moved when I impetuously pressed his hand. He led me towards the house, and as on the previous occasion we entered by the side-door into the large hall on the groundfloor. This time all the curtains and jalousies were opened, to let in the red glow of the setting sun; two chairs stood opposite the chimney, and from one of them the figure of the girl, so dear to me, arose and took a few steps towards me. She held a book in her hand and between its leaves I saw my letter. Her abundant hair was tied up this time and a black ribbon was twined through it. On her neck I again noticed my locket.

"Fabio," she said, "open the door towards the garden, and wait on the terrace in case I should have some orders for you."

The old man bowed respectfully, and obeyed. In the meantime we stood motionless beside each other, and my heart beat so violently that I could not utter a word. Her eyes were fixed on mine with a grave expression partly of inquiry, and partly of wonder.

A last she regained her full composure, and appeared to understand what a moment before had been unintelligible to her. She stretched out her hand which I eagerly seized, but dared not press to my lips.

"Come and sit down beside me," she said, "I have much to tell you. Do you see this portrait before us? It is my mother's; she died long ago. When I got your letter I sat down before her and asked her what answer I ought to give you. It seemed to me that she assented to nothing but the truth. And the truth is, that from the moment I saw you in the carriage, all my thoughts went with you, and there they will remain till I die." I cannot express what I felt at these simple words. I fell on my knees before her, seized both her hands and covered them with kisses and tears.

"Why do you weep," she asked and tried to raise me. "Are you not happy? I am full of joyfulness. I have suffered much, but now all is blotted out. Now I only know that we are firmly united and I can never again be unhappy."

She rose, I sprang up. Intoxicated with joy, I tried to press her to my heart, but she gently stepped back.

"No, Amadeus," she said, "that must not be. You now know that I am yours, and will never be taken from you by any other man; but let us be calm.

I have considered the matter during the long night that has passed. You cannot come here any more. I have promised it to poor Fabio. This is the first, and the last time that we meet here. If you repeated your visit I should soon have no other will but yours, and I will never dishonour my father's name. Listen, you must go to him, you will find no difficulty in introducing yourself in his house, so many young men," she added with a sigh, "even perfect strangers are received there. When he knows you more intimately, and has given you his confidence, then demand my hand. You may also tell him that we know each other and that I will never marry any other than you. All the rest leave to me, and above all promise not to speak of this to my stepmother; she does not love me, does not wish me to be happy. Oh, Amadeus, is it possible that you can love me as much as I love you? Did you not feel the first time we met, as if a flash of lightning had fallen from heaven, as if the earth trembled and the trees and bushes were on fire! I do not know how it occurred to me to throw a branch of blossoms on the stranger who slept underneath his umbrella. I could not even see your face; it was a childish trick, and I repented if it a moment later; yet an irresistible impulse made me look once more over the wall, and then when I saw you standing in the carriage and waving the branch of pomegranate blossoms towards me, I was seized as with a fever and from that moment you have always been before me whatever I do."

I had led her back to her chair, and holding her hand in mine, I told her how I had passed the last few days. She did not look at me while I spoke so that I could only see her fair profile. Every part of her face, even the pure and spiritual palor of her complexion, and the violet shade under her eyes, were full of expression. Then I too became silent, and felt the warm blood rush through the delicate veins of the small hand that lay clasped in mine.

Old Fabio discreetly looked in, and asked if we wished for some fruit.

"Later," she replied, "or are you now thirsty, Amadeus?"

"To drink from your lips," I whispered.

She shook her head, and looked grave, as she knit her finely pencilled eyebrows.

"You do not love me," I said.

"Far too well," she replied with a sigh.

Then she rose. "Let us walk round the garden," she said, "before the sun is quite set. I will pluck some oranges for you. This time I need not bid Nina do so."

So we walked on, and she holding fast by my hand, asked me about my country, my parents, and if the hair in the locket were my own. When I told her that my sister had given it to me, she enquired after her. "We will go and see her," she said, "she must love me, for I already love her. But we cannot stay there. My father cannot live without me, I am his only joy. You will come to Bologna with me, will you not?" I promised all she desired. Nothing seemed impossible to me now that one miracle had been performed, and she looked upon me with the eyes of love. After that she became exceedingly merry, and we laughed and chatted as happy as children, and ended by throwing oranges at each other. "Come," she said, "let us have a game at battledore and shuttlecock. Nina shall play with us, though she almost makes me jealous, by constantly speaking of you. See, how she slips away, as if she feared to disturb us. Might not heaven, and earth, and all mankind listen to what we say?"

She called her companion, and the good girl came up to us, gave me her hand and said: "I hope, you will deserve your happiness. I would have grudged her to any man but you. If you do not make her happy, Signor Amadeo, then beware!"

This menace was accompanied by so vehement and tragic a gesture that we both laughed, and she herself joined us.

On the lawn, where I had seen the girls at their play, we now all three threw the feathered balls, and were soon as much engrossed with our game, as if we had never had any more serious thought in our lives, and had not decided on all our future happiness an hour before.

Papa Fabio did not appear again. When the shade grew deeper the two girls accompanied me to the gate. I was dismissed without a kiss from those dear and lovely lips. I could only seize her hand through the bars and press a parting kiss on it.

What an evening! what a night! The people of the hotel probably thought I was somewhat crack-brained, or an Englishman, which in their eyes comes much to the same thing.

On my way back I bought a large basket full of flowers which was carried after me by the flower-girl. These I strewed about my room. I ordered several bottles of wine, and threw a five franc-piece to a violin-player in the street. Then I went to sleep in the refreshing night air which entered by the open windows. I still rememcer the sensations I had during my sleep, as if the vibration of the terrestrial globe as it proceeded on its aerial course were re-echoed by the pulsations of my heart.

Not till the following morning did I remember that some obstacles had to be surmounted before I could take possession of what was already mine. I must get introduced to her father; and would he confide in me with the same readiness that his daughter had done? Whilst I sauntered through the arcades of Bologna considering these matters, propitious fortune again came to my aid. I met the correspondent of our firm whom I had visited the second day after my arrival; he was greatly surprised, as he did not expect to find me still in Bologna. I alleged some news I had received from my brother-in-law, as an excuse for my prolonged stay. I said that a plan had been formed to found a branch establishment of our business in Italy, with particular reference to Bologna. My departure was necessarily delayed for an indefinite period, and in the meantime it was my duty to form acquaintances in town. Amongst the names of other distinguished families, I mentioned the General's. Our friend did not know him personally, but a young cousin of his, a priest was a frequent visitor at his house, and would willingly introduce me. "But beware of the dangerous eyes of the lady of the house," he continued, "for though she has not the reputation of treating her admirers with much cruelty, yet your attentions would be wasted, for the young count her present adorer, does not seem at all inclined to relinquish his conquest."

I joined in this bantering as well as I could, and we then made arrangements for an introduction.

In the evening of the same day I met the young priest by appointment at one of the Cafés, and he then accompanied me to the general's house which was situated in a very quiet street. It was a Palazzo of very unpretending exterior, but furnished most luxuriously within. Thick carpets covered the corridors through which we passed to reach the apartment where every night a small circle of habitués assembled.

Prelates of every rank, military men, several patricians, but only men, formed the society. The young abbate never tired of expatiating on the happiness of the fortunate mortals who were admitted to the intimacy of that house. "What a woman," he sighed. He seemed to hope that his turn would also come some day.

When I entered I first perceived the old General. He sat in an arm-chair, and opposite to him an old canon; between them stood a small table on which they were playing at dominoes. On a low stool beside the general lay a pair of scissors and some sheets of paper, on which were depicted little soldiers; these he cut out, when he could not find a partner for his game. A lamp hung above him, and in the full light, I again remarked the astonishing likeness of his features to those of Beatrice. I had hardly spoken a few polite words to the old gentleman, who responded to them with a childish and good-natured smile, when my companion hurried me away. I followed him into a small boudoir, where the lady of the house was reclining on

a couch, while a tall much adorned young coxcomb
sat on a rocking chair by her side; they both of them
seemed rather bored by this tête-à-tête. He was
languidly turning over the leaves of an album, and the
fair lady embroidering some many coloured cushion,
and now and then she caressed with the point of her
brocaded slipper a large Angora cat which lay at her
feet.

By the subdued light of the sconces, reflected by
numberless mirrors, I did not at first recognize in the
lady before me the fair devotee of that morning in
church, although the same mother of pearl fan lay on
a table near her.

She was more quick sighted than I, and started
up so vehemently at my approach, that she lost her
comb and her abundant hair fell over her shoulders.
The cat awoke and purred, the tall young man cast a
piercing look at me, and I myself was so startled as I
recognized her, that I was most thankful for my little
companion's volubility. She remained silent for a
while, and looked at me with that same stedfast gaze
—which had made me feel uncomfortable in the church.

Only when she observed the rudeness of the count,
who tried to ignore my presence, her face grew more
animated. In a low caressing voice, which was the
most youthful part of her, she invited me, after dis-
lodging the cat, to sit down beside her. Then turning
towards the young man; "You can look over the music
which I received to-day from Florence, count, I will
sing afterwards and you can accompany me."

The young exquisite seemed inclined to rebel, but a
severe look from her blue eyes subdued him, and we soon

heard him strike some accords on the piano in the outer saloon.

The young abbate was employed in cutting the leaves of some new French novel, so I alone was left to court our fair hostess. Heaven knows I envied them, aud above all the old canon at his game of dominoes. From the first words I exchanged with this woman, I felt an invincible dislike to her, which increased in proportion to the efforts she made to attract me. I had to summon all my prudence to keep up an appearance of politeness, and to listen attentively to her remarks. My thoughts were far away in the saloon of the villa, and between those glib and clever words, I still heard the soft voice of my darling and saw her eyes fixed on mine with a sad expression.

In spite of this absence of mind and heart, the fair lady did not appear to be displeased with my first attempt. She probably imputed my embarrassment to a very different cause, and the fact that I had sought to be introduced in her house, she certainly construed in her favour.

She praised my fluency in the Italian language, but remarked that I had a Piemontese accent, that I could not find a better opportunity of correcting this, than by frequently joining her friendly circle. Then she begged me to consider her house as my own, provided my evenings were not otherwise engaged. She had melancholy duties to perform, she said with a sigh, and a glance towards the adjoining room, from whence was heard the good natured laughter of the old gentleman as he had won his game. Her life, she continued, only began with the evening hours; I certainly was very young, and the society of a sad woman, grown grave before her time, would hardly attract me. But so sincere a friend as I should find in her was worth some sacrifice. I greatly resembled one of her brothers, who had been very dear to her, and whom she had early lost. She had noticed this likeness in the church, and for this reason, she warmly thanked me for my present visit. She cast down her eyes with well assumed embarrassment and then with a smile stretched out her hand to me which I slightly touched with my lips. "As a pledge of friendship," she said in an undertone.—Fortunately some new arrivals spared me an answer which could not have been sincere. The new comers were dignitaries of the church, men of the world, who treated me, as they would an old acquaintance. The count also returned and whispered a few words to her. She arose and we all followed her into the saloon where the piano stood. She sang the new airs and her Cicisbeo accompanied her.

Her fine voice poured forth trills and cadences and I could remark that between times she glanced towards the dark corner where I leaned against the wall, and mechanically joined in the general applause, at the end of every song.

My thoughts wandered to the villa where I had heard another voice so dear to me. Liveried servants entered noiselessly, and offered ices and sorbets on small silver trays; the music ceased and an animated conversation commenced. The old general now appeared leaning on his stick, and seemed delighted at having won six games consecutively. He asked me if I ever played at dominoes, and on my replying in the affirmative, he invited me to return next evening, and try my luck with him. He then called his valet as it

was his usual hour for retiring to rest. This was the
signal for departure. I obtained a significiant smile
from the lady of the house, and I hastened to leave
the rooms before the rest of the company. I longed
for solitude to shake off the unpleasant impressions of
the evening. Yet I could not get rid of these sensations till next day at dusk, when I again directed
my steps towards the villa. I well knew that I should
not be admitted, but I hoped, between the bars of the
gate, to catch a glimpse of her dress or of the ribbon
on her straw-hat.

I found her on the balcony alone, and her eyes
were turned towards the road as if she expected me.
For a short while we were contented to express our
feelings by looks and gestures. Then she signalled to
me that she would come down, and a moment later
she issued from the lateral door, and approached me
blushing with love and happiness. She gave me her
hand between the bars, but when I asked her if she
would not admit me, she shook her head gravely, and
laying her hand on her heart, she said, "Are you not
here, nevertheless?" We were soon engaged in ex-
changing sweet and childish words of love, till I told
her of my yesterday's visit to her father. When I spoke
affectionately of him, she suddenly seized my hand,
and before I could prevent it had pressed it to her lips.
I did not mention his wife, and her unseemly behaviour.
She understood my silence. "Return to him," she
said, "and do all you can to please him; he cannot
fail to love you." Finally, when I begged her for a
kiss, she approached her cheek to the bars, but hearing
the trot of a horse coming down the road, she speedily
fled. So I had to leave her with an unsatisfied longing

my heart. I confess that for the first time I doubted
e strength of her love. I knew how strictly girls in
ly keep back their feelings, only to give them more
e course when they are once married. But why
idge me a kiss from her lips even when separated
the bars of a gate. Then again I thought of all she
d said to me, and of the looks which had accompanied
r words and felt tranquilized.

Of course in the evening I punctually appeared in
e General's rooms, and he ordered me at once to
e dominoe table. The company was much less
merous than the day before. The old canon when
ook his place retired to a niche near the window,
d was soon snoring comfortably.

This time the lady of the house did not remain in
e boudoir, but sat on a sofa not far from our table,
eatly to the annoyance of her adorer who sat sulkily
posite to her. She had given him a novel, and she
de him read to her. He made many blunders, and
last threw down the book with an oath, common
this country but certainly not fit for drawing room
ciety.

The lady then rose and beckoned to him to follow
r into the next room, where a passionate but whispered
spute took place. We heard that she threatened
ver to receive him in her house again unless he
ered his behaviour.

The old gentleman who had been very happy at
s success in the game, listened for a moment. "What
n be the matter?" he asked. I shrugged my shoulders.
strangely anxious look passed over his face. He
ghed, and for a moment seemed irresolute as to

whether or not he ought to interfere. Then he sank back in his chair, and appeared to be lost in dreams. The canon awoke, took a pinch of snuff and offered his snuff-box to the General; this restored his equilibrium, and we resumed our game. When I at last rose to depart, he begged me to return soon; he preferred me as a partner, to the old canon. These words were spoken in a most amiable tone and accompanied by a cordial pressure of the hand. Altogether in spite of his weaknesses, he still retained the manners of a gen-leman of the old school. His wife dismissed me more coldly than the night before, but this seemed to me to be only for the count's sake with whom in the meantime a reconciliation had taken place.

I was right. The following evening, when the count was prevented by some excursion from appearing at his usual post, her efforts to lure me into her nets were redoubled. I assumed the character of an unsuspecting young man who from sheer respect neither hears, nor sees, nor understands anything, but she was evidently not duped by it. Probably the unsuccessfulness of her efforts provoked her, and incited her to conquer at any price my real or feigned coldness. She was so carried away by her vexation that she lost all command of her feelings, and could not master them even when the count returned. Of course all the rest of the company noticed how matters stood. The correspondent of our house did not neglect to inform me of the rumours which were current in the town. He congratulated me on my good fortune, and little guessed how uncomfortable I felt at his words. I perceived that I must no longer delay in declaring my real intentions.

A conversation I had with the young count pre-
pitated this decision.

One evening when I returned to my hotel I found
im waiting for me. He saluted me with frigid politeness
nd requested me in a curt, and concise manner either
> discontinue my visits at the General's house, or to
xpect an encounter of a different nature. Being a
ranger I was probably unacquainted with the customs
f the country, otherwise he would not have taken the
ouble of giving me warning.

I begged him to wait twenty-four hours, and he
ould then perceive how absurd was any idea of rivalry
etween us. He looked surprised, but as I did not
ive any further explanation, he bowed and departed.

Early the next morning, for I knew the old gentle-
an was up betimes, I asked for an interview with him,
nd was ushered into his bed-room, where he sat
noking a long Turkish pipe. He was rummaging in
everal card boxes in which all his treasures consisting
f cut out pictures lay around him. When he saw me
e stretched out his hand with evident pleasure, thanked
ie for visiting him in the morning, and offered me a
ipe. When I declined this he pressed me to accept
s a token of remembrance several cut out soldiers on
hich he set particular store. I felt heavy at heart
hen I reflected that my future happiness depended
n this poor old man. But to my astonishment the
xpression of his face completely changed when I men-
oned his daughter. He became grave and silent, and
nly the intent look in his eyes betrayed, that even on
iis theme, he could with difficulty collect his thoughts.
 concealed nothing from him. Beginning with our
rst meeting, I related every circumstance up to the

last hours. He now and then nodded acquiescence, and when I told him of my love for her his eyes glistened and he raised them heavenward with a deep emotion which shed a sort of glory over his features.

Then I spoke to him of my circumstances and expressed the very natural wish to take my young wife—provided he should entrust his child to me—to my own home; assuring him however, that I was quite willing to remain in his neighbourhood for several years, as I could never tear her from him. He seized both my hands when I said this, and pressed them with more vigour than I could have believed possible in so weak and worn out an old man. Then he drew me into his arms, and without a word kissed me till his strength failed him, and he sank back into his chair. After remaining so for a few moments he made a sign to me to help him to rise, and when he had regained his feet, he said: "I entrust this treasure to you my son, and thank my God, that I have lived to see this day. Come we will go and tell it to my wife. From the first moment I saw you I felt sure that you had a kind heart. If I had ten daughters I could not see them better provided for. But did you ever see such a naughty child? Fie, fie, Bicetta! meeting a lover when your old babbo's back is turned, but they are all alike when love is in question, and where their heart is concerned they are not to be trusted, no, not one!"

He sighed and his face took an expression partly of anxiety, partly of sorrow. Perhaps some recollection troubled his mind. A moment after he again embraced me, pulled my hair, called me a traitor and a hypocrite, and finally seizing my hand, he drew me towards his wife's apartment, which was situated at the other side of the house.

In the ante-room a maid advanced to meet us; she looked at me with wondering eyes, and only admitted the General to her mistress' room, after having first announced him. She then begged me to wait as her mistress was not yet dressed for receiving. I heartily rejoiced at this, though the time I had to wait seemed interminable.

I could not distinguish what was said in the adjoining room, but the General spoke in a louder and more commanding tone than I had ever heard from him before. A long and hurried whispering followed, till at last the door opened, and the General issued forth erect, and triumphant as if he had won a battle.

"Beatrice is yours my son, the affair is decided. My wife sends her best wishes to you! At first she made some ridiculous objections. You see a cousin of ours, a young fop who is now in Rome, said to her before he left. "Keep Bicetta for me, I will marry her on my return. This was only in fun, but you and I, we are in earnest, so you shall have her Amadeo. It is true," he continued, with a sigh, "that I let many things take their course, I am an old man, and the reins often drop from my hands, but on some occasions Amadeo, I take up arms again and then I am not to be daunted. I now solemnly promise you that Beatrice shall be yours. Come back this evening; you will find her here. Embrace me my son, make her happy; she deserves to be rewarded a thousand fold for the love she bears her old father."

He only left me at the top of the stairs after folding me once more in his arms.

When I returned in the evening, I found the house brilliantly illuminated. In the ante-room many people were assembled who eyed me with curiosity. In the drawing-room the old General sat in his usual place, and the Canon opposite to him, but to-day the dominoes lay untouched on the marble table, for on her father's knees sat his daughter, simply dressed, without any ornaments, only pomegranate blossoms in her hair. Her arms were twined round the old man's neck as if she felt uneasy in this society, and took refuge with her only friend. When she saw me enter, she glided from her seat and stood motionless as a statue before me till I took her hand. She cast a rapid glance at the sofa where her step-mother sat, brilliantly attired, her hair flowing over her beautiful bare shoulders, her round white arm reclining on a crimson cushion. She evidently intended to outshine the slender maidenly beauty of the young girl. At her side sat the tall young count, who had now recovered the phlegmatic insolence of a supreme sovereign. He nodded to me with a gracious condescension.

When I turned towards them holding my betrothed by the hand, I noticed a sudden palor on the woman's face, but she greeted, and congratulated me with a most winning smile; offered me her hand to kiss, and then embraced Bicetta who submitted to it with an impassive face; only the trembling of her hand told me what she felt.

After this we had to receive the congratulations of the company, and I admired my darling who stood the flow of shallow words with which she was overwhelmed with perfect calmness. The General contemplated her with an expression of great delight. He bade us sit down in the embrasure of one of the windows, where two chairs had been placed near each other, and then he proceeded to his game with Don Vigilio.

Bicetta and I soon forgot all around us. The hum of conversation did not reach us. The dim light of a lamp which swung on a chain across the street was bright enough for me to drink the deep draught of love from the eyes of my beloved, and from her enchanting smile. On that evening the company dispersed later than usual. Champagne was drunk, and an old archbishop who was passing through the town on one of his pastoral tours proposed the health of the betrothed. The venerable old man was particularly affectionate to me. He made me take a seat in his carriage and insisted on driving me back to my hotel. But hardly had we been a moment alone together, when the reason for this remarkable condescension appeared. "You are a Lutheran?" he asked. I assented, and he continued with a benign smile; "You will not remain so. The great earthy happiness you have found here, will lead you to a higher bliss. Come to see me to-morrow, and we can talk more about this."

I did not fail to appear, but he could not force me one step from the path which I had traced for myself. I demanded the same liberty of faith which I conceded to my wife. With regard to the children, she might decide for them, till they had reached the age when they could judge for themselves what was necessary to the welfare of their souls. The artful old priest seemed well pleased with this beginning, and to rely on the future.—As he was forced to leave the town, he committed me to the care of a younger keeper of souls; a member of a religious order, who set about the affair much more vehemently and clumsily so that to prevent further unpleasantness, I broke off all intercourse with him. This, I could perceive in the faces of certain of the frequenters of my future parent's house, was greatly taken amiss, but as the General's cordial manner remained the same, and the mistress of the house continued to shew me a cool amiability, I bore it with great equanimity.

My betrothed, who was aware of my feelings, fully coincided in my desire to cut short any further attempt of this kind. "What can they mean by it?" she said. "There is only one heaven and one hell for us; is it not so Amadeo? If I entered Paradise and found you not there, my soul would turn back, and not rest till it had found yours." When she spoke thus it seemed to me that I saw heaven open before me, and I could not believe that any danger threatened our future happiness, or even that any delay was possible.

The wedding was fixed for October. I had made up my mind to bear this interval of two months with all the patience I could muster. Only one thing made me uneasy; I had announced my betrothal to my sister, and brother-in-law, and had not received one line in return.

I knew them too well to fear any objection on their part; only some illness or some sorrow which they wished to keep from me could account for this silence. So in spite of the happiness which smiled upon me, I grew more and more uneasy. At last after three weeks of feverish impatience, the longed for letter from my brother-in-law arrived. He wrote that my sister Blanche had been dangerously ill after her confinement, and that the state of her health was still so precarious that he had not ventured to agitate her by the news of my engagement. If it were possible, it would greatly relieve him if I could come home for a short while.

"You must go," said Bicetta when I had silently handed her the letter. "You must leave this to-morrow. I will try and bear your absence as well as I can. But you must write to me when you arrive, write to me as often as you are able. How I long to go with you. But of course that is impossible. Give my love to Blanche; tell her that she already lives in my heart, and give her this kiss from her sister."

She passionately threw her arms round my neck and pressed her lips to mine. It was the first kiss she had granted me. Even when I had met her alone, and entreated her both jestingly and earnestly not to be so cruel, she had always remained inexorable. How often had I not felt hurt at this reserve, but then she had only to speak a word, or to stretch out her hand with that indescribable smile of hers, and my doubts and displeasure vanished.

I departed with the full persuasion that I should find nothing changed on my return. The old general took leave of me with evident distress; he could not cease to press me in his arms. His wife shewed great interest in the illness of my sister, and so completely deceived me that on my way home, I reproached myself for my former injustice towards her, and mentally begged her pardon.

Part of my luggage remained at the villa which had been my habitation during the last weeks of my betrothal; Old Fabio and my friend Nina faithfully ministering to my wants. I felt sure of returning in less than a month, and hoped to bring back with me my sister and her husband to the wedding. Nina in the meantime went up to town to keep Beatrice company.

Everything seemed to be arranged for the best, and this short separation to be a sacrifice to the jealous gods before I was allowed to enjoy complete happiness.

At home I found matters better than I had imagined during the anxious hours of my long journey. Blanche was out of danger, and it seemed as if the pleasure of seeing me again and the joyful news I brought her, hastened her recovery. Their accompanying me to Bologna however was out of the question. My sister could not leave her child, and my brother-in-law was detained by our business which had lately so much increased that we could not both be spared. Yet they hastened my departure, and indeed as matters stood my visit caused them more anxiety than pleasure, for in spite of our firm resolve to write to each other as often as we could, and though I faithfully adhered to my promise of never missing a single post, yet not a line had reached me from Bologna. During the first week of my stay I was inexhaustible in finding some natural cause for her silence. But when I had remained a fortnight at Geneva without a word either from my betrothed or any member of her family, I was tormented with anxiety. My only comfort was that no great misfortune could have happened to her without our correspondent in Bologna informing me of it, but then again, how could I know that he had not left Bologna, and should any letters have been lost or intercepted, might not his too have been among the number?

I felt that I must start for Bologna if I did not wish to go mad. The state of my feelings as I travelled day and night is not to be described. As I saw my face in the glass when I stopped to arrange my disordered toilet before entering Bologna, I started back. It was certainly not the face of a happy bridegroom, such as I had hoped to return.

It was early in the morning when my travelling carriage dashed along the well known road. I called to the postillion to pull up at the trellised gate of the villa. I jumped out with tottering knees, and rang the bell violently. Some time elapsed before my dear old friend Fabio appeared at the door. When he recognised me he started and without taking time to button his old waistcoat across his naked chest, he rushed to meet me with so disturbed a face that I called out in an agony: "She is dead!"

He shook his head and hastily unlocked the gate, but the fright had completely taken away his breath, so that I could only draw out word by word, a scanty unconnected explanation from him. He observed my pale face and worn out looks, and wished to spare me, instead of which he only cruelly tormented me by his dilatoriness. With many things which had been schemed in the dark, he was unacquainted, for he had only learnt the main points from Nina. I who well knew the actors never for a moment doubted who had taken the principal parts in this fiendish intrigue. Hardly had I left Bologna when that cousin from Rome appeared, and brought forward his imaginary claim to the hand of my bride.

Had he come by order, or would he have arrived of his own accord even had I not been absent I never knew. He cut a sorry figure Fabio said. A life of gambling, revels, and adventures had considerably reduced his fortune, but being the nephew of a cardinal, and of the old nobility, he was still considered a good match. Bicetta had always disliked him. He (Fabio) remembered that she had once boxed his ears for having ventured to kiss his little cousin. Upon which he had laughingly vowed to make her pay for it once she was his wife. Now the time had arrived when he hoped to realize his threat. The step-mother and all those who had most authority were on his side. They had frightened the poor old general by predicting for him all the torments of hell, if he married his only child to a heretic, till they had subdued and silenced him. But whenever he looked at Bicetta his eyes filled with tears, and he would sit for hours in his arm-chair, and sob like a child. He never spoke to his wife for he knew that she was at the bottom of it all.

"And Beatrice?" I asked, half maddened with rage and pain.

"Ah Bicetta," replied the old man, "who can understand her! At first when they urged her to renounce her heretic lover, she had answered: "I have pledged my faith to him in the sight of God, and I will keep it though I should die for it;" so they could not persuade her. Then when her cousin had come to pay his court to her, she had calmly told him: "Don't trouble yourself Richino it is perfectly useless; even had I never seen Amadeo I should never have loved you." Then when he attempted to take her hand and to play the gallant to her, she drew herself up and said in the hearing of Nina: "Miserable coward to lay hands on another's propecty! Go I despise you." She would not see him after that yet she never sheds a tear though the marriage is decided on, and she has quite left off begging and entreating her father, her step-mother, or any one, even God I dare say. She no more received your letters, than you did hers which I posted myself. It seems that the officials at the post-office know what is expected of them when the nephew of a cardinal wishes to carry off the bride of a foreigner. Still it is surprising that she should have resigned herself so quickly for she cannot possibly doubt your fidelity. Nina told me that they threatened to shut her up in a convent if she did not marry her cousin, and certainly a convent is not the proper place for our Bicetta, yet I should have thought it preferable to a marriage with that man, when her whole heart belongs to you. I for my part cannot make her out, and my daughter too is in a perpetual state of amazement.

So the good old man rambled on without venturing to look at me, whilst I lay completely stunned on one of the chairs opposite the chimney. It was the same in which we had sat our hands clasped in one another's the first evening of our betrothal. I was quite incapable of thought; every feeling even of love or of hate seemed paralyzed within me and all vitality to have ceased, as the movement of a watch stops when a blow has broken the spring. After a long pause I recovered my composure sufficiently to ask when the marriage was to take place. "This afternoon," replied the old man in a timid voice. Then I started up, brought to my senses by the nearness of this fearful and decisive event. Old Fabio seized my hands, and looked anxiously into my face.

"Merciful heavens!" he exclaimed, "what are you doing. You know not how powerful they are. If you were to appear openly in the streets, who knows whether you would outlive the night."

"I will go in disguise, I will stand face to face with this scoundrel, and tell him that one of us must die. You surely have a pair of trooper's pistols in good condition. They are all I shall want. Leave me now."

"First you must shoot me with them," he said, and clung so firmly to my arm, that I saw no possibility of freeing myself from his grasp without using force. "Think of Bicetta," he continued, "what would she say to it." "You are right," I replied, and felt as if I were again deprived of all energy. "I know not what she would say, but I *will* know, or I shall go mad. Let go my arm, and give me my hat. I will go to her; I will burst open the doors which keep her from me, and when once I have seen her then come what may."

But he would not let me go. He led me back to my chair and said, "you must surely be persuaded that no one so sincerely desires yours, and the Signorina's, and the old general's welfare as old Fabio, so you must listen to his advice, and not rush headlong to your own destruction. If you imagine that you can reach her apartment, you are greatly mistaken. The house is filled with servants on account of the wedding, and you would fare ill if you desired to see the bride with this face. Let me go to her; they cannot forbid me the entrance, although the Signora does not regard me with favourable eyes. If it should come to the worst, I can always send for my daughter; so if you will write a few lines I promise to deliver them, and they will certainly reach their destination with more safety than by the papal posts. Sit down here by this window and write a few lines and if I am not greatly mistaken in our Bicetta she will answer them. He ran to fetch me writing materials, but I was in such a wretched state that I could not even hold a pen, and the fury which raged within me drowned every thought.

"Never mind," said the old man, "there is no need to write. Is it not sufficient that she hears you have come? If she then still consents to this marriage, hundreds of letters would be of no avail."

With this he left me, but first I had to give him my word that I would not leave the house, which was now completely deserted, and that I would open the door to no one but him.

By this time day had dawned, and after bringing me some wine to strengthen me, the old man departed, and I remained alone in the death-like stillness of the house—I could not rest; I dragged myself into the garden, to the orange-tree of whose fruit she had given me, and to the pomegranate the blossoms of which had been her first love token to me. She was always before me, and the more clearly she appeared to me the less could I understand her apparent oblivion.

Though I was greatly exhausted by my night's journey, yet I could not swallow a morsel of bread nor drink the wine, but I sucked the juice of an orange, and felt so revived that I seemed to have imbibed hope and comfort with it. Then I returned to the house, ascended the stairs and slowly walked through all the apartments. In her little room all remained as she had left it; even the book which she had last read was still open on the table. I began to read from the same page where she had left off. It was an edition of the "Canzone di Petrarca" and I felt soothed and refreshed by their gentle harmony. I shoved a low chair into the balcony (it was the same on which she had sat as a child while playing with her dolls), and threw myself into it with the book in my hand. But after each verse my eyes wandered along the road in the hope of seeing a messenger appear. I had grown calmer however, and no longer dreaded the decision of my fate, yet I started wildly when the old man appeared.

"What news do you bring me," I called to him. But I knew all when I saw his sorrowful countenance, as he turned towards me, and I rushed down the stair case with trembling knees. "Read this," he said; "perhaps you will understand what it all means."

I tore the paper from his hand. On it were hastily scrawled these words: "My own dear love, what I am going to do, had to be done; do not try to prevent it, only trust in me. I shall never be another's. You will understand all when we meet again, and perhaps that may be before long. Whatever happens I am yours only for ever and ever." On the edge of the paper was added, "Remain concealed. If you are found out, all is lost."

Whilst I continued to stare at these few lines, the old man told me that he had not seen her himself. Nina had been the messenger between them; but even from her, he could not find out what he wanted to hear. She only told him that the Signorina had not shown the least astonishment at the news of my return. "I have long expected him," was all she said; and while her maid was bringing in her bridal attire, she had written the note quickly, standing at the window. Then she had charged Nina to enjoin the greatest secrecy on her father, and to tell him to take care of me. After that she quietly proceeded to unfasten her hair which had to be dressed for the wedding. "She wrote these lines," Nina added, "with the calmness of a person who is unable to live any longer for the very agony of his pain, and writes down his dying wish." She had always thought she knew her as well as she knew herself, but in these last days she was a perfect mystery to her.

Was it not the same with me? I who had fancied that I understood her better than any one else, could I understand her now, though I read the lines she had addressed to me over and over again a hundred times. Why if she would not belong to any one but me, why did she not fly to me, or take refuge in a convent till I had found means to liberate her. Why did not the boldest and most adventurous scheme appear natural and easy to her, rather than resignation to the fate which was forced on her, and to the bearing quietly those hateful fetters which death alone could tear asunder.

Still there was something in those simple words which sustained me, when I was on the point of despairing, and which silenced me when I was on the point of giving vent to a burst of indignation or despondency. I even slept a few hours, and could swallow a few morsels which my faithful attendant had prepared for me. Not a word passed between us; only when the hour of the wedding approached we had a violent dispute. I insisted on attending it, and he opposed this to the utmost. At last when he saw that my resolution was not to be shaken, he brought some of his clothes and helped me to muffle myself up in them, and then pulled an old torn straw-hat, which he generally wore in the garden, over my eyes. I will accompany you Signor Amadeo, for I fear that you will lose all command over yourself, and that you will require some one to restrain you. He might have proved right had not the wedding guests, and the bridal couple entered the church before we reached it, and the crowd been so great that they stood pressed together, spreading over the Piazza far beyond the church portal.

I bitterly reproached the old man for having deceived me with regard to the hour, but he vehemently asserted his innocence, and his ignorance of the hour.

So we waited amongst the crowd, and the sound of the bells, which were ringing loudly, lulled me into my former state of dull torpor. Suddenly the cry arose: "Here they come!" I should have sunk down had not Fabio supported me. I kept myself up, so to speak, by fastening my eyes to the church door, whence she was to issue forth. When she at last appeared I was surprised that I could bear the sight, that it even calmed me, although her husband was walking beside her. He was just the man I had expected to see from Fabio's description. A creature I could have felled to the ground at one blow. A smile hovered on his worn features which made my blood boil. He nodded with a triumphant, and lofty air to the people around him, and stroked the fair moustache on his thin upper lip.

She passed through the crowd without looking up, the expression of her face was inscrutable, and her eyes were veiled by her long lashes. A child offered her a bunch of flowers; she took it into her arms, and kissed it, and I could even perceive a smile on her lips. Had not the distance been so great, and Fabio watching me I should have pushed my way through the crowd, and asked her how she dared to smile on such a day. But the smile had vanished while I was reflecting on it.

They got into their carriage, and drove off, followed by the parents of the bride. The old General bending under the weight of his grief, at the side of his proud young wife. Then came all the dignitaries of the church who frequented the house.

"The Archbishop performed the ceremony," said an old woman beside me. "She would not marry him at first, but they say that the holy father himself urged her to it. Nothing more has been heard about that other one, the Lutheran."—"Aye, aye," replied another woman; "it seems that his sister has died, that is the just penalty for refusing to abjure his heresy." —And so their foolish talk went on around me. Fabio dragged me away, and led me by a bye path back to the villa. I let him do as he pleased with me; all my strength had left me. I was as unconscious of my actions as a man in a fever, or a sleep walker.

Even now, when I reflect on the past, I cannot understand how I bore that day. My nature, generally so impetuous, appeared to be completely subdued by the great bodily exhaustion caused by that hurried and sleepless journey from Geneva, and I submitted unresistingly to these horrible events.

When I reached the villa, I staggered blindly. Fabio forced me to swallow several glasses of strong wine in such rapid succession that I at last sank insensible to the ground.

When I recovered my senses, night had come on,

and it was some time before I could recollect where I was, and what had occurred. The clear sky could be seen through the high panes of the glass door, and the faint light of the new moon fell on the portrait of Beatrice's mother, who I fancied looked sadly down at me from her place above the chimney. Then only everything came back to my memory; then I remembered how terrible was the significance of this night, and what future these hours foreboded. Then a fearful agony overwhelmed me, and I was brought to the verge of madness. I cried out aloud and the unearthly sound of my voice as it echoed through the desolate house terrified me. I threw myself down on the cold stone floor of the hall, and there I lay writhing, pressing my face against the ground, and tearing my hair as if bodily pain could stifle the despair which raged within me. Every thought which sprung up in me, I willfully thrust back into the general whirlpool which darkened and confused my mind. I would feel nothing, think of nothing, but the terrible certainty that my heart's treasure was now in another's possession; I could not cease from piercing my heart with this thought, as though it were a poisoned dagger that would make it bleed to death. At last worn out with this self destructive frenzy I lay motionless in the dust. The cold stones of the floor cooled my burning brow, and my tears ceased to flow. After some time, I roused myself sufficiently to regain my tottering feet, and to crawl into the garden. At the fountain underneath the evergreen oaks I washed the tears and the dust from my face, and took a deep draught of the tepid water, which nevertheless cooled my blood.

I now considered what remained for me to do, but

could not come to any resolution. One thing, however, I determined on. I would write to her the next day, and implore her to end this dreadful uncertainty; to rend asunder the last tie which bound me to her. Then I remembered the words of her note, but of what avail were they now to me? Now that I had seen her come out of the church, and that day, and part of the night had passed without bringing me any comfort.

When I heard the clock strike midnight, and the moon disappeared I could no longer bear the awful stillness of the garden, and I returned to the hall. I lighted a candle and placed it on the mantlepiece; then I drew a chair near it, took a small volume of Dante from my pocket, and was soon deeply engaged in perusing the most gloomy and despairing canto of his "Inferno."

I had remained thus about an hour, when suddenly I thought I heard the key turned in the lock of the garden gate. My hair stood on end. I fancied in the first moment of terror that my poor darling had destroyed herself, and that her restless spirit now sought me to suck my heart's blood; but the next moment I had shaken off these senseless ideas, and regained my composure. I arose and listened attentively in the stillness of the night.

The garden gate was opened. I heard steps on the gravel walk—some one sought for the handle of the hall door; it opened and a youth in a black cloak and hat appeared on the threshold. Suddenly the hat fell back from the brow, and I recognized Beatrice. With a cry of joy we rushed into each other's arms, and clung to one another as though we could never be torn asunder nor our lips ever parted.

At last she disengaged herself from my embrace, and her tearful eyes turned on me with a sad mute gaze. "How pale thou art!" she said; "and this is all my doing. But now it is all at an end. I have kept my word. Here I am your own wife, and never another's, though I should suffer for it in this world, and in the next. Oh! Amadeo, why is this world so full of wicked people; why do they sully the purest, and revile the most sacred feelings! Why do they force us to lie, and to perjure ourselves in the very sight of God. We must say *yes*, with our lips, while our hearts say *no*. They have brought me to this, that I can only choose between two sins: either to deliver myself up to a man whom I despise, or to slink like a thief in the night to one who in the eyes of the world can never be mine. But God metes with another measure than these cruel and selfish people; is it not so, Amadeo? He cannot bid me break my faith to you. He never meant our destruction. I imprisoned in a convent, and you alone in the world, without love, or joy. He has destined you for me, and me for you, and now I am yours for ever. That other one dared not touch me. When we were left alone together, I said to him: 'If you ever try to approach me, to-day or at any other time, you will have been my murderer, for I have vowed before God not to survive the hour in which you dare to claim your right on me. I told you this before our marriage and you still insisted on its accomplishment. You then carried the point, now it is my turn.'

"So I left him, and shut myself up in my room

till I knew that every one in the house was asleep. Nina then brought me this disguise, and now I am here, Amadeo! The happiness of being yours would be too great if I had not to strive and suffer for it."

She clung to my neck and hid her glowing face on my breast. All the ardour and passion which she had repressed with maidenly pride, and had not even betrayed by a look, now burst forth in a sudden flame, and threatened to set my whirling brain on fire.

When we had at last recovered our power of thought, and speech, she told me what had occurred after my departure; the intrigues of her step-mother, the helpless efforts of her father to defend himself, and his child, against the ascendency of the clergy; her useless attempts to disarm and confound her enemy by the most unshaken sincerity. At last, when she perceived that they would mercilessly separate her from her father, and shut her up in a distant convent, from whence no letter from her could reach me, she suddenly determined on apparent submission to every thing for the sake of saving herself and me. "And, in fact, they only desired an outward victory. What do they care whether my soul is lost or not," she continued. "Did they ever blame the woman who bears my poor father's name for indulging all her passions freely? They are all of them the slaves of appearances, and they cannot bear to look truth in the face, for it would put them to confusion. Oh! Amadeo, how often did I form the resolution to fly to you, and then declare openly that I am your wife, and shall be so to eternity. But you do not know how powerful they are. Even if we started this very moment, and travelled day and night they would overtake us, and that would be certain death to you. Then my poor dear father also, he would not survive the separation, and such a one, from me. But do not grieve my love, we are now united and those who know our secret are faithful. Pardon me, for not telling you of my coming in my note of this morning, but I knew not for certain whether I should be able to accomplish my plan, or whether that wretch might not strike me to the ground on my refusal to acknowledge him as my master. And if I then had staid away, should you not have suffered greater tortures than in this uncertainty? You knew that I had pledged myself to you, and that I would keep my word; that I would be faithful to you, and never belong to any man but you.—I will return to you every night. The porter who is an honest fellow, hates his present master, but would have died for you."

She noticed that in spite of my happiness; my wife sitting on my knee, that I was silent and thoughtful. "Why are you so sad?" she asked.

"That we must obtain by fraud what is ours by right," I replied. "That we must hide in darkness, and mystery as if we committed a crime in keeping our vows!"

"Do not think of that," she said, and passed her hand across my forehead. "The future is unknown to us; we are only certain of the present hour, and of our own hearts. Why should we not thank God for it. He surely knows that it is best so. Come now; I am not going to sit here as your lady love with my hands folded, and leave it to others to minister to you. You must be half famished, and I too am hungry. I have tasted nothing since last night. I remember perfectly where Fabio keeps his provisions. I will go and prepare a wedding feast which will be more joyful than the last one was, where I saw that every drop of wine was turned to gall for my poor father."

She rose, and hastened to the cellar, and larder. In the meantime I pushed a small table into the middle of the room, and lighted up all the bits of candle which remained in the dusty chandeliers. When she returned with the plates and glasses, she stopped on the threshold with a joyful exclamation. Then she laid the table and filled the glasses with her own hands from the heavy wicker bottle. "Come," she said, "let us drink to our future happiness, if your sister were but here I should desire no other wedding banquet." After drinking this toast, she waited on me, helping me to the cold meat and olives, persuading me to eat, and doing the honours like a good little housewife. To please her I swallowed some morsels though I felt no hunger. She too would hardly take anything till I began to feed her like a child holding the choicest morsels to her lips, then she laughingly opened them and complied with my request.

"Now I have had enough," she said, rising. "I must provide a better couch for you than these cushions on the floor. Fabio never thinks about such things. An old soldier like him hardly perceives whether he is lying on the bare ground or on a feather-bed. To be sure the wisest thing for you will be to take possession of my little room upstairs, instead of remaining here where any body can look in, and betray you." She took my arm and conducted me thither after we had put out all the lights. As we passed Fabio's closet,

I stopped to listen if he moved. "Don't mind him," she whispered; "he knows that I am here. A short while ago, when I fetched the wine, I met him coming from the garden, where he had plucked the fruit for our wedding feast. He was nearly beside himself with joy on seeing me; he wept, and kissed my hands. Now he does not appear, for fear of disturbing us."

The day had not dawned when she reminded me that we must part. I insisted on accompanying her back to town, and when she saw the disguise in which I had ventured out the day before, she consented. She pulled her broad brimmed hat over her eyes and I wrapped her up in her large cloak. We then left the house, and proceeded in the direction of the town. We met not a soul—no lights burned either in the houses or in the streets—the morning star sparkled alone in the pale azure of the sky. A cool breeze came from the North. We hardly spoke a word during our walk. My heart was oppressed, and she too when the moment of separation approached, seemed to feel, for the first time, how unnatural was our position. When we reached the house, she clasped me in her arms with tears in her eyes and held me so for a while before giving the appointed signal to the porter. "Expect me to-morrow," she whispered, and disengaging herself from my neck she glided through the half open door, and I was once more alone in the darkness.

A bitter feeling came over me. So I had to resign her again, my own, my bride, who had vowed to belong to no one but me; to leave her at the threshold of a stranger's house, whose door was for ever closed to me. Here I had to stand at the entrance, and if the master of the house appeared, should have to hide in a corner, as a thief from the bailiff. What would be the end of it? Would a life of so full of bye ways and mysteries be endurable. Can that be called happiness which can only be obtained at the price of daily torment, and anxiety?

Before I reached the villa I had firmly resolved to put an end to this insufferable position. From that moment I felt easy at heart, and as I walked along the deserted road, could fully rejoice in the unalloyed happiness which had been granted me, and I considered in its minutest details how the plan which was to unite us for ever was to be accomplished.

In the garden of the villa I found the old man at work. I apprized him of my scheme, and though he thought the execution of it would be more difficult than I expected, he willingly agreed to do all I asked of him, and this was no slight sacrifice at his age, the more so that he would have to part with his daughter. But where Bicetta's happiness was concerned, he had no will of his own.

We both spent the day in preparations. More than once, while taking our measures, I had occasion to admire the circumspection, and the foresight of the old soldier. During the afternoon I slept, and at ten o'clock at night, I was stationed at the gate of the town through which she had to come. We had not settled that I was to meet her, so when I stepped out of my lurking place, she started back but instantly recognizing me as I pushed back my hat she gave me her still trembling hand, from underneath her cloak. So we walked along gazing at each other in silence, for we met several tardy wayfarers who were returning to the town, and feared to awaken their suspicion should they hear a soft woman's voice underneath that broad brimmed hat only when we had reached the villa, and its comfortable hall where lights were burning, and a rustic meal had been prepared for us by Fabio, she again talked freely. She told me how she had passed the day, how long and dreary it had appeared to her. Richino had treated her with a rigid coldness, hoping to mortify her by it, and to force her to make some advances, but before the world, her parents and their numberless visitors, he had assumed the manners of a happy young husband. In the evening however, he had bowed to her without a word, and had withdrawn to his apartment. "This cannot last," I suddenly said, after a long silence; It is as unworthy of you, as it is of me. We must put an end to it. Your decision alone is wanting. Mine is already formed."

"Amadeo!" she exclaimed, and her eyes turned towards me with a wondering look. "What can you mean? Separation! Oh, death rather than that!"

"No," I replied, "fear not; I do not demand what is impossible to me as well as to you. Leave thee my wife, my second self, truly that would be death! But our present existence, is it not worse than death? A life which must in time, kill the soul's freedom and dignity, and will sooner or later cause our ruin. But even if it did succeed, which is most improbable, if I could remain here concealed year after year, in what a wretched state should I not drag through the weary days; idle and solitary cut off from all society but yours; condemned to an aimless, useless life, consumed by the torture of an obscure, and worthless existence. But even if, in more favourable circumstances, I could

openly come to your horse as your declared lover I
would not do it; I could not brook this state of am-
biguity and falsehood. I must be able to acknowledge
my feelings, and openly take possession of what is
mine. Do you now understand me my darling?"

She nodded, and her eyes were pensively fixed on
the ground.—"I know how painful it will be for you,"
I continued, and took her cold and lifeless hand in
mine, "You feel that you must leave your father, perhaps for ever, if he cannot summon courage enough to
follow us; You must leave your country, and all that is
dear to you, and has taken root in your heart from
childhood upwards. You can no longer kneel in the
church on the same spot where your mother once
prayed—You dread the strange country all the more,
that you will have to enter it as a fugitive, and not
with the rejoicings and honours due to a bride. You
imagine that you would not dare to lift up your eyes
to those who love you. Is it not so Beatrice?"

She again nodded; then she looked up to me and
said, "I will bear all if it can make you happy."

"My own love," I resumed clasping her in my
arms; "You have full confidence in me, have you not?
You believe that I have carefully considered what I
owe to you, and to myself, and that I would not shrink
from any sacrifice so long as my honour is not concerned, and that it does not lower me in your eyes.
There is but one way of escape possible from all the
snares and fetters which our enemies have thrown
around us. You said truly that flight with the swiftest
horses would not save us: no, we must set about it
with more caution, if we do not wish to be overtaken.
I have spoken to Fabio, he knows all the ways to

Ancona as thoroughly as he knows this garden. He will be our guide. We shall travel on foot, dressed as peasants and only at night, once there, we shall embark for Venice. Fabio too leaves all that is dear and valuable to him, only for our sakes, in order that he may assist us to recover our freedom and happiness. Are you courageous enough Beatrice? Do you feel strong enough to undertake this journey at your husband's side?"

"I will follow you all over the world," she said, and pressed my hand; "You shall have no cause to complain; I can do all you expect of me."

I embraced her with great emotion. "Come, then, I said; let us take some food to strengthen us for the journey."

"To-night Amadeo? I implore you with all my heart, ask anything of me, but that I should leave this without once more seeing my poor father, without the sacred memorials of my mother which I keep at home. I promise you that nothing shall alter my resolution, not a tear shall betray me, when I kiss my father for the last time. I feel that without that, without bidding him at least a mute farewell I should find no rest, and the longing for home would kill me. As yet, we risk nothing. No one knows that you are here, no one sees me coming, or going. I shall not even acquaint Nina with our plan. To-morrow evening when I leave my home, it shall be for ever; that I promise you. Grant me only these few hours, and then, I shall be as entirely yours, as if I had fallen from heaven into your arms, and had no other home than your heart."
She looked at me with an imploring expression which I could not resist, although I felt uneasy at the slightest

delay. I gave way to her entreaties, and her gaiety then returned, and soon banished every care from my mind. We supped together; Fabio waited on us, and not a word more was said of our project. I then sent Fabio to his bed, and brought in the dessert myself, and a bottle of sweet wine which she liked to drink only a thimble full of, at a time, but even a few drops of it sufficed to give her pale cheeks a rosy tint. Who could have seen us, joyous as we were together, and have believed that we had obtained these brief hours of happiness by stealth, and were enjoying them clandestinely.

She then drew me into the garden. "Let me bid farewell to all my friends, to the pomegranate, the orange trees, the fountain. To-morrow there will not be time for it." We walked arm in arm into the garden. She drank once more from the marble fountain, put a few oranges in her pocket, and plucked a spray from the pomegranate. "These must go ¡with me," she observed, "in your home in the north, these things do not grow. I shall soon learn to do without them. And this shuttlecock,"—she picked it up as she saw it lying forgotten in the grass, "I will not leave behind. Our children," she whispered, and drew close to me, "shall play with it, and you will tell them how you exchanged your heart for one of these feathery balls."

We had now reached the place where I had once looked over the wall. There underneath the spreading branches of the trees, the sward had remained fresh, and soft, and the air was pure, and free from dust. "Let us pass the remainder of the night here," I said, "I will bring some cushions from the house." I returned and brought a few, and also a cloak for Beatrice. She wrapped herself up in it and soon slept calmly, but it was long before I could find repose. I listened to her gentle breathing, and gazed at her sweet face, with the closed eyes up-turned to the grey sky. She murmured some indistinct words in a dream. I could not understand them, but their soft tone still lingers in my ear.

At last I too slept; I know not for how many hours. When I awoke, the day had not yet dawned, but she was gone. A sudden fear seized me, why had she left me? I jumped up to ascertain whether Fabio, at least, had accompanied her. Hardly had I taken a few steps, when I heard the bell at the garden gate pulled violently. In that moment a fearful foreboding came over me, and forgetting all prudence, I dashed across the garden, and round the house towards the gate. Nevertheless old Fabio had reached it before me, and when I turned the corner, I saw him trying to lift up a dark figure which had sunk down at the entrance of the garden.

"Beatrice!" I cried and rushed to the spot. When I reached it, she just opened her eyes again, and supported by Fabio, she turned towards me with a look of intense anguish and despair, but directly she tried to smile again. "It is nothing Amadeo," she gasped out with a great effort, her hand pressed to her heart. "Do not be alarmed, I do not feel much pain. Are you vexed that I left, without awaking you? You slept so quietly, and I thought there was no danger. How could he have discovered that you were concealed here? Yes to be sure, I forgot to tell you what Richino said to me yesterday at table; he spoke in French to prevent the people from understanding him: "Do you believe in ghosts, Madame? If such things exist, they are welcome to roam about, but if living creatures take it into their heads to play the *revenants*, upon my honour, I will take good care that they are soon turned into real phantoms."

I fancied that these were only idle words. Alas, Amadeo, now I cannot travel with you; you will have to go alone, and in this very hour. Those two who were on the watch outside the garden gate, certainly expected you to pass. They called to me when I was ten paces distant from the gate, and asked for my name. I gave no answer, so they did what had been ordered them. They did not succeed however; see I can still walk and even speak. Leave me here and do not be uneasy on my account. I shall not die. When I hear that you are in safety then I will follow you. Go my darling husband—before the break of day—Give me your hand—kiss me."

Her voice grew faint; her knees could no longer support her. We carried her, insensible, into the hall, and laid her on a low couch. When we pushed back her cloak, and opened her coat, the blood streamed over our hands. I bent over her; she heaved a deep sigh, looked at me once again, and sunk back to rise no more.

Let me pass over that morning in silence.

When the sun shone through the glass door, it found me still kneeling beside her couch, and gazing on her pale face. Old Fabio crouched in a corner, and sobbed.

Suddenly we heard her name called from without. Nina rushed in, and with a loud cry, threw herself on the corpse. By her demeanour it seemed as if she had been struck a deadly blow. Then in the midst of her convulsive sorrow, she roused herself, and turning me she said, "You must escape; I hastened hither to caution you and Beatrice. A short while ago Richino entered her bedroom and sought her. I know now for what reason; it was to tell her that the man she loved was dead. He hardly expected it to end as it has done. When he perceived that she was not in her room, he turned pale as death, and went away. But believe me, he will come to seek her here, and if he finds those dreadful marks on the path—listen! I hear footsteps approaching—they are his. Fly! they forebode death to you." I replied not, but rose and stood by the couch of my dead wife.

The door opened and he entered . . .

Whatever he had meant to say, the sight before him turned him to stone. He staggered back, and clung to the door post for support. His cadaverous face was distorted by helpless horror. I saw that he struggled in vain for breath.

"What do you seek here?" I said at last. "You hoped to find me lying covered with blood; your servants did your bidding promptly, but unfortunately they mistook the person. So you are disappointed of your malignant pleasure. You could not crown your deed by awakening this unhappy woman, of whose heart not a particle was yours, with the tidings that her lover was dead, and would never return. What hinders me," I continued, approaching him, and clenching my hands with rage, and maddening pain. "What hinders me from crushing you beneath my feet, and casting you out of the house, so that you should no longer pollute with your breath this sacred dwelling of the dead. If you had loved her, miserable scoundrel, if you could extenuate your deed by a human passion—but you would have taken possession of her, you would have abased this noble soul to your own level, only for the sake of gratifying your low desires, and because you were incited by others. Go, I say, hide your face in eternal darkness. Assassin! I swear that if you dare to stretch out your hand towards the dead, or cast your eyes on her once again, I will tear you to pieces with my own hands! Away with you!"—

In the midst of this outburst of my fury, I was silenced by the expression of his face, on which an expression of intense pain appeared. It seemed as if the ground reeled underneath him, as if it were going to burst asunder and devour him. He did not look at any one; he tried to raise his head, but sank down on the threshold completely overcome and remained so for several minutes. I had to avert a sort of pity, which I should have deemed a crime. When I had regained sufficient composure to say a few last words to him, I saw him totter like a drunken man towards the gate, and leave the garden.

I then allowed Nina to take off Beatrice's man's clothes, and to dress her in the same white gown in which I had first seen her. There she lay smiling peacefully amongst the flowers which her faithful attendant had brought from the garden and the conservatory, and so she remained during the day. Nina had just concluded this last act of friendship, when we heard a carriage approach the gate. Her father sat in it, pale, and with an insane smile hovering on his withered lips. Fabio, with scalding tears, assisted him to leave the carriage, and led him into the hall. When

he saw his child surrounded by the apparel of death
he dropped silently on his knees, and pressed his forehead on her folded hands.   When at last we tried to
raise him, we found that a paralysis of the heart had
compassionately united him to his darling.

In the following night we buried them both.   No
one was present but Fabio, and Nina.   Don Vigilio
pronounced the benediction on the dead.   He told me
afterwards that Richino had appointed it so, and had
given orders that all my requests were to be complied
with as if I were master of the house.   He had received
no visitors, and aftei a violent scene with his mother-
in-law, had on the same day left Bologna for Rome.

The widow of the General entered a convent for
the time of her mourning.   I for my part when the
earth had closed over the two coffins, took horse, and
before the day had dawned was on my way to Florence.

A year after, I read in the papers that the widow
of the General had married the young count, her faithful admirer.   But though I often returned to Bologna
to visit the grave of my wife I never saw either of them
again.

BEGINNING, AND END.

BEGINNING, AND END.

IN the deep bay window of an otherwise brilliantly
lighted saloon, a single candle, supported by the arms
of a winged figure in chased silver, shed its faint
lustre.

This soft shade was increased by broad-leaved plants,
the last blossoms of the season, and by a slender palm-
tree whose delicate branches arched gracefully above
the entrance of this dusky bower. Two chairs stood
beside each other in the background, inviting to repose,
but only one of them was occupied.

The slender figure of a young woman reclined in
it, her head supported by her arm. Those who suspected her of retiring from the gay company to this
verdant hiding-place in order to attract attention or
cause a search to be made for her wronged her. She
thought not of the effect produced by the delicate half
shade of the palm-tree on her pure white brow, nor of
the soft moonshine-like reflex of the candlelight on the
shining waves of her dark hair. Neither did she take
advantage of the solitude around her, whilst a girlish
voice was heard singing to the piano at the further end
of the room, to indulge in those reveries which in the
summer time of life so often take their abode underneath the closed eyelids. In a word, she slumbered.
The music to which she had at first dreamily listened,

had at last lulled her to sleep like a tired child. She did not even awake when the song being ended, the old gentlemen around applauded encouragingly, the piano stool was pushed back, and the hum of the interrupted conversation again sounded through the saloon with renewed vivacity.

No one came to disturb her; she was a stranger in this society, and besides there was a certain expression of grave reserve in her countenance which did not encourage new acquaintances.

It was her fate to be considered proud. She knew it, but the little effort she made to dispel this error arose more from indifference than contempt. A familiar voice which addressed her by her name at last aroused her. She opened her eyes in some confusion and saw the master of the house standing before her, and by his side a stranger whose forehead reached up to the branches of the palm-tree.

"Allow me to interrupt your meditation, Madam," said the host with a smile. "I here present to you my friend, and cousin Valentine, who only returned to Germany a few weeks ago, and a few hours since became my guest. We must now try to retain him, and who could undertake this task with more success than our fair country women." -

He had long left them and, still they remained opposite each other without a word of greeting. His eyes were fixed on the red rose which adorned her hair, and only a slight movement among the palm leaves betrayed that the blood rushed vehemently through his veins.

The lady's face was raised towards him with an earnest expression, as if she were trying to solve a problem. Was the veil which sleep had thrown over her eyes, not yet removed? Was this meeting only the vision of a dream. But no, could a dream have the power of changing, as time had done, the well known features before her; of thinning the curly hair, and of drawing those lines above the eye-brows which she had noticed at the first glance?

The longer he delayed in addressing her, the deeper grew the blush that suffused her cheek. Several times her lips parted as if to speak, but still she remained silent, and fixed her eyes on the ground. Her fan slid on the carpet. He did not pick it up.

At last he said, "Madam Eugénie, permit me to call you so, for I have just arrived here and have omitted to ask our host for your husband's name; how strangely we meet in this life. I am truly astonished at my want of presentiment which never foretold me by a sign from heaven or from earth that I should find you here."

"A special motive caused me to undertake this journey," she hastily said. "I intend to put my son to school and I am told that there is one here in which he will be well taken care of. I arrived to-day after having spent a sleepless night in the carriage, and I must confess to you that just as you came up, weak human nature, against all good breeding, was on the point of making up for lost time. I tell you this because the cool, and absent way in which I received you must have seemed strange to so old a friend."

She stretched out her hand to him. "I thank you," he replied, and his face brightened, "for having remembered my small claim on your friendship. Pray continue to treat me on the old footing, and resume your repose, which I unfortunately disturbed. I will take care that no one enters the bower: I can keep watch behind this palm-tree."

She laughed. "No, I did not mean that. I am only too tired to converse with perfect strangers. Come, sit down by me, if you will be satisfied with my good intentions, and tell me how the past, and the present have fared with you."

"You will best be able to judge for yourself how it has fared with me when I confide to you my situation at the present moment. My friend has only invited me here for the sake of marrying me. He regards it as a duty. What do you say to that? In what a sad state must not that man be whose friends consider it their duty to render him harmless?"

"You alarm me," she replied with a smile. "When I first knew you, you were, if not actually harmless, at least far from causing so much mischief that you had to be laid in chains for the sake of the public safety."

"You are deriding me, Madam. Ah that talent of yours, how well I know it. This time however your darts did not touch me. My charitable cousin fears not for others, but for my own safety. He believes that if I continue to reside alone in the old castle which I have bought; abandoned to my own crotchets, only occupied in catching hares and helping the peasants in their agricultural affairs, which I do not myself understand, that I should sooner or later lose the little sense which he kindly presumes is left to me. You see he wishes to treat me homeopathically, dispersing one folly by another. Perhaps he is right. Those who have proved themselves incapable of regulating their lives properly, should be grateful, should they not, to their friends for taking the trouble off their hands, and quietly follow their advice; but I fancy sometimes that their kind intentions have come too late for me."

"Too late? I must combat that assertion. Fourteen years have passed since we last met, and if you did not then make yourself younger than you were, you can hardly now have reached the prime of life."

"Make myself younger! Good heavens! to do just the contrary would then have conduced more to my interests. But of what are you reminding me Eugénie?"

"Is your betrothed young, handsome amiable?" she quickly resumed; "I would not ask these questions which imply a doubt, if you had not told me that you had authorized your friend to dispose of your heart, and in these matters friends are not always to be relied on."

"You greatly wrong our most amiable host," he said laughingly; "Not only are these cardinal virtues not wanting, but all three of them are three times combined."

"Three times?"

"I mean in three different samples, as I have been told; so it will be difficult to choose."

"And each of the three young ladies is desperately in love with you? Then a twofold catastrophe is inevitable."

"Up to this hour none of my destined brides know of my existence. Their father——"

"So they are sisters?"

"Yes. A fair, an auburn, and a dark haired one. You see there is no possibility of escape; Every taste is provided for.   Early to-morrow the merciless disposer of my heart, and hand takes me in his carriage, and delivers me over to my destiny. They live in L... not quite four hours drive from this.   Horse dealing is to be the pretext.   The father who is the doctor of that small town, has a thorough-bred grey Arab in his stables."

"You go forth as Saul the son of Kish.   I hope you may return like him with a kingdom."

"If you but knew," he said pensively, "how little I covet that dignity: is not a king fettered by his duties?   To-day I am still free, so I take the liberty of sitting down beside you, and of talking with you of that happy time when I too was held captive, but by enchanting fetters."

She remained silent while he threw himself into the second arm-chair, and turned it so that he could see nothing of the company in the saloon; but only the plants before him, and the charming face of the young woman, lighted up by the solitary candle. Meanwhile the mistress of the house had sat down to the piano, and began to play a waltz; and soon the light branches of the palm-tree trembled in the whirlwind caused by the passing couples.   Eugénie silently watched the gay scene before her.   With her left hand she played with a gold chain, and in the right, held carelessly a large bouquet on her lap.

Valentine stedfastly gazed at her; when she observed it, she took up the nosegay and buried her face in it.   "You think it somewhat indiscreet on my part," he said, that I sit before you, as though I were admiring a fine painting; but is it not pardonable if I gaze with astonishment on that soft bloom which remains as fresh as though hardly a day had passed since our last meeting. If I banished from my mind the thought that fourteen years have gone over my head, and that I may be a married man to-morrow, I might easily delude myself into the belief that I am sitting in the conservatory of your parent's house, and have just laid aside the book in which I had been reading aloud to you, who were meanwhile watching the gnats dancing on the pond, or the falling of the leaves. In reality however, only youth can give us those hours of enraptured extasy, that entire blending of the soul with the soul of nature, when we are freed from the fetters of our own individuality only to be united, like a plant, all the more closely with the elements. When I walked home, still entranced, after one of those evenings, I felt as if I were carried along the poplar alley, as a feather is borne by the breeze. In later years we often call that feeling sentimentality, but even now I cannot laugh at it."

"If I smiled at it in those days, I now feel as if I ought to apologize for it. We girls are taught by our education to watch over our sentinents, and to be cautious in our enthusiasms. Now I may confess to you that I often only wished for Cora to disturb our reading hour by her barking, or for Frederick to summon us to tea, because I could no longer restrain my tears."

"You always had the firmer character of the two. The cement which has consolidated my nature has only grown hard in the bracing atmosphere of a stirring, and active life. But the names you have just uttered, what remembrances they bring back to me! My friend, and my enemy, Frederick, and Cora. That dear old

Frederick. I know that he heartily pitied me, a feeling which is said to be rare between rivals. You cannot be ignorant of the feelings with which you inspired him. He worshipped you as devotedly as a gardener, a servant, can worship his young mistress. He looked on his case as still more hopeless than mine, though with regard to our social position, his was by far the more settled of the two. The quiet sympathy of hopelessness united us.   Often when he had come to fetch us from the conservatory and you were skipping before us after your dog, and overtaking it, would catch it up in your arms, and kiss it, he would turn to me with jealous wrath, and say: 'Now, can you understand, Master Valentine, what pleasure our young lady can find in hugging that stupid brute?' With an indignant shake of his head; the hair of which he always arranged carefully, since he served at table, and could offer you the dishes. If you confess the truth, you will own that you only fondled that ugly creature for the sake of driving us distracted."

"Do not speak ill of the dead," rejoined Eugénie. "Cora sleeps the sleep of death, not far from the pond where the bench stands underneath the elm-tree; do you remember it?"

"How could I have forgotten it?   Was it not on that bench that I fastened your skates, when we started on that skating expedition with your cousin Lucy. How is your cousin getting on?"

"She is now a fine lady, with a large family. If she only knew that I have met you here! Not more than a month ago we were talking of you. She has a kind remembrance of you, and has not forgotten that bright winter's afternoon, when we first initiated you

in the art of skating, and she maintains that you
squeezed her hand on that occasion with more ardour
than your later behaviour warranted. Since then a
shade of fickleness darkens the otherwise favourable
recollection she has of you."

"Good heavens!" he exclaimed laughing; "so the
most harmless cannot escape suspicion. To be sure I
was not wholly guiltless, but as it so often happens I
must suffer for another sin than that which I really
committed. When you both held my hands to guide
my first steps on the slippery plain, I longed to express more to you by the firm pressure of my hand
than the mere desire not to fall. But you were always
inaccessible to any intelligence of that kind. You will
now bear me witness that I need not reproach myself
with regard to little Lucy. Ah! I still remember it all
as if it had been yesterday! I still feel the glow which
rushed through my veins, in spite of the cold December
wind; the enrapturing touch of your hand, which seemed
to linger with me for weeks after. Do not be displeased,"
he continued, "at my speaking so freely of all this. We
are no longer the same and can now talk of these things
as though they had occurred to some one else. Is it
not an innocent pleasure if I now tell you what so often
hung on my lips in those days, and was always repressed by that unlucky timidity of mine. We now meet
as good comrades do after having settled a debt."

"And which of us is the creditor?" she asked.
"Both of us," he replied. "Do you not think that I
too have some right to that title? If you but knew what
trouble you have caused me; how long your image stood
between me, and every enjoyment of life. But you must
have guessed it. When I used to watch for you on

your way to your drawing lesson, when my heart beat
at the sight of your checked cloak, and grey hat—and
when I passed you with all the equanimity I could
muster, happy in having been allowed to salute you,
did the unfortunate fate of the poor lad who so humbly
bowed to you never smite your conscience?"

"You are greatly mistaken my dear friend," she
said, with a charming look of merriment. "I blushed
whenever I met any one in that attire which I fancied
gave me the appearance of a scarecrow. The cloak
had long passed out of fashion, but my mother thought
it good enough for the drawing lesson. How many
tears of mortified vanity have I not dried with a corner
of that detested garment."

He laughed. "You see how widely our natures differ.
Fate did wisely in separating us. I for my part on my
travels through the world vainly sought for a similar
cloak which seemed to me to be the essence of all that
is beautiful. In France I once remarked at some distance
the same kind of checked stuff. I rushed after it, but
found to my disappointment that the wearer in no way
resembled the lady of my thoughts. Since that time I
am inclined to believe that it was the wearer and not
the garment which haunted the dreams of my youth."

During this conversation the music had continued
and the air in the apartment became hot and oppressive. The young woman agitated her fan, and
inhaled with parted lips the refreshing breeze from it.
She reminded her friend of a remark he had once read
in a French book on the affinity existing between certain blue eyes, and certain glittering teeth. He told
her so. "You see," he continued, "how freely I take
advantage of the privilege of friendship, telling you

every thought which crosses my mind, I make up for my long silence, and you will not take it amiss. Truly it seems that Providence intends to make me a good husband and father as on the eve of the important step I am about to take it relieves my mind from all anxiety regarding it. If I had not met you, I should never, even in the midst of every domestic felicity, have been able to rid myself of the fear that some day or other you would appear, and turn my head as you did years ago. Now that you know my intentions and that we have placed our friendship on a warm, and steady footing, I can start on to-morrow's expedition in search of a wife, with an easy heart."

They had both risen, and now admired the flowers. "How beautiful this candelabra is," she remarked. "Fortuna subjected by man, and made to give him light."

"I believe it to represent the goddess of victory. The ball on which fortune glides from us, is wanting here, but Victory remains faithful to the daring."

"In that case Victory by serving you on the eve of your expedition, foretells you good luck."

"I see you doubt my courage Madam. Certainly you above all others have a right to do so. But this time I hope to manage my affairs better than I did fourteen years ago. I intend to challenge my fortune, be it good, or bad, and force an answer from it. If she smiles on me, I promise you that to you first, I shall be the herald of my heroic achievement. But enough of myself as a topic; as yet you have told me nothing of your own life, and how the years have passed with you. I could not muster courage to make enquiries about you. After I heard that you were married, I studiously avoided every place where tidings of you could reach me. I am even unacquainted with the name of your husband. Will you introduce me to him. He probably has accompanied you here?"

"I lost my husband seven years ago."

He started—"My son is all that is left to me," she resumed, "and I must now part with him. He has become quite unruly from staying with my mother in the country, and even if I could find a tutor who knew how to manage him, I should be sorry to see him pass the merry time of youth without any companions of his own age."

"I long to see him," he hastily said, without lifting his eyes from the flowers in her hand. "So he has lost his father; poor child! When he has grown up you must send him on a visit to me. I will take him out hunting, give him my horses to ride, and if he should fall in love with my daughter, why in that case the beginning and the end would once more be united, although in a different manner from what I blind mortal, once dreamt. Would you consent to the match Eugénie?" and he stretched out his hand to her.

"With all due regard to the future father-in-law of my son," she replied gaily. "I should wish first to see the young lady herself, especially as you cannot even answer for her mother."

"Of course you must approve of the mother; I should never think of marrying her, if she had the misfortune to displease you! The wisest course would be!"—

The conversation was here interrupted by a young man, who hesitatingly approached the embrasure of the window, with the intention of inviting the lady to dance. She declined, alleging the fatigue of her night journey as an excuse, and then she left the bower, and mingled with the rest of the company. Valentine who had remained standing by the palm-tree, watched her figure amongst the others, and now and then he fancied he heard her voice. It appeared to him as if he had forgotten some question of importance, and he tried to recall it to his mind. At last he remembered that he ought to have enquired for her mother. He went in search of her to repair his neglect but he could not find her either in the saloon or in the adjoining rooms. She had disappeared.

It was on the second day after this meeting; a dense morning fog still filled the street but the air above was clear, and promised a sunny day, that in one of the rooms of the hotel, Eugénie sat at a writing-table, an unfinished letter lying before her. Her folded hands rested on the paper, and her thoughts strayed far away from the contents of those lines.

Now and then when a step was heard in the passage, she started up, and listened, but they always passed the door, and she remained alone.

Why did all her thoughts revert to the past, to that particular walk in the garden where the sunflowers and china asters grew, and the small fruit-trees threw long shadows across the cabbage beds. The sun was shining through the high hedge but the air did not resound with the song of birds. To-morrow when the day waned, she would be far away from this homely spot, and when she returned, the fruit-trees would be bare, and snow would cover the ground. The young student who walked by her side and was digging holes in the gravel with the point of her parasol, was fully aware of this. He had seen the travelling carriage in the court-yard, and watched Frederick fastening the valise on the box. When people start on a journey, who can tell if they will return, or at least return the same as they went. Is it not expedient then to exchange one's last bequests, especially if each is disposed to bequeath body and soul to the other.

If he had but known how highly he ought to value her condescension in leading the way to this remote and solitary corner of the garden. As she walked along, she upbraided herself with having thus far made advances to him. But she would not take a step further, now it was his turn to forward matters, and if he did not, she would never forgive herself for having done so much to loosen his tongue. For it had a high opinion of the dignity of its sex, this young head of seventeen, and if the unfortunate youth by her side, had choked with mute respect, she would not have spoken a word to help him. Was not this walk sufficiently secluded, and the sun at their backs; was it not the only time she had ever walked with him in the kitchen garden, and above all, had he not seen the travelling carriage in the yard.

On no account, however, was he to perceive that she had contrived all this for his sake. She talked eagerly of the approaching journey, expressed her pleasure at seeing her cousins again, and laughingly described every one of them.

They had reached the end of the walk, and had looked over the hedge, but he became more and more laconic. At last he quite ceased talking and she too became silent. Feelings of passion and mortification rose in her breast, and nearly choked her. Then she suddenly turned towards him, and colouring deeply said: "Let us now go back; and give me my parasol. I shall want it on my journey, and you will break it to pieces. I must hasten home, as I still have many things to pack. Do you know that I quite shudder when I think of how much my intellectual refinement will retrograde during my absence. I shall hardly remember the English kings in Shakespear's works, which you have taken so much trouble to impress on my mind. It is a pity, but what can I do? My cousins are not such pedants as you are. If I return—but who can tell whether my aunt will not keep me through the winter. Well, it may be a long time before we can resume our studies and if I pass my examination badly, this long absence must plead for me."

More than a year passed before they met again— When the morning arrived, the travelling carriage was ready to start and the ladies sitting in it, he approached the door of it and offered a bouquet. The mother accepted it with many thanks. Eugénie nodded gaily to him, and gave him her gloved hand. He did not see her pale face, and swollen eyes behind her thick veil. He closed the door and bowed. As the carriage drove away, Frederic turned once more towards Valentine, and across his honest face there passed an expression of pity for his less fortunate rival.

This had been in autumn. When they returned in the middle of winter, Valentine had left the town; he was occupied at a small court of justice in the country. Only in the following summer he once again rang the well known bell at the garden gate. On being told that the house was full of visitors, cousins, and others who were strangers to him, he charged the servant with a message that he would return another time; but a cold bow from her mother whom he met in the streets next day, showed him that he should not find all as he had hoped; so he never returned.

Was his absence regretted? Who could solve the enigma on Eugénie's pale face, when three years later, she married the man her mother had chosen for her. But now when her thoughts wandered back from the letter before her to those days of old, the words of a pensive song resounded in her heart: "There was a time when happiness was mine to give and take etc."——

The clattering of swift hoofs was now heard in the street, and she flew to the window. A horseman on a beautiful grey Arab galloped through the thick fog which closed behind him. Clouds of steam arose from the reeking nostrils of the horse.

With an agitated glow in her eyes, she watched the proud and manly bearing of the rider, and the ease with which he managed his restless horse. What a difference between this chivalrous firmness, and the soft pensive manner of his youth. Still she had recognized at their first meeting, that his heart had lost none of its fresh bloom; it was developed not changed. Had he this time divested himself of his former timidity, and spoken the binding words? She shuddered at the thought.

Rapid steps were now heard ascending the stairs. Her habitual self-command did not forsake her, and when Valentine entered the room, her face was calm in spite of the quick beating of her heart. She met him with a smile, and offered him her hand. "Good morning," she said: "so you have kindly kept your promise! The triumphant prancing of your horse has already apprised me that you return crowned with success."

"Eugénie," he replied, "you must highly value my visit of to-day, for I have made it in spite of my conviction that you will have a good laugh at my expense. My only acquisition by yesterday's expedition is this horse which I paid for in ready money, and this apple which I stole." And he laid a fine wax-like apple on the table. "I do not hold the booty obtained by your campaign so very despicable. I understand nothing about horses, but as you doubtless obtained the apple from the hands of your chosen one"————

"If I had but reached that point," he resumed despondingly; "the rest would be easy enough. You are greatly mistaken, however, if you are inwardly accusing me of having been again wanting in courage. It was the superfluity of it which in this case hindered my success. Upon my word, I would, without the slightest hesitation, have made a declaration to each of the three young ladies, one after the other."

"What a pretty disaster you would have caused." "I never expected anything of you but an ironical pity. Still—you may judge from this how thoroughly perflexed I am—I turn to you for help."

"You expect more of me than with the best intentions I can give you."

"Ah, but you can help me Eugénie. Now listen and I will give you an account of it all. My friend, and I spent a whole day in their company."

"That is either a very long, or a very short time as you take it."

"You are right. The time is long enough to fall in love with all three sisters, and much too short to decide which of them is to be preferred. The only way would be to take the whole batch from the nest."

"Are the nestlings so unfledged that they would submit to that?"

"To tell the truth I never thought of that. The chief thing for me is to get so enraptured with one of the sisters, that she should banish the other two from my mind. But at my age it is difficult to grow enthusiastic."

"Then all three are equally irresistible?"

"Quite so, all of them made to be kissed, and each of them a different style of beauty; so that when one sees them together one feels that one could never be satisfied with only one of them."

"Your account is given in too vague and extravagant terms. I wish to have it in proper order, and with every detail. First then comes the fair, then the auburn, then the dark one; or how do they follow in age?"

"I don't know."

"Well, then we will arrarnge them according to size, and begin with the smallest. Is it the auburn haired young lady?"

"I really cannot tell."

"You seem to have employed your time badly, or was it the triple fascination which had such power over your feelings from the first, that your senses left you?"

"Certainly I cannot excuse myself on that score,"

he replied laughing. "I do not remember a more disagreeable sensation than I had yesterday on my way to L... A visit to the dentist is a pleasure trip compared to it. Several times I was on the point of jumping out of the carriage, but then I reflected that my cousin's horses would soon have overtaken me, and then I should have been delivered over ignominiously into the hands of my evil destiny. For on this point, my friend, who is in every other respect so yielding, knows no mercy. So I plucked up courage, and thinking over all the evil that had ever befallen me in the course of my life I tried to find comfort by repeating that in fact it all amounted very much to the same thing. At last we arrived. I had stipulated from the beginning that my cousin should not say a word of my real purpose, either to the father, or to the young ladies. The doctor was not at home when we first arrived, so we only found the sisters of fate in the neatest of dresses, fresh and charming like three rose buds on one stalk. Yes in truth they equalled the three graces, and their manners too were far from being provincial. I could not tire of looking at them."

"The beginning seems promising."

When they perceived us, they left their several domestic occupations, and ran to meet my cousin. Then arose a delightful trio of merry girlish voices around us. Of course my share of their words, and looks of greeting, was at first only what civility demanded, and I was quite contented with this, as it gave me a good opportunity of quietly observing them. When I first entered the room, and perceived the dark haired young lady, who looked up from her work with large and wondering eyes, I said to myself; This is the one,

I always had a predilection for dark hair. The next moment however, I again wavered at the sight of the fair haired one, whose voice is as clear as a bird's, and her skin as white as the cherry blossom. Then the auburn haired one entered, grace and modesty personified. You will understand, that under these circumstances my countenance did not wear a very intelligent expression. However I was soon on very good terms with the three young ladies, and when they conducted me to the stables to show me the horse, I even took the liberty of lifting the fair one on its back, and led it about in the courtyard."

"Then it is the fair one."

"Not exactly; I only gave her a ride because she was the most courageous, and appeared to be very familiar with the grey Arab. She sat on his back with folded arms as calmly as if she had been on her sofa, whereas the auburn haired one clung to the mane with a charming timidity."

"So all three had to display their horsemanship; at least you can now judge of the weight of your future wife."

"No, the dark haired one was not put to the test. Their father had now joined us. He turned them out of the stable-yard, and charged them to provide for our dinner. Then we soon settled the bargain, and ratified it by a bottle of good Heidelberg wine. The doctor pleased me. He is just the sort of man one would desire for a father-in-law. Besides he is a good sportsman, an excellent judge of horses, and the best chess player in the neighbourhood."

"In that case your young wife will pass very amusing evenings."

"If it ever comes to that. But as I said before I lost my time, and opportunities, in a most inexcusable manner. In the afternoon we walked through the town to see the old castle in which the former king gave great entertainments, but under the present government it is quite deserted. The place where the orange-trees stood is now turned into an orchard. It was a pretty sight to see the delicious looking apples, and pears lying carefully assorted in great heaps on the green grass; and I never inhaled a more refreshing odour than was diffused over the spot. So we walked along; the three sisters in front with light straw hats and all dressed alike; then we three behind them. While I was examining them, the thought struck me that I was now in the same position as that prince who while keeping his father's flocks, was suddenly called on to award the prize of beauty to one of the three goddesses."

"So you appropriated to yourself this apple, hoping to extricate yourself from your embarrassment by a symbolical allusion."

"I certainly put it in my pocket with that intention; and as we rambled through the old park, and now one of the sisters, and now another walked beside me on the narrow path, I several times felt fully convinced that just this girl was the right one and I secretly grasped the apple. Then again when one of the others turned round towards me, or some word or sound of laughter reached me I hastily replaced it. So I did not dispose of it, and have brought it back with me.

Is it not provoking Eugénie, that when love was at hand courage was wanting, and now that I have gained courage, love is not forthcoming."

"You must not despair at the outset," she said,

encouragingly. "Your first attempt was not so very bad. Rome was not built in a day, neither can you expect to found your domestic felicity in so short a time. Are their names all equally pleasing to you? I lay much stress upon names, and can easily understand the feelings of that dauphin who would not wed a woman called Uracca."

"That cannot decide me either," he answered, despondingly. "Anna, Claire, and Mary, I know not which I prefer. No, my kind friend, I now look to you for assistance."

"To me, I cannot guess how I can be of use to you in this intricate affair."

"It is certainly a great favour which I require from your friendship," he replied with some hesitation. He had now risen, and had taken the apple in his hand. He threw it several times into the air, caught it again, and finally replaced it on the table. "You see," he resumed, "when after having passed a very restless night, I mounted my horse—my cousin had driven back the same evening—and as I rode through the fog in the frosty morning air, it occurred to me what a strange co-incidence, it was that just before deciding on the most important step of my life, I should meet you once more; you the only one who really knows me, and in whom I could freely confide, were anything wanting to your knowledge of my character. I recalled to mind all your kindness to me, and also all the harm you have done me, and I felt convinced that you really were my debtor, and owed me some reparation for all my misfortunes, and privations. What I further thought, Eugénie!——Well, that is not to the purpose now.—So I devised a plan which I hope you will not mar."

"What is it?" she asked absently.

"Would you consent to get into a carriage with me, and accompany me to L....? I would take you to the doctor's house, and then you could see the three girls side by side. The one to whom you gave this apple would become my wife. I solemnly promise you that I will not raise the slightest objection to your choice."

"You cannot give me full powers, and I could not accept them in such a case."

"And why so? I am quite convinced that I could be tolerably happy with any one of them; indeed, for that matter, if I did not think it presumptuous, I might simply write down their names, throw them into my hat, and draw my lot with closed eyes. It could not be a great prize, *that* has passed for ever; at least many things would have to be changed; but at all events I should not draw a blank. But why should it be hazarded, why should you think the responsibility so great, if I consult you as the friend of my youth, with the firm conviction that a clever woman can more easily fathom the depth of a girl's character, than a man ever can."

"But even if I consented to your adventurous scheme, under what pretence would you introduce me to the family?"

"I have also considered this point," he said, striking with his whip the many coloured pattern of the carpet. "I introduce you to the good people as my betrothed. In this way we are sure to obtain our end, for every girl, even the most undesigning, in the

presence of a bachelor endeavours to shew herself in
the best light. They are daughters of Eve. But if I
return to them as one already disposed of we shall
easily be able to find out which of the sisters has been
acting a part and, perhaps, I may even discover that
one of them has secretly monopolized my heart. Surprise often brings to light the true character."

He glanced at Eugénie who stood before him with
an air of quiet deliberation. She had let him come
to the end of his proposal, but now she shook her
head.

"Think of some other plan, Valentine. I cannot
consent to this one."

"There is no danger in it."

"Possibly, but I am neither skilled enough, nor do
I feel inclined to act that part, and were I suddenly
to drop the mask my embarrassment could hardly ex-
ceed yours."

"Consent at least to assume the character of a
sister."

She considered for a while. "If I agree to this,"
she said at last, "I only do so for the sake of proving
how little I can help you. The qualities in a girl,
which please or displease an old woman, are totally
different from those which seem important to a man.
I confess that curiosity has a share in my decision,
and above all the fear of your cousin, who would never
forgive me if I did not further his philanthropic plans
on your behalf."

"I thank you," he exclaimed joyously, taking her
hand and kissing it. "Now I am free from all anxiety.
A true friend is certainly one of the greatest blessings

under heaven. I will go this moment to the landlord, and order a carriage."

"Your wooer's wings must submit however to some delay. Or do you expect me to perform the part you have forced upon me in my morning dress and cap?"

"In truth," he replied, "I never noticed that. In my opinion you might boldly drive to L... in your present attire. The hair so pushed back under your cap, shows your fair temples to advantage, I am enabled again to admire those unruly meshes in your neck which in former days ensnared my poor heart, like a fish struggling in a net."

She held up her finger threateningly, and then said, while a sudden blush suffused her face: "Take care, else I will betray you to your future bride. Your triple courtship, however, excuses the disregard with which you treat the toilette of an old friend. Here are some books; amuse yourself in the meantime; I will be back presently."

She disappeared into the adjoining room and closed the door behind her.

He approached the table on which the apple lay, and after pensively gazing at it for a while, he suddenly gave it an angry push, which sent it flying over the edge of the table, and rolling across the carpet. He sighed, and as if to rouse himself struck his hand with his whip till it smarted. He then mechanically took up one of the books which lay in the corner of the sofa. It was a volume of Mörike's poems, and they exercised on him their powerful charm. He forgot all around him, and drawn on from page to page was soon completely absorbed in "The moonlit path of love once sacred."

Suddenly the door from the passage opened and a lad of about ten years rushed into the room.

"Mother," he cried, "will you allow me— — — Why to be sure she is not here," he then said to himself, and turned his sharp clear eyes inquiringly on the stranger. "Come here, my boy," said Valentine stretching out his hand to him. "Your mother is dressing in the next room. What is your name?"

"Fred is my name."

"Won't you give me your hand, Fred?"

The lad hesitated. "Who are you?" he asked partly embarrassed, partly defiant.

"I am an old acquaintance of your mother's. She will not object to your giving me your hand. So, that is right. Will you come to see me some day? I have four handsome horses in my stables. I will give you a small gun, and will take you out shooting with me. The first hare you shoot, you shall bring to your mother."

The boy's eyes sparkled, but suddenly he became thoughtful, and said, "I should like it very much, but I must go to school. This is my last holiday, and the two sons of the head-master have just invited me to go into the fields with them to fly a kite."

"Well, then you will come to see me in the vacation time. Would you like that, Frederick?"

"Yes, if my mother permits it."

"Go, and ask her, my dear boy. We will become fast friends, won't we?"

The lad nodded. Valentine took him up and kissed him. Then his mother called him into her room; and Valentine heard him, as he eagerly repeated what the strange gentleman had said to him. "He gave me a kiss," continued the boy. "Why does he love from the first moment he sees me?"

They continued the conversation in an under tone, and then the boy left his mother's room by another door.

Valentine approached the window, and watched him as he left the house, and joined his two play-fellows, who had been waiting below for him. His fair straight hair hung in masses about his shoulders; his round childish face beamed underneath the border of his cap. Yet the man at the window seemed to find no pleasure in the sight.

When Eugénie, dressed for the drive, entered the room, she found him still in the same position. She wore a dark green hat with a waving black feather, and a short grey cloak which closely fitted her fine figure. "I am ready, my friend," she said; "let us get into the carriage?"

He looked up in confusion. "The carriage?" he asked.

"Yes, the carriage which I suppose you ordered long ago."

"I confess," he replied, "that I have not yet done so. I did not expect you to be dressed so soon."

"You are certainly the first man to complain of that. Well, so it seems that I must provide for our departure."

She rung the bell and ordered a carriage. Whilst

her orders were being executed, Valentine remained standing near the window, and attentively examined the arabesques on the curtain. He perceived that she stooped to pick up the apple, but .did not anticipate her.

"Well, I think you ought to treat this fine apple with more respect," she said jestingly. "You see it has been already injured by its heavy fall."

"Perhaps it were best Eugénie to leave it where it is. The reluctant shudder of yesterday is already coming over me. Why must I try my luck at L... Why should it be one of the three sisters. Possibly I need not look so far to find what I desire."

"You ought to be ashamed of your vacillation," she answered with comical solemnity. "Is this the courage you boasted of? Come, rouse your spirits, and replace the stolen apple in your pocket. The sin you have committed by this theft, can only be expiated by the more difficult task of stealing the heart of one of the sisters. Come, I hear the carriage driving to the door. You have excited my curiosity, and I shall not rest till it is satisfied."

When the carriage had left the town, and was rolling smoothly along the even road, Valentine broke the silence. "I have become acquainted with your son, Eugénie," he said.

"You must praise him to me," she hastily returned; "I am a very proud mother, he is the very image of his father."

"I thought so," he resumed. "The face seemed strange to me. I only recognized the mouth. This mouth is strikingly like yours, Eugénie."

She turned away towards the carriage window, and her eyes wandered over the landscape, which had now contracted, so as to form a narrow valley surrounded on both sides by steep vineyards. The mist had entirely cleared away, and the wet tendrils and leaves of the vines sparkled in the bright sunlight. The river bordered with willows, and alders flowed smoothly by the road side, and small barges glided rapidly along the current. Nothing is so refreshing and enlivening as a drive on a fine autumn day. Valentine experienced its charm and soon resumed the conversation. He enquired after the health of her mother, and after a while Eugénie began to speak of her husband. "You would have been his friend, Valentine," she gravely said. "He was an excellent man, and a brave officer and he had a profound and unaffected admiration for all that is good and beautiful. Those who did not know him intimately thought him cold and indifferent, but inwardly, he was full of generous warmth which he kept for his family, his friends and those who were in want. My mother still grieves for him, as she grieved for my father. I hope that Frederick will some day resemble him in every respect."

Valentine was silent for a long time. At last he asked, without looking at his companion, "Have you never thought of choosing a second husband among the many suitors who no doubt have surrounded you?"

"No, my dear friend," she answered quietly. "Passions have never troubled me, and a marriage founded on esteem—it always is a lucky chance if one does not repent of it afterwards."

They had now reached a turn in the valley, and the unexpected change of scene interrupted the conversation. On the left hand where the vine covered hills receded from the river, lay a small town, the industry of whose inhabitants was testified by the smoking chimnies of many factories, and the roaring and clashing of the water engines.

A broad stone bridge led across the river, and high above the old gable roofed houses, rose the graceful edifice of a gothic church, whose perforated spire of delicate fret-work with the ornamented cross at the top, projected boldly into the clear blue sky, and was surrounded by swarms of pigeons.

"This is C...." said the coachman, pulling up his horses for a moment, and pointing towards the town with the end of his whip.

"Drive over the bridge," cried Valentine; "we wish to visit that beautiful cathedral before we proceed on our journey."

Eugénie looked at him enquiringly. "Let me manage it all," continued Valentine, turning to her. "We are sure of reaching the doctor's house in good time, so I propose that we rest here awhile, climb up to that steeple, and dine at the inn of the place; by this plan we shall not arrive just as my future father-in-law is sitting down to dinner. To-night there is full moon, so that our drive back, though somewhat late, will not be the less pleasant."

"Be it so," she replied, "I only stipulate that the rest of our plan remain as we had first agreed upon, and that the valiant knight does not seek a pretext to keep the apple again in his own pocket."

He laughingly promised it on his honour as a knight.

The carriage had now stopped before the cathedral.

They got out and desired the old portal to be opened for them. The grey-haired door-keeper slowly led them through the lofty nave and aisles, coughing and gasping at every step.

"The dank air of the church is not good for you, old lady," remarked Valentine. "Have you not a grandchild, who could serve in your stead, as a guide to strangers? You ought to sit basking in the sun. Go, and leave us to find the way by curselves."

"Showing the church is all well enough," replied the old woman, "but I can no longer drag myself up the steep stairs of the steeple; so if the lady and gentleman wish to climb up there, they will have to go by themselves. You cannot miss the way; one flight of steps follows the other, till you reach the upper gallery; once there, you will have had enough of it."

Valentine looked at Eugénie. "Shall we try?" he asked. She nodded, so they passed through the narrow portal, guarded by two dragons hewn in stone and they began their ascent; leaving their old conductress below. Up there the scanty warmth, and light of the autumnal sun could not penetrate, and the dim cool twilight which prevailed, inclined them to silence. As they ascended the winding stairs, Valentine watched the little feet, which so nimbly mounted the steps before him. He felt as if he could not but follow them, even if they chose to venture out on the steep roof, which now and then was to be seen through the apertures. He heaved an involuntary sigh. She stopped on one of the landing places, and turning looked smilingly at him. "You are out of breath it seems."

"On the contrary, I feel as if I had too much of it," he replied.

"Do not squander it, methinks you will yet want it. See how high above the world we are already, and still the gallery over the nave is much higher."

"I believe you are in fact leading me straight to heaven, Eugénie."

"Gently, gently, you must first deserve it," she replied laughingly.

"And if I carry it by storm?"

"It remains to be seen whether you are as exempt from giddiness, as such a titanic achievement would require. But I would rather you now walked before me; for the stairs grow narrower, and narrower, and I fear I shall lose courage if I see no one in front of me."

He complied with her wish, and pensively ascended the steps before her. Only the rustling of her dress against the wall told him that she was still behind him. So they reached the first gallery which ran round the base of the spire, and entered the interior part of it. "Don't let us stop here," she said, "I will not look around me, till we have reached to the very top. Meanwhile we can admire what is above us. Look how curiously, this pointed airy tent of stone closes around us; a cool bower. It is a pity that the wooden pillar which supports the small upper staircase, somewhat disfigures it, and mars the effect of this beautiful sculptured rosace. But to be sure without it, we could not reach the very point of the spire. Come now, let us proceed in our ascent."

They soon stood beside each other on the aerial summit, and gazed with exulting awe into the fathomless depth below them. The numberless denticulations and ornamented pinnacles of the cathedral, the hundreds of chimnies and roofs, the neat market-place with its quaint looking old town-hall, the swarms of people in the streets, every thing appeared small, strange, and silent as if it were a world of pigmies. At a little distance the river basked in the sun, resembling a silver snake, and its ripples glittered like scales in the light. Further down the valley in the grey distance, above the vineyards rose the clear and cloudless outlines of blue and purple hills. As they stood beside each other, and leant over the stone parapet, he gazed intently at her purely cut profile, which she had heedlessly exposed to the sun. Her eyes were still fixed on the world below her; the wind had dishevelled her long hair and the loosened tresses brushed Valentine's cheek. She did not notice it; her parted lips eagerly inhaled the freshening breeze, her delicate nostrils dilated, and the blood flowed more rapidly through her blue veins.

"Are we not amply repaid for the fatiguing ascent," she asked. "How beautiful it is here. The further we are separated from our fellow creatures the dearer to our hearts they become. I can easily imagine that if a fierce misanthrope filled with animosity and hate were to ascend to these heights, with the intention of precipitating himself over the parapet, he would be suddenly softened and converted, after looking on these humble roofs, underneath which thousands of people bear the sufferings and toils of this life, and are contented if they can only see the sun, and the sky, and the golden cross on their steeple."

"There certainly is a purifying virtue in the air of higher regions," he replied in a low voice. "We are freed from the oppression of daily petty considerations and customs, and are drawn nearer to the Creator. We feel as if we were called to rise above the world, part of which we survey at our feet. Even the most faint-hearted must feel the wings of his soul expand, and that which he dared not utter or even think in the midst of the din, and cares of every day life, here spontaneously flows from his heart to his lips."

Suddenly the sound of trumpets and flutes reached them from below, and they saw a band of music followed by a crowd, slowly advancing in solemn procession, as it issued out of one of the narrow streets, and marched across the market-place. The brass of the instruments sparkled in the sun and some of·the people wore bouquets in their hats. "Apparently a wedding," remarked Valentine. "But where is the bride?" interposed Eugénie. "It rather seems to me to be one of those expeditions which now daily proceed to the vintage accompanied by singing and music. But you have just mentioned weddings; that reminds me of the great aim of our excursion. Come let us descend." He appeared not to have heard her. "Eugénie," he said, "if we had stood up here fourteen years ago, all would have been different."

"Who can say if it would have been better. I am inclined to think that all that happens to us is well, and for our good."

He had pulled out the apple, and held it before him on the stone parapet.

"Do you really believe that Eugénie?"

"Yes, I do."

"And if I had told you then, what escaped from my

lips, the first evening we again met, what would have been your answer?"

"That question, is a matter of conscience, my dear friend," she replied, carelessly, "which even up here a hundred feet above the every day world you are not justified in asking. Before I could give you a clear and concise answer, I should have to read through some chapters in the book of my life, which I have not perused for many a year." "And that truly is a trouble which I cannot expect you to take," he replied in a pained, harsh tone. "Besides it would be useless labour as the writing must have long since faded. I forgot that though the chapters in my book, end in a blank, yours have a continuation." Saying these words he leant over the parapet, and the apple he held in his hand rolled as if by accident over the edge. In its fall it struck one of the many pinnacles which surrounded the spire, and broke into several pieces, which flew, describing wide curves, into the street.

"What have you done Valentine?" exclaimed Eugénie; "where shall we be able to steal another apple? Only fruits of stone can be plucked here. But now let us hasten down."

"You are right," he replied, indifferently, "here every thing is of stone; I did not think of that." Then he remained silent till they reached the streets. The gloom however, which had settled on his countenance, could not hold out against the unconstrained gaiety of his companion. His brow cleared before they had taken many steps on their way to the inn. She had taken his arm through the narrow tortuous streets, her cloak, which in the warm sunshine had become too heavy for her, hung loosely from her shoulders. As they walked along, they joked merrily at the smell of the new wine, which met them at the entrance of every cellar and courtyard and even pervaded the precincts of the old dilapidated church, and at the large vats which obstructed their way.

When they reached the inn, the hour of the table d'hôte had passed, so they sat down alone in the large room, at a small table, where they were amply provided with the best wine of the country; but Eugénie wished for a bottle of that year's vintage. She said she longed to taste that beverage the scent of which she had so abundantly enjoyed during her walk—

When she had tasted it, she praised the sweet and turbid drink.

"It resembles first love," remarked Valentine, "beware of its strength; it will turn your head."

"At my age there is no danger of that," she replied, smiling. "I am an old woman already, and take my daily nap after dinner. To-day this bad habit will be of great service to me."

She then retired to a room prepared for her, and Valentine remained alone in company of the wine and his thoughts. The uneasiness of the morning had passed, and he no longer pondered on what would be the end of all this. The voice of a good genius secretly whispered in his ear that fate now smiled on him. He looked around, as if to ascertain that no one was near, and then hastily took a sip from Eugénie's glass, with the devout superstition that it would help him to divine her thoughts. As however no enlightenment on this point was vouchsafed him, he consoled himself with the thought that without doubt, she was asleep at that moment, and so could think of nothing. He represented her to himself reclining on the sofa, her small feet crossed, and her head drooping on her shoulder. A sensation of happiness thrilled through him; he felt as if he must hasten upstairs, kneel before the fair sleeper, and press her hand to his lips. But he soon rejected this thought, lighted a cigar and patiently waited for Eugénie's appearance. It certainly seemed as if the new wine had confirmed its reputation, for more than an hour passed before the door was opened, and his fair companion re-appeared.

"Good morning," she exclaimed, "how long have I slept? truly this wine though it seems so harmless, is even in its cradle as powerful as an offspring of the gods. It will be late before we reach the home of your fair ones."

"We never can reach it late enough," he replied, laughing. "Think of what you promised me on your honour as a knight," she said, with a menacing gesture, "and hasten our departure. What a careless mother I am, instead of spending my poor boy's last holiday with him, I stroll about the country making the acquaintance of new wine, and old churches."

In spite of Valentine's efforts to hasten their departure the day had waned before they reached their destination. The fog had gathered again, when the carriage slowly ascended the hill on which the town was built, and rattled over the bad pavement. Valentine lifted Eugénie from the carriage when it stopped at the inn, and silently walked by her side through the streets to the doctor's house. She remarked that he was greatly agitated, and she almost felt pity for him, but they had already mounted the stone steps which led up to the neat little house, the knocker had sounded, and a moment afterwards the door was opened by a stout little man with large gold spectacles.

"Why, what's this!" cried the merry old gentleman, pushing back his spectacles. "What gives me the unexpected pleasure of seeing you so soon again? I hope there is nothing wrong about the horse——but I see you have brought company with you, and I have left you standing out there in this rude manner. You must excuse me, fair lady; you see we are still barbarians in this remote corner of the world. I beg you will honour my humble roof. But now tell me seriously my dear friend *is* there anything the matter with Almansor? Unfortunately you will find no one but myself at home, my dear Madam; my daughters will be inconsolable when they hear that during their absence ——but I will send for them this very moment; but stop a bit! why confound me, I remember now, I have already sent for them, they will be here in a few minutes. To the left Madam if you please, will you kindly walk in here, most honoured guests?"

They entered the room, the door of which the lively little man had opened for them. In the centre stood a table laid for four, on which there were cold viands and a bottle of new wine. The whole was lighted up by the faint twilight which stole through the window. "Now you can judge for yourself, my most honoured friend, how we are treated by our children," resumed the doctor. "Those naughty girls of mine run away, and leave their papa to wait for his supper. We will play them a trick however, nothing but the empty dishes, shall they find on their return. But what a fool I am, inviting you to supper without considering that this scanty meal is in no way fit for such charming visitors. Unfortunately the cook is gone to summon them, so there is no one to——But please to be seated at least, take off your hat and cloak, and make yourself comfortable—Welcome to L. . . most honoured lady. Now my friend *do* tell me has the horse?"——

"I can relieve your mind on that point my dear doctor," Valentine at last interposed. "I value Almansor's excellent qualities more than ever, since he has found favour in the eyes of my betrothed, to whom I have the pleasure of introducing you." Eugénie bowed to their amazed host. She checked the words which had risen to her lips, and only a severe look reproved Valentine for this arbitrary assertion, so contrary to their treaty.

Had the little doctor entertained other hopes since yesterday's visit? Had he attached greater importance to it than mere horse-dealing?—With a low bow he stammered forth his congratulations, and thanked Valentine for honouring him with this visit. However he soon recovered his jovial equanimity and laughingly said: "Well, you are the most complete hypocrite and false hearted friend! Did you not on this very spot abuse matrimony so vehemently, that you even alarmed, and terrified such an old widower as I am? and then to come next day accompanied by your betrothed—— Well, she certainly is bewitching enough to convert a heathen.—Pardon me, pardon me, Madam."

Valentine laughed. "I can assure you, doctor; that none but you are responsible, if after all my yesterday's heresy has been retracted."

"I? you are joking."

"No, I am speaking in good earnest. For you have, or rather your horse has been of great assistance to me in winning this fair lady's hand. This morning when mounted on Almansor, I rode up to the window behind which stood my beloved one, the sight melted the hardness of her heart, and she acknowledged herself conquered. Hardly had I recovered my senses, which were somewhat confused by this unexpected victory than I declared that you should be the first person to hear of our engagement, so we ordered a carriage and drove to L... and now permit your grateful and overjoyed friend to embrace you."

"Ah!" exclaimed the delighted doctor, "my fancy for horses has caused me many vexations, but this master-stroke of Almansor's makes ample amends for it all. No my dear young lady, you need not take it amiss that your betrothed has divulged your secret. I esteem you all the more highly since I find that you acknowledge a man to be only complete on horseback. Now leave it all to me, my eye ranges all over the country, and if some day I should find a lady's horse worthy of cantering by the side of Almansor——"

"It shall be *mine;* let us shake hands over it, doctor, and the first time I ride with my wife, you shall accompany us."

"Agreed," cried the little man, and energetically shook hands with his guest. "But where are those girls, confound them; just when all is ready to celebrate this happy event they are wanting."

"Are your daughters on a visit in the town?" asked Eugénie.

"Yes, my dear young lady, they have been invited to one of the autumnal grape gatherings, by a friend of mine, who has daughters of the same age. I have no doubt, that the affair will finish off with a dance; however I exercised my paternal authority, and strictly enjoined them to come home before evening. I will not again allow them to dance at this season of the year, for every time they have done so, they have brought home bad colds. Now they will miss your delightful visit, and it serves the disobedient hussies quite right—but they really must come I will have them fetched home instantly! halloo Henry! he shouted to a farm-servant, whom he had seen passing, from the window; "just run over to the Kitzinger garden and tell Margaret to bring them home immediately. Now you see," he continued, turning to his guests, who sat side by side on the sofa without looking at each other, how little respect a father enjoys. You must educate your children with more severity. Ah! if my wife still lived, it would all be different."

Eugénie blushed and remained silent, but Valentine exclaimed: "No, no Doctor, don't disturb your daughters in their merry making. It is true that I have praised them so much to my dear Eugénie that she will not leave L... without having made their acquaintance, but there will be time for that to-morrow, for the moon does not make its appearance, and I hear that we shall be well provided for at the inn of the Crown."—"Are you not of my opinion darling," he said turning to Eugénie, and suddenly approaching his lips to hers.

"Valentine," said the young woman, and drew back quickly, "you seem to have forgotten what you promised me."—"Now what do you say to that Doctor? She reminds me of my promise, and does not keep hers. Eugénie have you not vowed to agree to all my wishes, and are you justified in refusing a kiss to your betrothed. Come now let us seal our engagement as students seal their fellowship. We have not yet done so."

"That is right!" exclaimed their host. "This is only new wine, but in the cellar...."

"Don't trouble yourself my dear friend; is not new wine sweet, turbid, and intoxicating like first love. And you must know, Doctor, that the fair charmer before you has been worshipped by me from the time I entered college and though fate parted us in later days. 'Old love fades not,' as the people say, and you know that 'the voice of the people, is the voice of the gods.' So we will perform the sacred act with none other but new wine. Fill your glass, Doctor!"

He had risen with these words and again turned towards Eugénie, with two full glasses in his hand. She sat on the sofa suffused with blushes, and her eyes fixed on the ground. Maidenly confusion sealed her lips, she tried to speak, but could not utter a word, so she took the glass mechanically. He then knelt before her, twined his arm within hers after the fashion of the students and emptied his glass at one draught. She took a sip from hers with half averted face. Valentine then threw away his glass and kissed her lips.*

"That's right," said the doctor. "You need not blush fair lady, if an old man like myself is present at

* This is an old custom at the German universities when a new comer enters the Fellowship—they call it "Brüderschaft trinken."

The Translator.

so solemn an act. All I ask as a reward for my good offices, is that I should be permitted to assist at the wedding."

Valentine silently nodded, and remained standing for a while before her, pensively gazing on her calm brow.

"My dear Doctor," he then began, "you must make some allowance for two people who are nearly out of their senses with joy. It is no trifling matter, I assure my dear friend, when one's betrothal is only of a few hours standing; particularly as this cruel lady love of mine tormented me so relentlessly with her wicked tricks, and her apparent indifference struck me dumb, and made me feel as timorous as a bashful youth. It was so years ago, when she was still in her mother's house, and I used often to think that I should no longer be able to stand it, but must plunge into the water to cool my smarting wounds. Then when we again met after many years of separation she was just the same. How often, by some jesting word has she not checked the confession which hovered on my lips, that my feelings for her had remained unaltered; and who knows how all would have turned out, had it not been for you, my dear Doctor. Now, however, you see she has quite changed, and you would never believe how much of subtleness and womanly art lies hidden beneath those demure eyelids."

"Nay, you calumniate me, dear Valentine," she said, and raised her beautiful moist eyes to his. "It is only natural that I should not show my feelings so openly here, in a house which is yet strange to me, though it may not appear so to you."

"And whose is the fault, if not mine," cried the doctor, "or rather of those disobedient damsels who leave all the duties of a host to me." "Well, where are they? what are they about, why are they not with you Margaret?" he angrily asked the cook who had now entered the room.

"You see, Sir, the master and mistress of the house pressed the young ladies to stay for the evening," replied the old woman staring at the two visitors with wondering eyes. "They promised that the young ladies should not dance too much, and Miss Clara thought that if I put it in that light to you Sir! ...."

"Deuce take it," cried the doctor, in a passion, "but they *must* come home immediately!"

"Nay, my dear Doctor," Eugénie said, entreatingly. "Pray do not burthen our consciences with this cruelty."

"Heaven forbid," Valentine hastily added. "To-morrow there will be time enough."

"Well, let us go after them," proposed the doctor, "what do you say to closing this eventful day with a dance?"

"Are we not better here," replied Valentine, "we do not know your friends, and would greatly prefer remaining another hour under your hospitable roof if you will permit us to do so. Is it not so Eugénie?"

She nodded. The old gentleman then rubbed his hands delightedly, and declared that he had not felt so pleased for many a year. He sent the maid into the cellar and the larder and made her bring all that was to be found in the house, in spite of the entreaties of his visitors not to make so much ado for them. When they were at last sitting gaily and comfortably together, the doctor exclaimed with a look of satisfaction: "Now if the girls but knew what they have missed by their disobedience!"

Valentine smilingly looked at Eugénie who had now completely recovered her usual calm demeanour and gave with composure her opinion on the subject of the future arrangement of their life, which Valentine had proposed, and played her part admirably.

When the clock struck ten, she arose. "I am afraid, we can await your daughters no longer;" she said, "to-morrow, when they have rested after their dancing we will return."

"I will not detain you," replied the doctor, "for I verily believe that they will not come home, till I go and fetch them myself. That is the way they treat their old father. I will forgive them, however, this time an account of the pleasure they have procured me of having your society all to myself. But I rely on your promise to return to-morrow, and perhaps, you will understand my paternal weakness when you see these naughty daughters of mine."

So they all set forth; the doctor had insisted on accompanying them to the door of the hotel; there he left them, and they silently followed the waiter who carried the light before them. He opened two adjoining rooms and after wishing them good night disappeared.

Valentine stretched out his hand to Eugénie. She pressed it, and said calmly, looking up at him,

"Good night to you, my dear friend, sleep well, and au revoir to-morrow."

Then she entered her room and closed the door behind her.

After remaining quiet for some time he knocked gently at the door which separated the two rooms.

"Eugénie," he whispered.

"What do you want?" she asked.

"Your good night of before, was against our treaty."

"Against what treaty?"

"That which we solemnly ratified with the doctor's new wine."

"I think we have had enough of this acting I only agreed to the pledge because I thought it lay in my part."

"Can we not continue in earnest, what we began in jest. At all events it was a solemn vow made before witnesses."

"Well, then I will make up for it to-morrow morning, and now once more good night." But no movement showed that she had turned from the door. So after a pause Valentine began again,

"And all the rest may I not consider it as true?"

"What do you mean?"

"Well, all that we acted this evening."

"That is a good deal."

"Eugénie."

"Well."

"Can that be too much which alone can give me back the life and happiness you have taken from me a thousand times?"

"When I consider . . . . ."

"Oh, Eugénie, say that I may throw myself at your feet, that I may kneel before you. Do open the door—!"

"Gently, gently, my dear friend. You certainly deserve some punishment. What! is this all your courage? You can only speak out what weighs on your mind behind the shelter of a closed door! I will bet anything that you have even put out the light hoping that the darkness may give you confidence. You dare not acknowledge your love for me in the face of day. You are a poor hero indeed. But I will now confess to you that I have owed you a grudge for many a year."

"You are jesting again, Eugénie."

"No, this time I am thoroughly in earnest. If in former years you had as little courage as now, why at all events could you not have been as cunning. Was there no door then behind which you could have owned to me what now comes too late!"

"Too late? No, Eugénie; where are the years that separate us from that time? Is it not the same timid lad of those days who now stands here, and implores you to lighten the darkness around him with a heavenly ray from your eyes. Can you leave me to despair?"

He waited some time for an answer. Suddenly the door was noiselessly opened, and she stood before him smiling, but with tears in her eyes.

"One kiss freely given you, as a token of forgiveness for all you have made me suffer," she said.

He folded her in his arms and she softly passed her hand across his brow, saying: "Here, there are many lines, but our hearts are still fresh and youthful, and to-morrow we will begin life anew where we left it off fourteen years ago."

She pressed her lips to his, and with his arm round her waist, he led her to the window. The moon had dispersed the fog, and a gentle autumnal breeze wafted the scent of the grapes through the open casement.

"Let us drive back to-night, my darling," she said. "I could not sleep now, and the air is quite mild. Go, while you order the carriage, I will write a few lines to the doctor, and tell him not to expect us to-morrow: Is it true, Valentine, can it be true, that we have at last told each other what we knew years ago?"—

THE END.